ORACLE
DREAMS
TRILOGY
BOOK 3

Pagan FIRE

LUCKY CROW PRESS

TERI BARNETT

Pagan Fire
Oracle Dreams Trilogy: Book 3
Published Internationally by Teri Barnett
USA
Copyright © 2020 Teri Barnett
teribarnett.com
Lucky Crow Press

Previously published as Pagan Fire
by Lachesis Publishing Inc.
© 2010 Teri Barnett
Significantly revised and re-released as Pagan Fire
by Lucky Crow Press © 2020

Editor: Joanna D'Angelo
Exclusive cover design © 2023 Joanna D'Angelo
Interior design © 2023 Indie Book Designer

PRINT ISBN 978-1-7328138-7-8
EBOOK ISBN 978-1-7328138-6-1

This is a work of fiction. Names, characters, places, and incidents are either the product of the author's imagination or are used fictitiously, and any resemblance to any person or persons, living or dead, events or locales is entirely coincidental.

For my sons, Aron and Daniel
You are the best and I'm grateful to be sharing this life's journey with you

CONTENTS

From the molten depths
of the earth,
through a portal of
jewel green water,
the goddess rises.

She speaks
and her thick, honeyed voice
penetrates the heavy veil
of cool clear liquid.

She smiles
and grants magic
to those
she would love.

~Teri Barnett

PROLOGUE

Tintagel, Cornwall, Isle of Great Britain
November 865 A.D.

"'Tis a fine night for a child to be born," Manfred cu Llwyr whispered, lost in thought as he warmed himself before the robust fire which burned brightly there. Shaking himself out of his reverie, he strode to the thick oak and iron door that led outside.

Opening it with a loud scrape, he made his way down the unheated corridor. As he moved, his body cast shadows tall and thin before him from the glow of torches mounted high on the wall. The straw scattered about the stone floor for warmth and cleanliness offered a muffled crackle beneath his feet.

Once out of doors, he rubbed his hands together and raised his eyes to the sky. On the horizon, the setting sun cast a red glow and turned the gray winter clouds to indigo. Manfred sighed and his breath hung in the air before him.

He stopped near another fire—one of many lit this night in celebration of the feast of Samhain—and leaned against the timber and stone wall of the keep. He looked out past the fence—hand-hewn stakes of wood sunk deep in the ground—surrounding his *burh*. A fine mist hovered about the treetops, its long fingers beginning to touch the ground.

It all belonged to him. As far as the eye could see, from the lush green rolling hills to the thick forests shaded dark by the coming night.

The sharp tang of the sea, not quite a mile away, rose on the wind and tickled his nose.

The Samhain bonfires scattered along the hillsides broke the shroud of mist and night. His churls would soon be starting the dedication of animal sacrifices to the gods, goddesses, and denizens of the Other-world. It was their sincere belief these offerings would cause the deities to look upon the people favorably and see them safely through the coming winter.

He hoped their prayers would be heard, thankful the portents hadn't indicated a harsh winter on the way. If this had been the case, a human sacrifice would have been in order. And though it would've been his duty to see it through, he was loath to take a life.

Manfred's "new way of thinking" was a constant point of contention between himself and the High Council of Bards, Ovates, and Priests. It was even worse with his twin brother, Eugis, who saw Manfred's beliefs as a threat to their very way of life.

A woman's scream pierced the growing darkness and Manfred swung around. He let his breath out slowly, clenching his fists until his nails dug deep in the callused flesh. Nestled deep inside the hall in their bedchamber, his wife was laboring to bring forth their first child. He unclenched his hands and cast a log on the fire in front of him. Silently, he sent a prayer to Nuada for Rhea's safety.

By the gods, he was fearful of losing her. She had come into his life like a bright shining light, at a time when he thought love was perhaps beyond his grasp, and she enchanted him. She was truly a child of the hills, with her thick black hair and freckled cheeks. She wove wondrous stories of meetings with the Tuatha de Danaan themselves, the very fays who lived in these emerald hills! And who was he to dispute her? He'd seen enough of magic in his own life to know it existed.

Lost in his thoughts, he didn't notice the little boy approaching. The child stopped before him and tugged at Manfred's long white tunic. The copper and stone adornments chimed together. The move-ment startled him, and he glanced down. He'd forgotten he was still wearing the heavily embroidered and jeweled priest's robes. As the Chief Dyrrwed Bard for his clan, he should be at the Samhain celebration now, reciting the stories of the Ulster Men, Cu Chulainn, and the other heroes and deities.

Ah, but he couldn't leave Rhea's side for long as she struggled with the birth. If only for his own sense of well-being, he needed to be close to her. Too many women died while laboring. He would stay and make certain the midwife and priestess in attendance drew upon all of their powers to keep his wife safe from harm while the baby fought its way into the world. And a fight it truly was. Already a full day had passed and still the babe remained in its mother's womb.

"Dylan mac Connall. What is it?" Manfred squatted down to be eye level with the boy. "What can I do for you this evening?"

The boy didn't answer, but only watched the older man.

"I would've thought you'd be at the feast with the others." Manfred smiled as he looked at the child. Hair as black as the night sky and eyes to match, the boy was so serious for one who'd seen only four winters. But he'd always been that way. Even as a wee babe he didn't cry out or raise his voice. He only seemed to look out on creation with sober curiosity.

Dylan pursed his lips together, then spoke. "I told Da I needed to be here with you and the Lady. He said it would be all right, as long as I didn't get in anyone's way." Dylan's father, Fox mac Connall, was the leader of the neighboring lands and Manfred's oldest and most trusted friend.

Manfred smiled again and ruffled the boy's hair. "But the festivities have only just begun. Have you had your fill of our good cook Hazel's honeycakes so soon?" It was just like the child to do something out of the ordinary, the opposite of what everyone else was doing. Single-minded though he was, he was a good boy and a more-than-able student, well on the path to becoming a powerful Dyrrwed priest. Already, Manfred had been able to teach him a hundred verses and tales of their people, the Dumnonii. Of course, there were literally thousands more, but so far, the boy had memorized each and every one he'd been taught. No small feat for a child his age.

Dylan shrugged. "I was at the festival, warming my hands near the fire, when I heard someone calling my name." He pulled his hands up inside of the thick brown woolen cloak he wore as if, with the telling of the tale, the small fingers remembered how cold they had been. "I walked into the woods, down the path where the two tall stones stand watching the stream. I heard my name again." His eyes met Manfred's. "Then I saw a lady there."

Manfred grinned. "And what sort of lady did you find?"

"A wet one, Sir. She was just lying there under the water, smiling up at me. Then she started to talk, and her voice sounded like music. She told me I should be here, with you." He pulled his hands out of his cloak and tossed a green pebble up into the air with one hand and caught it with the other. When he showed his palms, the stone had vanished. He pushed his black hair out of his eyes and looked at Manfred again.

Manfred's grin faded. He took the boy by the shoulders and looked at him carefully, judging the truth of what was said. Dylan's gaze never wavered. Manfred ran a hand through his silver streaked bright red beard. Had he heard correctly? Had the raven goddess of the water, Morrigu herself, spoken to the boy? Manfred sucked in his breath. *It truly is a special night.*

At that moment, to his left, one of his churls came lumbering out of the barn, wiping his hands on a bit of ragged cloth. To his right, the midwife appeared at the door to the keep, a soft bundle in her arms.

"The new foal has arrived, my Lord. She's as white as a fair summer cloud, she is." The churl grinned broadly, displaying two rows of uneven teeth, then turned and walked back to the barn.

"An' I 'ave more news fer ye, Sir. Yer child has finally come." The midwife placed the babe in his arms and pulled the blanket away from the small face. As she did so, a hawk flew overhead, crying to the night. The midwife jumped, then made a quick sign for protection.

Manfred stared up at the bird and a shiver ran along his spine. All the signs were present: The appearance of a goddess. The birth of a white foal at the same moment as the babe. The hawk...

It could only mean one thing. The child would be triply blessed by the gods and goddesses, with the powers of healing at its command.

"How is Lady Rhea? Did she fare well?" he asked, his voice a ragged whisper.

4

"Oh, Sir, she done jest fine." The midwife smiled kindly. "She's a-sleepin' already."

He looked at the sky again as the hawk continued to circle overhead, now joined by what appeared to be a large raven. "Morrigu," he whispered.

Sparks from the fire lifted with the wind and mixed with the stars. Still the birds flew steady. When Manfred realized the midwife was still speaking to him, he shook his head to clear it. "What was it you said?"

"I says I'm very sorry it's a girl-child. I know how disappointed ye must be." She pulled her homespun shawl tighter around her shoulders as light snowflakes began to fall.

Manfred waved her away impatiently. "Nonsense, woman. Girls have their value, and my daughter will aspire to greatness." He puffed his chest out. "She will be a leader of the Dumnonii. Nay, of all the Keltoi tribes." He gestured to the sky. "Tell me you don't see the signs!" Manfred lowered his hand. He ran a rough finger down the babe's cheek and stroked the downy thatch of dark red hair covering her head. "Leave the babe with me and go watch over my wife in case she wakes."

"But, Sir. It's gettin' much too cold fer the child to be out here." She glanced around, as if hoping for someone to support her position. "Sir?"

Manfred's expression grew dark. "You heard me. Off with you." When she hesitated, he barked, "Now!" The midwife took a step back, then turned and ran into the hall, her shawl trailing behind her.

He chuckled, then gazed down at his new daughter. "Dylan," he whispered as he crouched down. "This is an important lesson and I want you to remember it. Look at this babe. Life is sacred. It should never be taken from another in vain or for the purpose of calling up healthy crops." He sighed. "There are those who disagree with me on this matter, but, as your teacher, it's important to me that you understand."

"I'll remember, Sir." Dylan leaned forward, his eyes wide as he looked at the baby. "She's beautiful. Prettier even than the lady in the stream."

Manfred laughed. "Of course, she is. And, because of your vision, I have decided to name her Maere, after the water spirit."

Dylan smiled proudly. But as he continued to watch the babe, his smile faded. He touched the child's tiny hand and whispered, "I swear by all the gods and goddesses that I will protect her for you and the Lady Rhea." He raised his eyes to Manfred. "Always."

CHAPTER ONE

Eighteen years later
April 883 A.D.
Tintagel, Cornwall, Isle of Great Britain

"Come," *the woman's voice bade.* "Come to me."

Dylan mac Connall opened his eyes and rose from the herb-and-grass stuffed mattress which served as his bed. Dylan strode to the window and pushed back the homespun curtain. To the west, the full moon was still high in the sky. The breeze caressed his face, as gentle as a maiden's touch. Quietly, he dressed and, on silent feet, made his way to the door of the sod-and-timber cottage that had been his home these past ten years. He smiled at the sound of soft snores coming from the room at the other end of the humble abode. His adopted mother and mentor, Hekate Athelred, known to him simply as Kate, was sound asleep. How many times had he slipped out just this way? If she knew about his nocturnal wanderings, she kept it to herself. If she did know, would she warn him against it?

"Come…" the voice whispered again.

It was her. As it had always been these past four years. He'd just reached eighteen summers when she'd come into his life once more. He'd been in a deep sleep after a long day assisting Kate with drying and storing the herbs and powders she used in her potions, balms, and poultices for healing and her magical incantations.

When he'd turned *eighteen, a beautiful voice had began to call to him in his dreams. The melodic whispers woke him from his sleep and awakened in him a restless yearning…*

The buzzing sound of insects vibrated in his ears, urging him forward. He walked in the direction he was being drawn, the same as he'd done so many years ago when Kate had rescued him.

It was night then, too, when he'd evaded capture by Eugis's men. They had been hot on his trail after the Samhain massacre, after he'd lost Maere and everyone dear to him, after he'd witnessed the murder of her mother and father and his own Da. He'd survived the treachery only by diving into the thicket and tumbling down a steep hill. They thought him dead and left him where he lay.

The buzzing intensified; his senses heightened. He pushed his way through the dense covering of bushes at the edge of the clearing, through the trees and saplings. Then, the faint gurgle of the stream and the tangy scent of the sea touched his spirit and he understood.

Morrigu was here.

He hadn't seen the goddess since the night Maere was born, but he always sensed her presence nearby. He somehow knew, deep inside, that she guided him. Cared for him. Perhaps loved him.

"I'm here," he whispered. A raven cawed in the distance, in response. Its raucous song came closer and closer until it seemed to come from all around, enveloping him. Dylan looked up. Sitting in the branches of a sacred oak was the bird, as large and unmoving as any he had ever seen. It stared hard at him and he stared back.

"What is it you cry so loud and hard for, Friend Raven?" he said. "What is it that brings you here to me in the middle of the night?"

The bird cocked its head to one side and the white moonlight touched its eyes. "Caw!" it screamed again.

"Were you, too, awakened from a dream-filled sleep and lured to this very spot, the same as me?"

In response, the raven let loose with a furious beating of its wings, descended from the branch and landed on the ground in front of Dylan. It took a step forward and, as it did, slowly grew taller and taller, its very shape transforming before his eyes.

Dylan took a step back, his gaze transfixed on the sight before him. He'd *seen much of magic over the years, during his lessons with Kate. Water flowing in reverse, lead turned into gold and back again, fairy folk and all manner of strange beings. But he found —to his own surprise—that he was unprepared for the shape-shifting raven.*

As he watched, the bird continued to metamorphose. It beat its wings again and they changed into shapely arms. It stomped its orange claws on the ground, and they turned into long, well-formed legs. It tilted its head from side to side as if its neck ached, and the feathers and sharp yellow beak were slowly replaced with a woman's face. The cheekbones were high and angled, the eyes slanted at the outside corners. The hair, as black as the feathers, cascaded down her back. Everything changed but the color of the eyes. They remained the same luminous silver as the raven's own.

"Who are you?" Dylan said. His throat was tight and dry, and the words were more of a croak than actual speech. Wide-eyed, he stared at the naked woman that stood before him. Her breasts were creamy and ample, her hips round and full.

"I am Morrigu," she said, her voice low and husky. "Do you not know me?"

Recognition dawned on him. "Forgive me, goddess. I saw you but once and I was only a child then." He spoke quickly. Morrigu's temper was legendary among the people who still followed the old ways. It could be deadly to cross her.

Morrigu's eyes roamed over his tall, lean frame. "Not so much a child any longer." She smiled and the moonlight reflected off her wine-red lips. She ran her tongue across them, wetting them, drawing his attention to their fullness.

"Why is it I never saw you again?" he said. "I've sensed you, knew you were here—"

She took a step nearer. "The moment wasn't right."

Her musky scent rose on the air and floated to Dylan. The aroma entered him like a potion. It silenced his tongue and he couldn't speak. He continued to watch her as she approached.

Morrigu reached up and ran a long fingernail down the side of his face. A thin trail of blood seeped through his skin where she touched him. "Until now."

Dylan opened his mouth, then closed it, still wordless. He shifted uncom-

fortably as the damp ground chilled his bare feet. What was going on here? Was he dreaming?

"No. No dream," she said quietly. "I've been waiting for you all these years. Waiting for the perfect time to show myself to you." She reached for his hands and placed them over her breasts. With gentle motions, she showed him how to knead them, how to pull at the dark rose peaks and tease them to hardness.

"Tell me, Dylan mac Connall. What do you want more than anything from this lifetime?"

He dropped his hands to his side and his face hardened. He found the full strength of his voice and answered, "Revenge."

She tossed back her head and laughed, the sound a spell in itself. It stroked and taunted him. He felt desire begin to burn in his loins. Desire for the goddess and desire for the death of the man who had destroyed his life.

Morrigu's eyes locked onto his. She touched his shoulders and forced him to his knees. "Remember this feeling," she said. "The desire for revenge can rage as hot as the desire for a woman. But do not let one interfere with the other."

He looked up at her, puzzled.

She laughed again. "For now, do not fret over what I say. You will have time enough to ponder the meaning of my words." She leaned over him and dangled a full breast above his lips. He took it in his mouth like a ripe peach and suckled. Morrigu wrapped her fingers in his black hair and pulled his head tighter against her bosom. "Sweet Dylan," she moaned, "you shall have all that you wish from me. I will teach you the magic of love. And one day, in the future, I will set you forth on your quest for vengeance..."

He arrived at the clearing as he had so many times before. And she appeared to him once more, in all her dark, voluptuous glory.

"You are here," she purred, sauntering up to him, her naked form bathed in moonlight.

"Aren't I always?" he replied.

She laughed and her long inky black hair shook with the movement. "You are a devil, you know that?"

He stood silent. Still. He'd learned not to show eagerness. He'd learned everything there was to know about pleasuring a goddess.

And in those first years, he was eager indeed, and couldn't wait to be in her arms. Believing that she loved him. Foolish boy that he was.

Morrigu didn't love anyone, possibly not even herself. She would play the coy maiden one night and the seductress the next. She was elusive and fickle Morrigu was, calling out to him every night for a sennight and then disappearing for months at a time. Eventually he'd learned to accept who and what Morrigu was. She could not be controlled, only handled.

Morrigu twined her arms around Dylan's neck, pressing herself against him.

"Tonight, I will release you from the shadows that keep you here. Tonight, I will tell you where Maere is."

His chest clenched. Finally, after all this time, he would know the truth. He'd endured Morrigu's quicksilver temperament as he continued to learn his own magic, biding his time, knowing she would one day tell him where Maere was.

"Don't you want to know this very minute?" She ran her finger along the scar on his cheek, her mark. "Don't you want to see your betrothed again after all these years? She will be eighteen soon. Ripe for the plucking. And you, my darling, will be the one to pluck her…"

"You know I do." He considered the goddess. "Will you tell me now?"

Morrigu pulled him to the ground. "Soon."

As he lay there, half asleep, Dylan ruminated over Morrigu's words. She'd spoken so carelessly about Maere and her prophesied powers. Maere, his childhood friend, the young girl who'd made the world a magical place and had been taken away from him and hidden away at St. Columba's by her evil uncle Eugis, in a horrific act of betrayal.

Dylan had no idea what kind of person Maere had grown up to be. Did the shock and horror of that long ago night forever alter the fiery spirit of the child she'd been? Would she still have that fearless sense of adventure or would she be forever changed?

Now that he knew where she was hidden, he could cut his ties with the goddess and forge his own path forward.

Soon, I will see you again Maere. And all will be as it should have been.

CHAPTER TWO

St. Columba's Abbey
Glastonbury, Isle of Great Britain

The form of a man emerged from the darkness of the fog, his body a lean dark silhouette against the swirling gray mass. The moonlight touched his hair and it glowed blue-black in the night. Stars danced about him and the very trees themselves tipped and bowed as he passed.

Walking—nay, gliding—he moved with purpose and determination along the road leading toward the abbey. The evening offered him a cloak and he wore this mantle proudly, becoming one with the nighttime.

On silent feet, he approached the old, ivy-covered stone walls of Saint Columba's as if it were a cornered animal. He paused for a moment, glanced about him, and then resumed his advance.

His breath billowed about his head, obscuring first his face as he passed through the quiet walls of the abbey itself, and entered her small cell.

The young woman, deep asleep, struggled against the bed linens entangled around her limbs. He grinned as he watched her slender legs push and kick while her hands pulled and tugged, until she was finally free of their unrelenting grasp.

He reached for her, the feral glow of his eyes penetrated the blackness and touched her with their intensity. "Come to me," he rasped, his fingers inches from her face. "Come to me."

The young woman bolted upright. Her chest heaved as she tossed the offending linens to the floor. Sweat beaded her forehead and dripped down the lightly freckled cheeks of her otherwise fair skin. Her back was damp as well. Her heart beat so fiercely against her breast she feared for her life. She clutched at her throat. She couldn't breathe. She glanced frantically around the small room. The walls seemed to move in toward her, threatening to crush her. Panic set in. Where was he? Where had he gone? Was he still here?!?

"Sisters!" she screamed. "Help me!"

Within moments, Abbess Magrethe shoved open the cell door and rushed to the young woman's side. "What is it, Maere?" She searched her face. "What troubles you so?"

Maere huddled against the wall at the head of her small cot, her knees drawn tightly to her chest. Her dark copper hair tumbled over her shoulders, clinging to her damp skin. Slowly, she raised her green eyes to the abbess's and peered at her through the long, wild strands. She tried to speak, but the words caught in her throat.

"It was another nightmare, wasn't it?" Magrethe asked, as she set her candle gently down on the nightstand. She drew Maere to her.

Maere nodded and began to sob. "Who is this man who haunts my sleep? Why won't he let me rest?"

"If only I knew," she murmured. Magrethe held Maere out at arm's length and searched her face once more. "Was it the same dream? Was he coming for you?"

"Aye, Mother. He's close, too. I saw him outside the abbey walls. He walked right through them." Maere's voice shot up a notch. "He was here!"

"Poor child," Magrethe sighed. "If you had not been having these dreams for so many years now, I would believe the pleasures of the flesh were calling to you." She released Maere and picked up her candle, lighting Maere's with it. The light cast tall shadows on the wall, mimicking the woman's motions.

"You believe that's what these dreams mean? That I am thinking of being w-with a man?" Maere rolled the edge of her gown between her fingers as tears fell onto the fabric and stained it. "If that were true, why does he appear as if he is hunting me down, like a deer or a fox?"

The small flame flicked and sputtered. "I know he wants me dead." She turned her eyes away from the light. "Why does he want me dead?"

"I cannot explain the Devil's lure, but it's widely known he seeks young women such as you, those nearly ready to take their vows."

Maere rubbed her eyes furiously. "I appreciate your counsel, Mother." Maere let her head fall gently back against the wattle-and-daub wall. "If you think this is Lucifer's work, then I must do penance. I must seek forgiveness for bringing this demon to me."

"Maere, you've been disturbed by these images for more years than you've been a young woman, so this may not be the case with you." She sighed. "I'm sorry I know not the answer, child." The abbess drew the young woman to her breast again. She stroked Maere's hair until Maere was calm and her breathing even. "I think it would help if you prayed about this. Perhaps a fast and meditation might bring the answer to you.

Maere remembered the glowing red eyes. They were animal-like, fierce in their determination to seek her out, more frightening than anything she could ever remember seeing before. "Do you really think it would help, Mother?"

"With God anything is possible. You know that, girl." Magrethe patted Maere's cheek, then helped her get back under the covers of the straw-filled mattress. "For now, try and sleep. It's almost time for Matins and Sister Aubrey will be most put out if you doze off during prayers."

Dear Aubrey—her lined face—came to Maere. The image of the old nun tapping the sisters and novices on the top of the head with a thin willow stick as they fell asleep during the two-thirty a.m. service made her smile.

"There, now, that's much better," Magrethe said, as she stood and blew out the candle.

"Thank you, Mother," Maere whispered.

Magrethe nodded as she left the small cell. She stopped outside the doorway to talk to the sisters who had gathered there, curious what the commotion was about.

"It's the night terrors again, isn't it?" whispered Sister Bernard harshly. "It's the pagan soul in her, I tell you. The girl is tainted." The tall, thin nun made the sign of the cross over her breast.

"Really, Bernard," another scolded. "Her mother and father may have followed the old ways, but she's been with us many years now, raised since but a small child to be a good Christian."

Magrethe frowned. "Enough of this," she quietly ordered, shooing them away with a wave of her hand. "Everyone, back to bed. Maere's fine and there will be no more of this discussion tonight." She offered one last glance at Maere's now-sleeping form, Sister Bernard's words echoing in her mind.

Pagan soul.

Tainted.

With a shiver, she closed the creaking door behind her.

CHAPTER THREE

The iron chapel bells clanged loudly, proclaiming time for Matins. Maere pushed herself up and out of the bed. Her bare feet landed on the cold stone floor without a sound. Yawning, she stretched and rubbed her eyes. It seemed as if she'd only just fallen back to sleep after that terrible dream. She shivered, feeling the eyes still upon her.

"Oh, Mama, I wish you were here," Maere whispered as she sat back down on the cot. She hugged her arms around her waist, tears filling her eyes. Sweet Mary, but it'd been such a long time since she'd even thought of her mother. Too long, she realized. She searched her memory for anything she could hold onto—eyes that smiled, the curve of a cheekbone. Did her mother smell of the cooking fire or of sage and lavender and heather? Did she look like her, with dark copper hair and freckles across her nose?

Try as she might, she couldn't recall much except the remnants of a warm smile and comforting hug. Maere rubbed her eyes again. Why did those cursed Vikings come to their land, wreaking death and destruction? And why did it have to be her family who was struck so brutally, leaving her orphaned and alone?

If only she could remember, perhaps she could begin to understand what happened that night when her mother and father were murdered. But even now, with nearly ten years passed, she only knew of their fate at the hands of the Northmen because Abbess Magrethe had told her it was so. She sighed and hung her head. Her mind was hazy to what life was like before coming to St. Columba's. Abbess said it was because of the shock of witnessing such an evil act. Maere had prayed many a night, until she was hoarse, asking the Virgin for intercession. She so wanted the memories to return. Still, her pleas went unanswered.

Maere thought she recalled an uncle, but wasn't sure it was a true remembering, or rather the result of abbess mentioning him from time to time over the years. Magrethe said Eugis was a kind man who had taken her in when Mama and Papa were killed. As he was unmarried, he had thought it best Maere receive her education at the convent. He'd promised to return for her when she turned eighteen and take her to an arranged marriage.

In her heart of hearts, Maere secretly hoped in the span of the years she'd been here he'd forgotten about her and would let her be. Then she'd be free to take her vows and join the sisters as one of them. They were all dear to her and, in truth, the only family she'd ever known. She sighed again. Or, at the very least, the only one she could remember.

"Blessed Madonna," she prayed as she stood and pulled on the rough tan habit of the novitiate, "Please guide me that I may know what to do." With a long, tired breath, she fastened her black mantle over her shoulders with a simple silver clasp. Then she braided her long hair into a single plait.

A sharp rap sounded at the door and sent her thoughts scattering. "Maere? You'll be late!"

"Yes, sister. I'm almost ready," she called back. She arranged a short veil on her head. As she readied to leave the room, Maere paused at the door, the conversation with Magrethe the night before on her mind. Could it be what the older woman said was true? Could it be she'd actually invited the Devil himself into her dreams? That he was inducing her with thoughts of the flesh? If it were the Devil's work, then surely there would be some sign. A flash of red eyes flickered in her mind's eye, a startling reminder of her dreams. Fear overtook her.

I'm so tired of being afraid all the time.

Everything made Maere skittish—dark corners, a loud pop and crackle of a log in a hearth fire, even a bird taking flight from a tree branch made her knees wobble.

The Devil be damned, I must get over my fears or I will never live a peaceful life.

Her hand on the door, she realized there were other young women at St. Columba's who were plagued so with thoughts of men and the flesh. For their penance, the priest had stripped them to the waist and beaten those ideas out of them with a leather whip. She shuddered as she imagined herself bared for the world to see, the sting of leather tearing into her soft flesh. She instinctively crossed her arms over her full breasts, held almost flat by the binding cloth the sisters insisted all the women wear.

Why in heaven's name did the abbess have to suggest such a notion?

No! I refuse to tell the priest.

Courage! I must not allow every wee thing to strike fear in me.

She slipped on her suede sandals as the bell rang again and rushed out of the room.

After Matins, Lauds, and Prime, the sisters gathered in the dining room at eight for a silent breakfast of hot cider and thick crusty bread. They sat elbow-to-elbow on hard benches at a table long enough to seat all twenty of them, ten on either side. The only sounds in the white-plastered room were wooden sticks beating against the clay cups as the sisters stirred their drinks. The thick sweet liquid stuck to the sides of the vessels, and chunks of apple had to be scooped out with bits of bread. It was good and filling, exactly what was needed for a cool day.

The sunlight broke through the window and across the table. Maere turned her head, squinting horribly, as the rays hit her directly in the eyes.

Two of the novitiates seated across from Maere giggled. "What are those terrible faces you're making?" Seelie, one of the girls, whispered.

Maere glanced up at her friend, then pulled her veil down to shade her face. "It's the sun. You know it hurts my eyes."

"I know you like to complain!" Seelie said, louder than she intended.

"That's not true," Maere said, even louder.

"Seelie. Maere," Abbess Magrethe called out their names. They stood up from their seats.

"You both know better than to speak during the morning meal. You are supposed to be reflecting on the scriptures you heard earlier today." Magrethe stared at her charges. "For your punishment, the two of you will clear the table and wash the dishes by yourselves." She looked around the room. "Any of you who were assigned to this duty can help in the yard. We'll be clearing a new garden plot near the well." With that, the abbess stood, dusted the crumbs from her apron, then turned and left the room.

As soon as everyone finished eating, they filed out of the dining area, one by one, and headed through the heavy timber doorway which led outside. There, they would see to their separate duties of planting the garden, feeding the livestock, or boiling the laundry over a large open fire. Maere hated that job the most. There was something about the size of the flames and incredible heat that stirred an uneasy emotion within her. Whenever it came her turn to wash clothes, she begged and pleaded to be given other duties. After a while, the sister in charge of scheduling the weekly duties must have grown weary of Maere's pleading because she began to assign her other tasks.

Maere scooped up a willow basket half-full of bread and cradled it in her arms. "Why do you mock people all the time?" she grumbled to her friend. "It's not Christian, you know."

Seelie laughed. "I'm sorry, my friend." She affectionately squeezed Maere's arm. "Forgive me?"

"I suppose I'll have to, since you asked." She quirked her lips and headed for the kitchen, calling behind her, "Of course, if you hadn't asked, I wouldn't've had to now, would I?" Maere dropped the basket on the well-worn wooden counter then paused for a moment. Her smile faded as she looked out the small window over the soapstone sink. Beyond the outer walls was a thick stand of trees. She felt the eyes again, watching, boring into her. She made a quick sign of the cross over the center of her chest.

"Maere, I was speaking to you."

Startled, Maere spun around and almost dropped the heavy clay cup she had absently picked up. She clutched it tight to her chest, then set it down on the counter. "I'm sorry, Seelie. What was it you were saying?"

"I asked if you've seen the new monk who came to visit the

convent yesterday." Seelie held her arms out to her sides and twirled around. Her long blonde hair, unbound, fanned out around her from beneath her small veil. "He's so young and handsome," she sighed.

"Of course, I haven't noticed him. I have more important things to do with my time." Maere rolled her eyes and placed the cups into the round washtub. She dragged an iron bucket of water over to the hearth and hoisted it onto the hook to boil. She wiped her brow then returned to the dining room for more dishes. Seelie was always on the prowl for handsome young men. Of course, she never admitted it to her confessor, so she'd yet to be beaten as penance for it. "Why do you ask?"

"Why do I ask? Is there something wrong with you, girl? Have you no eyes in that head of yours?" Seelie followed Maere back into the kitchen with several trenchers in her hands. "Can you honestly tell me you've never noticed a man or thought what it might be like to be with one?" She set the plates down and put her hands on her hips. "Don't lie to me now, Maere cu Llwyr. I've known you for too long."

Maere's back stiffened. She fumbled and dropped one of the cups on the floor. With a loud clatter, it broke into a several large pieces. Her friend crouched down and picked up the shards. She put them in the refuse barrel and turned back to Maere. "I'd say that answers my question," she said, dusting her hands on her apron.

"You have to swear not to tell," Maere cried. "Promise me!" she all but shrieked. Seelie might be a friend but even *she* didn't know the details of her dreams. If anyone other than Abbess Magrethe even remotely suspected she kept seeing a man in her sleep, why, who knew what might happen to her?

"Is there something wrong in there?" one of the sisters called through the kitchen window as she walked past. "Did I hear something break?"

"Everything is fine, Sister Emmanuel. Nothing to worry about," Seelie answered. She looked at Maere and smiled. "I'll strike a bargain with you, sister. If you pretend that I'm in your cell tonight, praying, I won't tell any of them your secret thoughts."

"You want me to lie?" Maere asked, incredulous. She had given to telling tall tales as a child. The abbess told her once she talked on and on about big cows who watched her wherever she went. About the fays and other little people she'd seen dancing in the forest and about a young boy who was her best friend. But, thanks to the good sister's help, she'd long since outgrown that childish obsession of spilling forth whatever fanciful thought flew into her head.

Seelie shrugged. "Either that, or I'll have to have a talk with Father Ambrose when he comes to visit. I'm certain he'd be most interested in hearing about this affliction of yours." She narrowed her eyes and smiled tightly. "Now, are we in agreement?"

Maere wanted to shake the evil out of the girl. How could she call herself a friend and then threaten to betray her in the next breath? It was difficult enough for her to control the temper she felt brewing a good deal of the time as it was. It rested just below the surface of her skin and threatened to bubble up when she least expected it.

Abbess always told her to avert her bad thoughts to the Virgin Mary and ask her for forgiveness. But Maere knew the other sisters whispered her temperament came from being tainted as a child, raised wild by the Keltoi. But it was better to hold her tongue than have to face the priest and his whip. She sighed. "Agreed."

Seelie's face lit up and she clapped her hands together. "I knew I could count on you!" She turned to leave. Maere touched her arm and she turned back. "Yes?"

"There's one thing you must tell me before I'll lie for you, Seelie. Where exactly will you be during the time we are supposed to be practicing our prayers?" Why'd she even bother to ask? She knew the answer before the girl spoke.

"I'll be with the young monk." Seelie leaned forward and giggled. She whispered into Maere's ear, "We've made arrangements to meet in the old hermit's cave near the outer wall. And when I return, I promise I'll tell you every last detail."

CHAPTER FOUR

Dylan cast a final glance to the sky as Morrigu's raven form disappeared from sight. With a sigh, he pushed open the door to the cottage. The rising orange-red sun glowed in the morning haze, warming his back as he stood in the portal.

Kate glanced up from where she sat at an old worn table in the center of the plain room, squinted against the filtered sunlight, then returned to her work. The clatter of the wood mortar against the clay bowl as she ground plants and roots grated against the stillness of the morning, and Dylan's nerves.

He walked in, ducking his head to avoid the dried herbs hanging from every rafter, nook, and cranny. As he pulled out the chair opposite the old woman, the pungent odor of garlic and rosemary filled his senses. So many days and nights he'd spent in this very seat, since that first night when she'd found him running from his would-be captors. The rhythm of Kate's work, combined with the warmth of the room, took him back to that time. Back to the night he lost all that was dear to him, everything and everyone he loved…

Just a boy of twelve, he stood between the dying flames of the many Beltane fires, clutching Maere's white mantle to his breast. It was all he had left of her; all he'd managed to grab when Eugis rode off. Dylan tried to pull Maere off the horse, but it was too big and too fast for him.

How did this come to pass?

Why did they murder his father and Maere's parents?

Maere!

His newly betrothed had been stolen from him, dragged off screaming into that Beltane night.

The people of his village, chased away by Eugis' men, had fled. Dylan became sick and disoriented, vomiting over and over onto the hard ground until there was nothing left in him but the bitter taste of bile. He'd watched, in dazed silence, as the fluids his body had given up flowed into the hot coals of the sacrificial fires, simmering and then evaporating in the heat.

Eugis's men returned then and spied him where he lay. "There he is! Grab 'im!"

Dylan's escape was blocked by the Beltane fires to his left or right. He scrambled to his feet, kicking up dirt behind him, and bolted for the forest. He ran fast and hard as the attackers followed. The low underbrush and sharp brambles tugged at his stocking covered legs. The plants tore the fine woolen fabric of his ceremonial robe into shreds, and his skin along with it.

He gave a quick glance over his shoulder. *Sweet Danu*. They were so close he could see the horse's nostrils flaring, the steam rising in the pale moonlight their heaving flanks.

"Don't let the bugger get away! We'll have the gods to pay if we don't kill 'im dead."

Kill me?! Why?!

A steel band of fear tightened around his chest. Frantic, his eyes darted from side to side, looking for some refuge from his pursuers. He splashed through a shallow stream, sending water flying high, soaking the edge of his garment. His breath came in short, ragged gulps. His lungs were near-to-bursting as the horses and their riders gained on him.

He glanced behind him again. One of the men was leaning forward, his arm stretched out, dirty fingers flexed, just inches from Dylan's face. Another minute, and they'd have him.

In that instant, Dylan saw a dark opening in the brush. Could he make it? The man's hand caught his shoulder and the boy stumbled. In a last burst of speed, Dylan's long legs pushed him forward into the unknown...

He'd tumbled straight into Hekate Athelred's keeping. And it was here he'd stayed. It took many months, but he'd healed from the physical shock of the murders of his loved ones, of Maere's kidnapping, of his own near brush with death. Thanks to Kate's curatives and wisdom.

Then Kate began to teach him about magic. And he'd listened and learned while she explained to him the various levels of power, their rewards, and their dangers. She always insisted on telling him the bad along with the good. What was burned most clearly into his memory, though, was when she woke him from a nightmare the night after his escape and rocked him back and forth as he poured out his grief. Once he had calmed down, she held his face in her hands, and gently wiped his tear-streaked face. The wisdom in her eyes wrapped itself around him like a healing balm. "The magic is strong in you, Dylan mac Connell," Kate whispered. "It sings in your blood. In your soul. It fills you with strength. Remember this always: True magic comes from within. If you possess it with honor, no one can take it away from you, no matter how hard they may try."

Dylan blinked back the moisture forming in his eyes and poured himself a cup of water from the pitcher on the table. He would miss this place terribly. He looked around the room, impressing every detail on his mind. The small window beside the kitchen cupboard outlined with the flowering vines he himself had painted for his mentor. She had been more than that. Kate had been his mother, too. His gaze landed on her. Finished with the herbs, she now sat on the rocking chair next to the stone hearth. She was adding the final scrap of cloth to the patchwork quilt she'd been working on for the past fortnight. He cleared his throat. "It's time I left."

"I know," she said without looking up.

It wasn't like her to be taciturn. He'd decided long ago that there must be something inside of him that attracted boisterous instructors. First there had been Maere's father, Manfred cu Llwyr, with his booming voice and jovial nature, Kate with her raspy laugh when he'd mastered some new element of magic or her quick shriek and a swat to the ear when he didn't. He smiled slightly when, in his mind's eye, he saw her that first day shaking a finger in his face, telling him to be quiet so she could talk.

He learned back then that Kate had promised Manfred to watch over Dylan and Maere in case anything happened to Dylan's father or himself. Unfortunately, she had not made it in time to rescue Maere as well, but she had kept Dylan safe in those first few years when he was still a boy and vulnerable.

And, as a boy, he'd believed Morrigu watched over him. Now, though, he knew the truth. It had always been Kate. Kate had taught him everything she knew and he'd been a good student, learning to commune with the trees and command knowledge from them.

He sighed and moved to the chair across from her. If he didn't embark on his quest to get Maere and plan for vengeance against Eugis cu Llwyr, he might not make it in time. After Morrigu had given him the knowledge she had also given her blessing. Not that her blessing mattered to him as much as Kate's did. Dylan leaned forward and rested his elbows on the table. "Tell me. How did you know?"

Kate waved his question away and folded up the quilt, setting it on the table next to her. "Be careful of Morrigu. She may be an eternal beauty, but she is still a goddess whose notions change with the wind."

He blushed under the whiskers he'd yet to scrape off. It hadn't been quite an hour since he'd been with Morrigu. His cheeks burned brighter as he thought of the intimacies they'd shared.

"You must think clearly as you begin your journey to find Maere. Do not dwell on thoughts of the flesh, especially when it comes to *that* one."

Dylan knew Kate honored the goddess, but he also knew she'd had her issues with Morrigu in the past.

"She gave me her blessing to seek my revenge against Eugis."

"Is that what you want from this lifetime?" Kate shook her head. A long strand of gray hair fell out of its bun and touched her wrinkled cheek. "No wonder Morrigu sought you. Though she can be a loving goddess, she feeds on war and hatred. Why do you think she took you and taught you the ways of the flesh when you passed eighteen summers? Let this need for revenge go. Invite the light into your spirit." She tilted her head and her eyes met his. "You yourself have seen how dangerous the lure of evil is."

He jumped to his feet and roughly shoved his chair against the table. "We've had this discussion more times than I can count, Kate." He ran a hand through his black hair and turned his back to her. "Why do you think I was spared that night? Why do you think I survived Eugis's evil plot? So I could live a quiet life and pretend I never saw the agony in my father's eyes and in the eyes of Manfred and Rhea as they were slaughtered?" He spun back around. "Was I spared so I could simply forget Maere as she screamed for me—as Eugis dragged her off? He slammed his fist into his palm. "I tell you, Kate, this is something I will do. Something I *must* do."

Kate bowed her head for a moment then looked up at him again. "I won't fight with you, Dylan. You're a grown man. I believe I've taught you well, in spite of your temper." She gestured toward his room. "Go on, son, and pack your things."

Dylan nodded, then made his way to the rear of the cottage and pushed back the long curtain that served as the door to his room. Walking over to his desk, he straightened the parchments into a neat pile and checked the ink stoppers to be certain they were stuck tightly in the jars. He crouched down and pulled a rough linen sack from under the mattress.

He opened the bag and began stuffing his clothing into it when he saw a flash of white. He tipped the bag upside down. A length of cloth with a gold-and-garnet brooch pinned to it came tumbling out. He slowly picked it up. Tears gathered in his dark eyes again as he buried his face in the fabric, the agony of losing Maere renewed.

He took a deep breath then stuffed it back into the sack, followed by a tunic, two pairs of stockings, a pair of sandals, and the parchments. When he had gathered everything he owned, he stood and wrapped his mantle over his shoulder.

Dylan took one last look around the room, his room. How was he ever going to repay Kate for everything she'd done for him? She'd taken in a sorry boy and helped him grow into a man. He went to his desk and pulled out a parchment, one he'd been working on for many nights now. He hadn't realized until now that it would become his farewell gift to this wise and kind woman. He picked the sack up and left the room.

"Kate? I have a gift for you."

"I love presents." The old woman clapped her wrinkled and work worn hands. "What is it?"

"You are an impatient one, aren't you?" Dylan said, with a smile. He placed the manuscript on the table in front of her.

"Oh, Dylan. Your work is the most beautiful I've ever seen. It's full of grace and meaning." She pointed at the inked and painted interlacings of colorful animals devouring each other as they traveled around the page. In the center was a raven, its head held high, as if it dared anyone to challenge it. "It is as though the goddess herself guided your hand as you drew."

He shrugged. "I suppose, but I didn't know it at the time I was painting. I tell you, Kate, the images come to my mind and I have to draw them. I've tried to ignore them, but they threaten to drive me to madness if I do."

Kate nodded, her pale eyes glittering. "I understand. It's part of your gift." She gently placed the parchment on the table then looked up at Dylan. "I have something for you as well." She smiled as she handed him the thick colorful quilt.

"Ah, Kate, I am honored. It's a beautiful blanket."

"It will keep you warm on those cold nights on the trail. And when you rescue Maere, you can wrap her in this blanket and know that there is magic and goodness watching over you both.

Dylan smiled for a moment, then grew serious. "I've seen Maere, in my dreams. Some nights, I send my spirit to her dream world, but I never knew where she was until Morrigu revealed the truth to me. She's living at St. Columba's Abbey in Glastonbury. It's only a week's walk from here."

His teacher smiled proudly. "Good work." She poked him in the center of the chest with her finger. "I'd wish you luck, but I want you to remember we make our own luck."

Dylan leaned down and wrapped his arms around Kate. After a few moments, he pulled back. Avoiding the old woman's keen gaze, he made a point of checking his sack to make sure he had everything he needed. If he did look at her, he would surely weep like a little boy. Clearing his throat, he stuffed the blanket into the bag and tossed it over his shoulder. He walked to the door and reached for the latch, then turned back around to face her. "To say thank you is not nearly enough," he whispered.

"Yes, it is. I know what's in your heart. You've been like a son to me and I'll always be thankful for the time we've had together." Kate clasped her hands in front of her. "I've a last bit 'o wisdom for you. though, Dylan mac Connall. You've been hidden away in the woods for a good many years. Your magic is untested. At nearly twenty-two winters you may think you know everything, but you don't. Don't forget: You *are* mortal."

With a nod, he turned to leave.

Sweet Danu, I know.

If he had been anything but mortal, he'd have been able to prevent those tragic deaths. He'd have had magic enough to pummel Eugis into the ground and rescue those he loved.

Would he have enough magic now? Dylan set his mouth in a firm line as he gazed out past the trees and east toward the horizon, toward Glastonbury.

Only time would tell.

CHAPTER FIVE

Maere sat in bed, her head resting against the whitewashed wall, the Gospel of St. Mark spread across her lap. She stared at the ceiling as if she would find relief from the evil plaguing her in the uncomplicated criss-cross of hewn wood. The exposed timber rafters slanted high and disappeared into the flat boards and rushes which formed the roof of her small room. There were times she wanted to follow them and disappear as well.

A slight draft crept in from under the door and the candle on the bedside table flickered, sending elongated shadows dancing across the walls. An even stronger draft blew in through cracks in the window shutters. The flame sputtered, then grew strong again. Maere gently closed the precious volume—only one of two copies the convent owned—and placed it on the table. Where was Seelie? The girl should have been back by now.

Maere leaned forward and pulled her woolen shawl up and around her shoulders. Why in heaven's name had she let the girl talk her into such foolishness? She never should have agreed to lie. Seelie shouldn't be cavorting around at night. And especially not with a monk! What would become of her soul? Not to mention Maere's own soul for lying.

The worry ate at her insides and made her head hurt. She picked up a cup of water from the table and took a sip. A sound from outside startled her, making her spill the water onto her nightgown. Her ears pricked up, setting all her senses on edge. A muffled scratching was coming from outside the window.

Maere's first thought was to investigate, but she hesitated when a second thought entered her mind. What if it was *him*—the Devil himself—come to claim her for helping Seelie lie? Then she heard the noise again, followed by a woman's voice, weak and barely discernible.

"Maere?" A pause. "Maere?"

She dropped her shawl and hurried to the shutters. She pulled them open and peered outside. There was no moon to light the grounds and she strained her eyes to see with what feeble light the candle could offer. There, huddled in a tight ball under the window, was Seelie. Maere reached out her hand to her friend. Gingerly, Seelie stood and leaned through the open window into the room. With Maere's help, she made it through the opening, falling to the floor once inside.

"Sweet Mother," Maere cried. Seelie's habit was torn and covered with dirt. Her eyes were angry purple bruises, almost swollen shut. Blood seeped through her clothing, staining the lower half of her habit. Maere dropped to her knees, frantic. "Seelie! Who did this to you?"

Seelie turned her eyes away and stared blankly at the wall, whimpering. Her breathing was fast and shallow, her skin clammy.

"I'll go for help."

With a firm grip that belied her condition, Seelie grabbed Maere's arm. "No," she whispered. "They can't know. I don't want them to know."

Maere's eyes moved frantically over her friend. Seelie's face was growing paler and paler as the blood continued to flow bright red. How was she going to make it stop? And why wouldn't Seelie say who had attacked her? Oh God, no, she thought, as her entire being filled with horror. "It was the monk, wasn't it?"

"I had no idea," Seelie murmured. "No idea at all." Her eyes fluttered, then closed. "He was so handsome."

"Handsome? That's all you can say?" Maere raged, her voice low. She waved her hand. "He's all but killed you, girl, and you can only talk about how handsome he is?"

"It was my fault. I shouldn't have tempted him." Seelie let out a ragged sigh. "He told me I was an evil woman to lure him away from the monastery and I should be punished. I should have left when I had the chance. Before—" Seelie began to sob.

"Oh, Seelie. Is that what he told you?" Maere asked, incredulous.

"You're not evil." Maere's whole body shook and she looked up, fighting to control the anger roiling inside of her. She wanted to run out into the night and find him. She wanted to show the others what he'd done to her friend. She wanted to see him punished for the deed. Maere swallowed back the bitter taste for vengeance that threatened to shatter her composure. She must tend to her friend right now. There'd be time enough later to deal with the man.

"Maere?"

"Aye?"

"I can't feel my body." Seelie coughed, hard. Bright red blood trickled down her lips, staining them the color of summer berries. "I fear he's killed me." As the words tumbled out of her mouth, Seelie's head rolled to one side. Her eyes lost their focus and went blank.

"Seelie?" Maere gently shook her. "Seelie?"

Seelie's eyes remained blank.

"Dear Lord, no," Maere whispered. She leaned back on her heels and, in that moment – as rage and anger like she'd never known washed over her – something broke loose inside of her. She clutched her stomach as it crackled fiery hot inside her belly. She jerked when it traveled down the length of her legs, up her spine, and out to her hands. It reached her brain and flashed brightly in her mind's eye, blinding her for an instant. The top of her head tingled and hurt and her hands burned.

Instinctively, Maere reached for Seelie and clasped her friend to her breast. She placed one hand over the young woman's eyes, another on her friend's belly. The space around them glowed green, then white. A strong breeze which seemed to come from the very center of the room whipped the bed linens. The candle fell over and burned itself out. Bursts of light shot out of Maere's fingertips and into Seelie's body. The jolt lifted them both from the floor. Another burst. Another jolt. A loud sucking sound filled the small cell. Seelie's mouth fell open and the light entered her, leaving the room dark.

Seelie stirred and slowly raised a hand to her head. "M-Maere?" she whispered.

Maere jumped, startled out of the light trance she'd fallen into. She studied Seelie's face. The bruises had vanished. She looked at the floor.

The blood was gone. Seelie's torn habit was the only evidence of the ordeal. Maere's hand flew to her mouth. Sweet Jesus! What had happened?

What have I done?

Before Maere could even begin to think, a loud knock sounded at her door. She quickly grabbed a blanket from the bed and tossed it over Seelie. The door to the cell flew open. Abbess Magrethe, followed by several other sisters, pushed their way in. "We heard a terrible noise and saw a bright light coming from under the door." She looked around the small room. "What's been going on in here?"

"If I only knew, dear Mother," Maere murmured. Her face felt so hot and feverish. "I swear I would be most happy to tell you."

The abbess stared at the younger woman. "I beg your pardon?"

"What I meant to say was—" Maere glanced around the room. "Seelie here, she tripped and fell when we were studying. She knocked herself out and is just now coming to." She took in the candle on its side. What was becoming of her? The lies were beginning to flow so easily. "The light you saw must have been from the candle when she knocked it over." Maere stood and pulled her friend to her feet, careful to keep the blanket tight about her, lest they see the damaged clothing. Maere gave Seelie over to the care of Sister Jane, who helped the novitiate out of the room. The other sisters followed. Except Magrethe.

She circled Maere, considering her. With a practiced eye, she again looked around the cell. "True, the candle is lying on its side." She righted it and relit the wick with the candle she was carrying. She touched the spilled beeswax and it stuck to her finger. She turned to face Maere. "I'm going to ask you a simple question. I expect an honest answer.

Maere bobbed her head. "Of course, Mother."

"Have you been practicing magic?"

Maere's eyes widened. She stumbled back a step as her knees threatened to buckle. "N-no. Never. Why would you ask me such a thing?"

Magrethe sat on the edge of the narrow cot and patted the spot next to her. "Sit by me." Maere complied. "The signs are here, girl. I've seen it before, the lure of the Devil. His empty promises catch the eye of a young novitiate. She seeks to strike a bargain for power and the Devil is all too happy to assist." Magrethe shrugged her slender shoulders and shook her head. "Often, it's nothing more than idle curiosity." She glanced at her charge. "Given your heritage, I simply had to inquire."

"My heritage?" Maere asked. "What of my heritage? What haven't you told me, Mother? Is there something about my mother and father that I should know? Is it because I am Keltoi?"

"Too many questions for this late hour." Magrethe's blue eyes darted back and forth. "Besides, there's no need to delve into the past, girl."

"But I truly want to know," Maere said softly. "Perhaps if you told me everything you know it would help me to remember."

"You've been told of the Vikings who murdered your mother and father. And you know your kin were of the Keltoi tribe Dumnonii, that they practiced the old religion." Magrethe stood. "We've discussed their heathen ways, and how your fine Uncle Eugis brought you here to us so you could be raised a Christian."

Maere started to speak, but the abbess raised a hand, her mouth set. "I will not discuss it further. As I said, none of it is important anymore. You know what you need to know. What matters is that you've grown into a fine God-fearing woman. Now, I'll ask you again to tell me. What really happened here tonight?"

Maere swallowed the ache in her throat, forcing down the other questions she wanted to ask. It would do no good to push the abbess any further. Despite her diminutive size, she was a strong stubborn woman who rarely, if ever, budged after making up her mind. "I've already told you, Mother." She fidgeted with the sleeve of her gown, then focused her eyes on the dark silhouette of the tree line beyond her window. "Seelie fell."

"Well, then." Magrethe slowly let her breath out. "It's late. I won't bother you about it anymore tonight." She turned to leave the room.

When she reached the door, Maere called out to her. "Mother? The things you said last night about the Devil and my dreams have been on my mind." The image of Seelie's still form, covered in blood, flashed before her eyes. She blinked and looked at the abbess. The surge of power that had shot through her body was still vibrating within her. "I think it might be best if I did enter into a fast and meditation. Perhaps the Blessed Virgin can help me through my nightmares."

"I'm most happy to hear you say that," Magrethe said with a smile. "Fasting and meditation are the gateway to truth." She folded her hands in front of her.

"I think I should enter an anchorite for a short time," Maere said with a shuddering breath.

Magrethe took a step forward. "Now, Maere, have you thought long and hard about this? Locking yourself away in a stone hovel is an extremely hard cross to bear, especially for one as young as yourself. Are you prepared to take such a drastic step?"

As she considered Magrethe's words, Maere thought about everything she'd seen lately. Her mind filled with the image of a dark man with glowing eyes, rising from the mist. He disappeared and was replaced with the sight of Seelie, first bloody and dead, then suddenly brought back to life with a touch of her hand. And there was the fire she always dreamed of, as tall as a man, hungry and devouring everything in its wake. She shook off the visions. God knew what she needed most now was time to think and pray, time to sort out what was happening to her.

"I'll only stay for a month. Certainly, an answer can be found by then." A cold chill ran up her spine. "And the Lord will surely protect me in my hour of need." She was filled with a sudden foreboding. She looked at the abbess again, tears forming in her eyes. "Won't He?"

Magrethe smiled and nodded. "Of course, He will." She turned and quietly closed the door behind her.

Maere walked to the window and, with only a quick look outside, snapped the shutters closed. With a click, the iron latch fell into place. She sat on her flat straw mattress and stared into the candle flame. Then her attention was drawn to the place the stub had fallen earlier. Maere reached out and ran her fingertip over the now-hardened beeswax. A raised figure had been left there—the likeness of a raven in flight.

CHAPTER SIX

Following the morning meal, the residents of the abbey gathered behind the large sisterhouse, close to the wide stone wall protecting the grounds. Here, nine hermitess dwellings stood. The homes were small, constructed of large flat rocks laid at right angles to each other to form the sides. The roofs, made of timber and thatch, were so low it was impossible for any but the shortest woman to stand upright once inside.

Aged women who, upon their husband's deaths, had chosen to enter into a life of prayer and contemplation now occupied seven of the anchorages. Most had been there for several years and had never once left the small hovels. Not to bathe, not for bad weather, nor to meet with visiting relatives. Not even for illness, no matter how life-threatening. Every day, one of the sisters tended their needs, bringing water and food.

In exchange for the opportunity to pray ceaselessly and offer consultation to pilgrims, the anchoresses had each bequeathed to the convent all their worldly goods. It was a special honor to have these holy women stay with the sisters. The greatness of an abbey was partly measured by the number of anchorites it attracted.

Maere stood quietly outside the small building which was to be her home for the next month. One-by-one the sisters and novitiates, their arms laden with simple gifts and necessities, gathered to bid a temporary farewell to their friend. Though some might still speak with her on a limited basis, touching or eye contact was strictly forbidden during the time she would be ensconced here.

Sister Joan presented a thick woolen blanket she'd woven from the convent's supply of shearling. "I know it's spring, but the nights will still be chilly afore you join us again," she said. Maere smiled and the elderly nun patted her on the cheek. "Good luck to you," Joan whispered. "I'll be praying for your soul."

Other sisters followed with presents of dried apples, herbs, and more blankets. Maere humbly accepted their offerings. She glanced up as the line drew to an end. Seelie stood a few feet away in a patch of wildflowers. Her blonde hair was neatly braided and shining nearly white in the morning sun. Her cheeks were pink and glowing. Seelie rushed to her friend's side as the last sister walked away.

"Are you feeling well today?" Maere asked as she took her friend's hands into her own. She studied Seelie's face. There was absolutely no sign of the battered and abused young woman she'd seen only last night. Had she dreamed everything? Did her friend's injuries exist only in her imagination?

"Aye. Very well indeed."

"Do you remember what happened?" Maere asked, her voice low. Could Seelie's mind have forgotten the horror as easily as her body had?

Seelie nodded, her expression serious. "Enough to know I won't be behaving the same way again. I don't know what you did, girl, but I feel as if the face of God has looked on me and put my soul to rest." She smiled, her eyes aglow. "It's a miracle, it is. I feel as if the cares of the world are gone from my mind."

Maere hugged her tightly. When she released her, they both had tears in their eyes. "I don't have any idea what happened last night in my room, but I can't say I'm sorry it did." She gestured toward the anchorage. "My hope is I'll discover the meaning of what transpired while I'm in there."

Seelie nodded. She bent down, picked up a small basket of yellow flowers and handed them to Maere. "I'll keep you in my prayers. And don't fret. Just as you promised to protect me, I'll protect you. No one will ever know."

"Thank you," Maere said, relief washing over her. "If anyone should find out, I'd be beaten for certain. And who knows what else."

She turned to face the small building and took a deep breath. It was time she entered and begin her period of meditation. She dropped to her hands and knees as the entry was low and could only be accessed by crawling on one's elbows. Maere pushed the gifts into the opening, gave the world behind her one last look, then crawled into the passage.

Once inside, she stood, and hit her head on the ceiling. With a grimace, Maere leaned slightly forward and rubbed the sore spot. She wasn't as tall as some and still the anchorage ceiling was too low for her to stand straight.

Still rubbing her head, Maere looked about. The room was completely bare except for an uncomfortable-looking straw mattress covered in homespun, a spindly wooden chair, a waste bucket, and the items she'd brought with her. To her left was a narrow window carved into the thick plaster-coated and whitewashed wall. A black wool curtain, embroidered with a white cross on both sides, hung loosely over it.

As she was looking about, someone passed by, casting a shadow through a small hole in the fabric. Maere jumped. She didn't expect anyone to come so soon. She waited near the window for the person to begin talking, as it was improper for the anchorite to start a conversation. It was the duty of the one seeking advice to initiate the contact.

"Maere? It's Abbess Magrethe."

"Yes, Mother?"

"I wanted to tell you to have faith. I'm most certain the Lord will guide you in this endeavor."

"Thank you, Mother," Maere said. "I will not lose heart." She watched as the shadow moved away without replying, then went to the task of arranging her belongings.

The room was barely large enough for the meager items that served as furnishings, let alone for what she'd brought with her. Maere lightly tested the seat of the chair with her fingers and a spider climbed out of the middle of the woven rushes. It moved slowly, as if awakened from a long nap. She cautiously touched the seat again and the insect sprung to life. Its long legs darted in front of it and it rounded the back of the chair in no time, disappearing from sight.

Maere frowned. "Well, Sir Spider, I suppose I'll be looking before sitting from now on." She bent to retrieve the rough homespun sack with her belongings and emptied the contents onto the mattress. From the bag, she gently removed the tiny wooden cross she'd made shortly after arriving at the convent. She ran her fingertips over the dark wood, the knife marks of her carving still evident. Abbess Magrethe had suggested she make it as an exercise to focus her mind. Busy hands, happy heart, she repeated again and again.

But Maere's heart had been anything but happy. Eight winters old she was when she'd first arrived. She didn't remember anything about those first dark months at the abbey. Magrethe had told her she'd cried and cried and then slept and slept and finally had awoken. It would take many more months before she even spoke a word. And then one morning Magrethe took her out for a walk in the spring sunshine and a butterfly landed on Maere's hand, making her smile. The abbess had told her it was the very first time she'd seen her smile in since her arrival, and a lovely one it was.

Maere clutched the cross in her hand, her eyes blurred with tears. That simple act of making the cross served to rescue a little girl from a sadness so deep it had threatened to drown her.

Maere tried over and over since then to make peace with the fact she might never remember the cause of that deep sadness. Even now, it still appeared from time to time. During those rare moments when her mind wasn't occupied with prayer or her hands with chores, it would creep in from the edges of her memory. As water followed the moon, so did melancholy follow an idle mind.

She took a deep breath and carefully hung the cross on a peg pinned into the stone over the mattress. She tilted it first this way, then that, adjusting until it hung just right.

On the peg next to it, Maere looped the necklace she'd somehow managed to keep all these years. Magrethe tried to take it from her that first day, whispering something about pagan relics and the ungodly ways of the Dumnonii. Maere always wondered if she was one of these people. She'd heard enough whispers among the sisters to believe she must be. But like the night before, the abbess was loath to answer detailed questions.

Despite Magrethe's efforts, Maere was able to keep possession of the only reminder of her life before entering St. Columba's. She had no idea what the circular citrine stone looped on a leather thong meant.

The only tangible link to her past, she often wondered if it was a gift from her parents. Or perhaps it was something she'd made herself as a child? She sighed. All Maere knew for certain was it gave her comfort when she was distressed and reminded her she once had a mother and a father.

Putting away the rest of her things, she stretched out on the mattress. "Saint Jude Thaddeus, dear patron of lost causes, is there any hope left for me?"

She hoped there was. Weary from the day, she closed her eyes and let sleep take her.

MAERE AWOKE LONG after the sun had set. She stood and walked to the window. Dare she? She wondered for only a moment before venturing a peek outside. A sliver of the waxing moon appeared high in the night sky, surrounded by a thick smattering of stars. It was late and the sisters would be in bed, fast asleep, waiting for the bell to ring time for prayers.

She pulled the curtain closed along its smooth wood rod. Now what? She was no longer tired. She paced for a bit, then decided she should pray. Tugging at her habit, she knelt in the center of the room and made the sign of the cross over her breast. She pressed her black wooden prayer beads to her lips.

"Our Father, which art in heaven." She stopped. A formal prayer didn't seem appropriate. She needed to say exactly what she was thinking. It might not be the polite thing to do, where God was concerned, but Maere was determined to find the hidden meanings of her distress. She decided to pray to the Blessed Virgin to intercede on her behalf.

She raised her eyes to heaven. "Forgive me, Mother, for addressing you so informally. I don't know what to tell you first. I only know that for some reason, I'm suddenly frightened by everything." She looked down. "Well, maybe not so suddenly. We both know I've always been overly nervous about the silliest things." She looked to Heaven once again. "But I tell you, this time it's different. It's as if the Devil himself is after me." She shook her head. "I just don't know what to do about this affliction…"

She sat quietly and hoped for some sort of sign. Her eyes focused on the wall in front of her. An image flashed in her mind. Maere blinked. It came back even stronger. She tried to clear her mind again, but this time the picture stayed. She watched, transfixed, as the scene unfolded as if it were projected onto the wall and not of her mind…

A tall thin man in flowing white robes was riding a pale gray horse. She squinted. There was something familiar about him, although he wasn't the same red-eyed demon who usually haunted her nights. This was someone, or something, else. He was riding hard, sweat flying from his brow like a shower of rain. He rode first in one direction, then pulled his horse around and rode in another, as if he were searching for something. Something he'd lost and couldn't remember how to find.

"Dear Mother, what is happening?" she whispered, unable to tear her eyes from the sight. Tears streamed down her cheeks.

The man rode closer and closer, until his face was clearly revealed. He had bobbed gray hair and dark eyes, which seemed to pierce through the night. His gaze scanned the countryside, before turning on her. Then he laughed, the sound seeming to fill the anchorage, though Maere knew it was only inside her head.

"There you are, Maere cu Llwyr. Have you missed me?" His voice was nothing more than a soft hiss. "Don't worry. I'll be there for you soon."

Maere closed her eyes tightly and covered them with her fists. She began to sob as the face dissolved from sight. "Oh dear God, am I going mad? What evil is this that haunts me?" She fell forward, prostrate on the compacted dirt floor, her body shaking as she cried uncontrollably. "I beg you, Mother so blessed. Please. Please. Intercede for me. Have mercy on my immortal soul."

CHAPTER SEVEN

Dylan looked out into the distance as he walked, taking note of a pillar of smoke rising from the next hillock beyond his vision. It twisted and drifted on the wind, suddenly filling the air with the stench of burning animal flesh. A noise up the road sent him a few steps into the tree line. The fire meant one of two things: Either the farmer had diseased livestock, or those Norse scavengers had been through here recently.

The sound of clopping horse's hooves, mixed with intermittent curses, reached Dylan's ears and he quickly stepped deeper into the cover of the forest. He watched in stunned silence as a group of Vikings rode by, dragging prisoners behind them. A few older men, a young woman, and several children were joined with ropes tied from wrist-to-wrist, the lead held tight by one of the riders. They came from the direction he was headed.

His heart froze in his chest. Had the abbey been raided? There was no way to know, but he wouldn't see his journey to Maere delayed even a moment longer. The strong oaks and pliable willows parted their branches as he entered their shared world, dipping low and brushing away his footprints as he passed. A chance encounter with anyone could prove a problem that would serve to keep him from his betrothed. And ten years had been long enough to wait.

Truth be told, if any Vikings came upon him, they probably wouldn't be interested, a lone poor traveler that he was. He had nothing to steal, but there was always the chance he might be taken as a slave. Or he might meet pious pilgrims on a journey of faith, much too eager in their zeal to convert him to the new religion. Dylan snorted. This Christianity was surely a scourge on the land just as powerful as those raiders from the north.

It baffled him his countrymen could lose the faith of their forebears so easily, could come to believe one god was able to care for this entire world. As vast as it was, it was obviously too large an endeavor for one deity. The old ways made much more sense to Dylan, with a particular god or goddess assigned to a specific duty. At least then one knew whom to pray to, whom to ask for what you needed.

Dylan leaned against a tall willow, its long thin branches dusting the forest floor around him. He closed his eyes. *I must focus on Maere.* It was the beginning of her eighteenth year and Eugis would be on his way to retrieve her. Ripe she'd be for the taking, and her uncle wouldn't hesitate, intent on ripping her power from her.

Keltoi legends spoke of a girl born under the triple signs of the goddess, a girl who would carry with her the great power of healing. And Dylan had been there to see the signs with his very own eyes, that cold night so long ago, when Manfred held Maere out to him.

Dylan touched the willow and smiled, remembering how she hunted the fays, those little people of the hills and woods, intent on catching a glimpse of their small forms. It seemed an entire lifetime had come and gone since they'd played in the forest as children. Full of mischief she had been, much like those same fays she sought…

"*Psst!*" *Maere had half whispered, half shouted for him.* "*Dylan!*

He could still hear her—see her as if from far away —as she waved one hand behind her, beckoning him, the other shading her bright green eyes. The dapples of sunlight littering the forest floor had found their way through the thick foliage and straight to her. She dropped her hand and shifted over a few feet.

She'd always hated the bright light, he remembered. She'd come to believe the sun goddess was out to make her life miserable. Dylan laughed in spite of himself as that day came to life before him.

Maere glanced cautiously out of the corner of her eye at the rays, praying to the moon goddess for protection. "*Please, Nimue, keep Bel at bay,*" *she pleaded quietly under her breath.*

She again called impatiently to her friend. "Come h – e – e – e – r – r – r – r – e."

Dylan carefully picked his way along the path Maere had made through the damp underbrush, his awkward feet stepping as lightly as they could over the fallen branches. "What is it?" he demanded, lowering his voice when she raised a finger to her lips. "I was practicing my recitations when you called. And if I don't have my new verses memorized for tomorrow night's Beltane feast, your father will have my hide." He rubbed his behind and chuckled. "What little I have left."

"Shhh! Keep your voice down!" Maere whispered. "Oh, please, Dylan. They'll hear you!"

"Who'll hear me?" he asked, dropping to his knees. He scooped up a handful of pebbles and looked around. "I see no one, Maere." He let them sift slowly out of his hand and they formed a small pile on the ground.

She pointed directly in front of her friend. Tall willow trees, their thin yellow-green branches trailing low on the ground, surrounded a small clearing. Wildflowers of white and purple were just beginning to bloom and dotted a smaller circle in the middle of the trees. Maere rubbed her hands together, barely able to contain her excitement at the find. "They will."

Dylan leaned over, his cheek almost touching hers. "Move it, you." He pushed her out of the way to get a better look. A blackbird jumped from one of the willows to a hawthorn growing nearby. It snatched a dark red berry then flew off. Dylan tugged impatiently at his brown tunic, then leaned back on his heels, hands on his knees. He gestured toward the spot. "You called me all the way over here to see a silly bird?"

"Of course not!" She pushed him back and looked at the clearing again. She studied the base of the trees and the circle of flowers from where she sat. Finally, Maere stood and shook the green moss off her skirt. "Well, that's just fine, it is." She leaned over Dylan and pointed a finger in his face. "You scared 'em, you foolish, noisy boy. No wonder they ran and hid. Why, I heard you comin' myself when you were still half a mile away." She snorted. "A fine priest you'll make. How are you goin' to cast secret ceremonies when everyone'll know where you are just by the sound of your big silly feet?"

Dylan squared his shoulders and raised his chin. "I am not a boy. I've lived through almost twelve winters."

45

Maere stuck out her tongue and rolled her eyes. "A wee babe, you are. I'm surprised you're not cryin' for your Da."

It was Dylan's turn to stick out his tongue. He then crossed his arms over his chest, a burst of maturity overcoming him, and considered the girl coolly. "As usual, Maere, I have no idea what you're talking about." He looked back at the clearing. "Just who, or what, have I scared off?"

Maere spun around and eyed him. In a fury, she rammed her shoulder into Dylan and shoved him backward as hard as she could. His gangly legs shot out from underneath him and he hit the ground with a yelp. He slowly pushed himself up on his haunches and rubbed his backside, groaning. "What'd you do that for?"

Maere stood over him, hands on her hips. She wrinkled her freckled nose and looked down. "For frightenin' the fays, that's why. They were gatherin' toadstools, for dinner no doubt, and you shooed them away." She sighed, wistful. "Why, I believe I even saw the queen herself there, with her long golden hair a-flowin' behind her." She lifted her own bright coppery tresses up over her head and let them float down.

Dylan scrambled to his feet. "I shooed them away? You were the one hollering for me to come see what you'd found."

"Doesn't matter," she sniffed. "If you were the least bit concerned, you'd have come a whole lot quicker and been a whole lot quieter." With a flip of her skirt, she turned and stomped away.

"Fays, indeed," Dylan said, half-aloud. "Well, I've never seen one!" he shouted after her. "I think you made it up, I do!"

Maere shot him a look over her shoulder, her eyes narrowed. Without a word, she continued to walk toward home…

The woodsy chiming of wind-rustled leaves brought Dylan back to the present. Would Maere be the same girl he'd known? Full of fire and life—a force of nature—she was. When she made up her mind, there was no stopping Maere cu Llwyr. Or had the sisters of the abbey forced the spirit out of her, made her docile and tame? The Maere he knew wouldn't let anyone or anything change her or her mind. Eugis had tried, threatening beatings if she didn't do as he'd said. Manfred had always stepped in, though, and protected his daughter from his twin brother. Now it was Dylan's turn to watch over her and protect her as he had promised.

He swiped at his eyes. There had been so much friction between Eugis and Manfred back when he and Maere were young. Intent on the events surrounding Maere's birth and the belief she was blessed, Eugis demanded Manfred betroth him to the girl. Ignoring his brother's desperate bid for more power than was already afforded him as a Dyrrwed high priest, Manfred instead betrothed her to Dylan during the Beltane celebration. The very same night Manfred and Rhea and Fox were murdered.

While Dylan knew in his mind there was nothing he could have done to prevent the slaughter, his heart told him otherwise. And so he'd grown into a man, his entire being intent on taking back what was stolen from him. He'd not let Eugis win this time. He *would* marry Maere before her uncle had the chance.

He shook off the thoughts of the past. It would do no good now to ponder what might have been. The day had moved into night and tomorrow would see him at the abbey. Dylan pulled a blanket from his pack and spread it on the ground, on the soft leaf-littered floor surrounding the tree. Lying down, he wrapped the wool cloth around his shoulders and consciously forced his body to relax.

Dylan took a deep breath and let it out slowly. Another deep breath and he searched his mind. Where was she? Another breath and he moved deeper into a trance. Yes. His spirit found hers. She was asleep. He inhaled again and, as he exhaled, he sent his essence to Maere, sent his spirit to her dreams.

MAERE SLEPT PEACEFULLY on the narrow anchorage cot, her chest gently rising and falling. She sighed and rolled from her side to her back. A thin ray of moonlight found its way through the window, carried in on the cool night breeze as it pushed and tugged at the curtain.

She sighed again, her full lips parted. A voice entered her dream. *I've missed you.* And in an instant, she was in the forest, near a gentle splashing stream. She kicked the covers away, falling deeper into the dream.

She knelt at the water's edge and looked at her reflection. Her long copper hair fell over her shoulders and danced on the liquid surface. The perfume of night flowers filled the air around her. A dragonfly darted by. Maere held out her hand and it landed on her palm.

Sensing another's presence, she looked beyond her hand. There, at the forest edge, was the shadowy form of a man. He held his arms out to her.

Maere stood. "Come to me," he whispered. And she went to his open arms eagerly, without hesitation. He held her close, stroking her cheek, murmuring words in the old language of the emerald hills that were her home. She inhaled his woodsy scent. No, she thought. *This* was her home. *Here.* With *him.*

Slowly, Maere opened her eyes. She laid still, staring at the ceiling. Tears streamed down her cheeks. Who was he, this man? The Devil in disguise? Her breathing quickened. She heard Abbess Magrethe's words, the Devil comes in many forms. What did it say about her that she felt so comfortable with him?

She was evil, she was, seeking the arms of Lucifer. Maere could find no other explanation as she lay there sobbing.

CHAPTER EIGHT

"Greetings. Is there an occupant within this anchorage?"

Maere stirred as the words entered her dreams and awakened her. She groaned with effort as she pushed herself to her feet. After falling asleep on the cold, hard ground, every bone and muscle in her body ached.

"Aye," she answered, her voice a raspy whisper. "I am here." She raised a water skin to her parched lips and quenched her thirst. All the crying she'd done the night before had left her throat raw and tender. She took another sip, splashed some in her hands, then over her face to soothe her sore eyes. She rose and stood near the window. The sun's rays were just beginning to cast an outline around its black covering.

"Is everything well with you? Should I fetch a sister to help?"

"Of course, I am well," Maere answered, her voice growing stronger. "Why do you ask this?"

"You sound near to death's door. You may not be seeing things all that clearly."

Maere bristled. Death's door, indeed. If he only knew what she'd been going through. Wait a moment. Her mouth fell open as she realized she was talking with a man. And not a very old one, by the sound of him.

She cautiously placed her palms flat on either side of the window and leaned forward ever so slightly. The stone wall was cool and rough beneath her hands and smelled of damp earth. She wrinkled her nose and squinted her eyes as she tried to peek past the edge of the curtain. What kind of ridiculous rule was it anyway that wouldn't let you look at the person you were speaking with? Maere pulled back, aggravated.

She couldn't see a thing. And she couldn't very well push the curtain aside. Someone would see her for certain if she did.

Maere took another drink and cleared her throat. "What do you need?" she finally asked, a little afraid of the answer. Could it be the man she saw last night? Or was it the red-eyed demon? Had he found her already?

"Ah, you sound much better now, but very young. Are you certain you're old enough to be offering consultations?"

She could hear the amusement in his voice. This curbed the fear that had begun to swell within her, quickly replacing it with annoyance. Well, lucky for him she was inside this anchorage, praying and performing charitable duties, or she'd be forced to give him a tongue lashing for sure.

"I'm only recently enclosed, but I assure you I will help in any way I can," came her reply, though she wasn't certain how she managed to be so polite. "Perhaps you could tell me who you are, Sir. What is it you seek at St. Columba's?"

"To tell the truth, I am only a poor pilgrim on my way west," he said. "West to Tintagel." There was a pause before he added, "Have you ever been there?

Something in the name of the region stirred Maere's blood. But why? Should she know of this place?

The man interrupted her thoughts. "Draw back the curtain," he bade, echoing her own desire. "I would like to see to whom I am speaking."

Maere looked sharply at the embroidered white cross. As tempted as she was to comply, she couldn't. "I'm sorry, but I cannot. It's not allowed by the law."

"By whose law?"

"It's the law of the Church. The law of God." What an odd manner of pilgrim, that he wouldn't know the proper etiquette for approaching a hermitess.

"Of which god do you speak? Anu? Lugh? Or one of the others?"

Maere took a step away from the window, her eyes wide. "I don't know what you're talking about."

The man laughed, the sound sending a chill up Maere's spine.

"How can you not know? Have these Christians cleansed your brain so thoroughly you would forget the tales of the Dumnonii?"

"I know nothing of which you speak," she insisted, close to tears. What was he saying? She was pagan? That she should know these things?

"Answer these questions for me, Anchoress. Is your hair dark copper like a chestnut horse? Are your eyes as green as the sea?" His voice grew gentle. "Do light brown freckles dance across your fine nose and high cheek bones?"

Maere put her hands over her ears. How did this man know everything about her? "Stop it! I tell you. You must leave!"

He pressed on. "Can you deny you are Maere cu Llwyr, daughter of Manfred and Rhea?" His voice was smooth, but there was no denying the strength beneath it, as if he were daring her to lie to him.

Maere's hand flew to her mouth and she stumbled against the chair, knocking it over. How could he know her name? Before she could reply, she heard the sound of feet crushing their way through dried leaves.

"Good day, Pilgrim. Is there anything I can help you with on this beautiful spring morning?" Abbess Magrethe asked.

Thank God, Maere thought, for the dear lady and her careful ways.

"No, thank you. I was just leaving. Peace to you, Anchoress. Please accept my gift." He pushed a rolled piece of parchment past the curtain. "May God have mercy on your soul."

Maere's head reeled as he spoke the words which had become a litany for her. Over and over she repeated them last night as she cried. Until, finally, she'd fallen into an exhausted, dreamless sleep. Her hand shook as she took the offering. More rattling of leaves told her he was walking away.

"Maere?" the abbess called. "Appears a good thing I thought to check on you this morn, what with already receiving your first visitor. I hope you weren't caught unawares at being approached so quickly."

She swallowed. Unawares was barely a fitting description for what she was feeling at the moment. Her insides were all in a knot and she felt feverish.

"Maere?"

"I-I'm sure I'll be fine. It's just, as you said. He did surprise me. I wasn't expecting anyone so early."

"Good day to you, then," the abbess said.

Maere stood still, firmly rooted. Her hearing keen, she listened while the older woman walked away. When she was certain the abbess was gone, she righted the chair and sat down.

Slowly, she unrolled the thin skin. Her face blanched. Her hand flew to her mouth and she cried out. The painted image of her own face stared back at her. Green eyes, dark red hair—even the freckles on her nose were there—just like he'd described to her earlier. In the background were several images: To the right, a dark-haired man, partially obscured. To the left, an older man, gray-haired, wearing a white robe. A fire burned in the foreground. Above her, the full moon, and above that, a raven's head, its wings sweeping out to serve as a frame for the entire painting. Whether the gesture was protective or possessive, Maere couldn't be certain.

She let the parchment fall out of her hand. It made a scuffing noise as it hit the floor and rolled back onto itself. She closed her eyes and leaned back wearily. She must be losing her mind. There could simply be no other explanation. What else would explain why a man— someone she'd never met—would come and give her such a drawing? And how did he know of the two men in her dreams? Two men — obviously bent on evil—whom no one else could see?

She shook her head. Of course, maybe none of it had happened. Maybe she'd imagined everything. Seelie had never been hurt or raised from the dead with a touch of her hand.

Maere laughed bitterly. None of it mattered, anyway, because one thing was obvious: The Devil had tainted her soul and meant to claim her as his own.

CHAPTER NINE

The sun peeked in through a small tear in the black curtain, then disappeared. It cast a thin ray again that struck Maere straight in the eyes. She squinted and shifted to her left a little. The sun went away only to return a few moments later. It found her again, there on her knees, and she moved back to her right. What was this cat and mouse game the light insisted on playing with her? And why did she feel there was an old animosity between her and the sun?

Maere pulled her attention back to her prayers. She'd been praying all night, ever since the strange man had visited the day before, ever since her dreams of demons and devils coming to claim her. If only she could heal herself as easily as she had healed Seelie.

There's a thought.

Perhaps she could do just that. She glanced around the anchorage. The sun seemed to have lost interest in her for the moment and was now focused on her golden citrine necklace where it hung on the wall over her mattress. Perhaps there was some logic to this healing idea? Maere sat back on her heels and rubbed her hands together. She spread the idea before her again and looked at each and every word.

If only I could heal myself.

Why hadn't the thought occurred to her before? Now, what was it she'd done when Seelie came to her?

Maere pushed her hair off her shoulder and raised her right hand. She placed it carefully over her forehead, covering her eyes. She crossed her left arm over her breast. "Heal," she whispered. She waited. Nothing happened. "Heal," she said louder this time. Nothing happened. "I said 'heal'!" She shouted so loudly she must have frightened the birds away from the tree outside her anchorage, for she could hear them take flight.

Well, that was fine. She could bring her friend back to life but couldn't dispel her own demons. She shook her head, close to tears once more. *What a mess I've gotten myself into.*

Maere pushed herself back to a kneeling position and folded her hands in front of her. It was the Moon's Day and she'd vowed to stay praying until some guidance was offered to her. She prayed long and hard, to anyone who might be able to free the pain from her soul. She prayed to Jesus and to Mary, to Saint Joseph and even to Saint Columba himself.

"Tell me, dear Lord. Whom shall I trust? Who can I turn to with the truth of what agonizes me?"

"Anchoress?" An old man's voice, as dry and without life as the dead leaves littering the abbey grounds came through the window.

Startled, Maere jumped. She didn't expect an answer quite this quickly, but if it was the Lord's will..."Yes? Who's there?" She directed her voice toward the window.

"It is Father John. I've come to hear your confession today."

Her heart filled with panic. Now faced with the possibility of revealing her innermost thoughts, she wasn't certain she was brave enough to speak out. She took a deep breath. Oh, she was a coward for certain. "I would be most happy to wait if you'd like to see to the other anchorites first," she offered sweetly. "After all, it's not as if I'm going anywhere."

The priest chuckled. "You're the last on my rounds, dear child. Come to the window that I might give you my blessing." He cleared his throat. "Together, we'll seek absolution for your sins."

For your sins.

The words echoed in her brain. What would he think of her sins once he heard them? Would he be able to forgive her in the name of God? Slowly, she rose, her knees stiff, and approached the window. She straightened the brown wool tunic she wore as she walked. "I am here."

"May almighty God bless you in the name of the Father, the Son, and the Holy Ghost," Father John said.

As he spoke, Maere made the sign of the cross, touching first her forehead, followed by the center of her chest, her left shoulder, then her right shoulder. She replied, "Amen," as he finished, then added, "Forgive me my sins, oh Father, and grant me peace."

"Go on, child," he said. "Tell me what troubles you."

"Should there be something troubling me?" Maere asked, her voice an octave higher than normal. Her eyes widened and she distractedly fumbled her hair into a braid.

"Everyone has troubles. And everyone has sins, from a newborn babe to an old man," he said, patiently. "Now, will you seek to confess your misdeeds before God?"

Maere squeezed her hands against her stomach as it rolled and rumbled. How could she tell him what she'd done? How could she put it into words without dying of shame and embarrassment? "I don't know where to start, Father."

"The beginning is always a good place."

"True," she conceded with a slight smile. "If I only knew how all this began, I'd be happy to divulge it to you. As it is, all I know is that almost every night I'm visited by a man."

"A man?! A man comes to the anchorage?" the priest all but bellowed.

"No. No, Father. It's not like that at all. I see him in my dreams," she explained quickly.

"Hmmm. In your dreams, you say," Father John repeated, his voice growing calm again. "What does he do there?"

"He mostly watches from a distance, but the disturbing thing is—I know he's coming for me. And I know he'll be here soon." Tears filled her eyes. "What should I do?"

"How can you know this, that a man is on his way here?" Father John's dry voice took on a demanding urgency. "Have you been casting the stones? Are you practicing magic?"

For the second time in as many weeks, someone had asked her if she was performing magic. How had her life turned so completely upside down? She sighed. "It's not magic telling me he's coming. It's my gut. I feel it right there, like a cold lump of iron." In her mind's eye, Maere saw a strong hand reach into her and pull out the iron.

.ingers molded the metal, turning it over and over in its palm. .ien it finally glowed fiery red, the hand pushed it back inside her. .ier stomach burned just thinking about it. She pushed the picture away.

"You speak of strange things, girl. I am compelled to tell you I fear for your immortal soul."

Maere bowed her head, silent.

"Do you have anything else to say before I give you your penance?"

Maere dug her fists into her eyes, took a deep breath, then let her hands drop to her side. She'd come this far already, she might as well tell everything. "I dreamed he was here again last night," she said, her voice catching as she spoke. "I dreamed he, he—" She couldn't go on.

"He what?"

She raised her eyes heavenward and blinked back the tears. "He held me, intimately."

"I see," Father John said. "And tell me this, did you enjoy the act?"

"Enjoy it?" Maere repeated, embarrassment giving way to incredulity. "What does this have to do with anything?"

"Answer the question," he demanded.

"I, I don't know. When I was sleeping, I suppose I did. But when I woke up, I realized the evil which had possessed me." She swallowed hard and her cheeks burned hot. "Why do you ask such a thing of me?"

"The measurement of the sin for this dream is by how well you enjoyed indulging in the pleasures of the flesh. If you had said it was distasteful to you, then it wouldn't be as great a sin. Since you found it enjoyable, you'll have to accept a higher degree of punishment," he said, his patience obviously exhausted. "I'm sure you know, for this sin the penance is a sound beating."

Maere hung her head and wrapped her arms around herself. To be flagellated in front of the entire community of sisters and brothers? "When?" She had fallen so low.

"We'll assemble in the usual place, behind the chapel. I will discuss this with the abbess. Someone will come for you at sunset."

Maere heard him take a step away from the anchorage, the cawing of a bird rang out in the distance. "Is there no other way?" she whispered after him.

"Absolutely none."

DYLAN LAY ON HIS BACK, watching the play of light amidst the pine branches in the forest near St. Columba's Abbey. It was hard to be here, so close to Maere, but forced to wait until the right moment.

She would be grateful, he decided, to be removed from the stricture of the convent. To be able to run free again would be her greatest joy, of this he was most certain. He smiled to himself.

He reached up and pulled a small cone from a branch. Dylan closed his hand tightly around it for a moment. When he opened it again, the pinecone had been transformed into a miniature replica of its mother. With his free hand, he made a little hole in the soft needles and planted the tree there. As he worked, a raven flew overhead, loudly beating its wings before landing nearby.

"Do you realize what they have planned for her tonight?"

He leaned back, resting on one elbow. His eyes met Morrigu's, as she transformed into her human form. "Tell me."

"They will beat her," she said, her voice smooth and without emotion. There was even the hint of a smile on her face as she slowly moved toward Dylan, her hair swirling around her naked form. Laying down beside him she trailed her fingers up his chest.

He stiffened. "How do you know? Why are they doing this?"

"I know because I heard the girl's confession." Morrigu licked her lips, then leaned over and ran her tongue along his cheek, tracing the silvery scar of her mark. "And it's because of you she'll be hurt."

Dylan sat up, leaving the goddess where she lay. "What do you mean 'because of me'? How could that be?"

"Now, now. Don't play games with me. I know you've been visiting her." She pouted. "Do you think I didn't see your spirit leave last night as you sent it to the anchorage?" She raised herself up on her knees and ran her hands through her long black hair. "You've stirred a great fear in the girl. Now, they want to beat the fear out of her."

"That doesn't make sense. There was nothing fearful in the dream." He shook his head. "I don't understand."

"What you don't understand are these Christians. They fear what happens between a man and a woman. It is one of their greatest fears. They run from the power of it." She pouted. "I find it distasteful and I don't mind telling you, I long for the old days when men and women shared freely the pleasures of the flesh and my brothers and sisters enjoyed what I gave them." She caressed his cheek, then ran her hands lightly over her breasts. "Come, Dylan. Worship me."

Dylan stood so abruptly she toppled over. "I have to get to Maere."

Morrigu lay back on the moss, fanning her midnight hair about her, exposing her nubile form completely. "Leave her to the sisters and priests for now," she purred. "Nothing will happen until dusk." She opened her arms, the sunlight bathing her breasts in a warm glow.

"You realize, Dylan, she's almost of age? She doesn't need to be your concern any longer."

His eyes locked with the goddess's. "Her coming of age is *exactly* what I need to be concerned with. If Eugis should get to her first—"

"I'm certain you have nothing to worry about." Morrigu's lips curved up in a sultry smile. "Besides, I need you more at this moment than she does." Morrigu ran her hands over her breasts and down her belly.

Dylan's gaze traveled the length of her creamy curves. At one time, he would have leapt on Morrigu in an instant, eager to pleasure her for as long as she wanted. She had taught him everything about the intimacies between a man and a woman and for that he would be forever grateful.

But now, looking down at her petulant beauty, he almost felt sorry for her. Kate was right. Morrigu was as fickle as the wind and her only thought was for herself. He had to make haste, but nor did he want to offend the goddess. He sighed and crouched beside her. He leaned over and kissed her softly on the lips. "Thank you, my goddess, for everything you have given me. But I must go. I cannot allow anything to happen to Maere."

Morrigu frowned and crossed her arms over her chest. "I prefer you concern yourself only with me at the moment, Dylan mac Connell."

She eyed him, but he didn't falter. "If, as you say, Maere is in danger, I must save her."

"Remember this was your choice, to leave me for her." Morrigu stood and began to shift into her raven form. "Off with you, then. Go and rescue your maiden."

In a fluid movement, Morrigu completed her transformation and, letting out a loud caw, flew high into the treetops and disappeared from sight.

CHAPTER TEN

Maere sat cross-legged near the anchorage opening she'd crawled into only a few days earlier. Thin pink rays of dusky light filtered in through the narrow hole. She leaned forward, resting her elbows on her knees, and watched as dust danced and twirled in the fading beam.

Her fingers absently played with the citrine disk necklace she'd slipped on a moment before. The golden gem was smooth and warm beneath her touch and her thoughts drifted to her mother and father. Still disturbed by the words of her visitor and the drawing he'd left behind, she suddenly recalled that he had known her mother and father's name! How had she missed that?

Wearily, she rubbed her eyes. Given the chain of events following his visit, she supposed it wasn't surprising she'd let that detail slip by her. Maere tried to conjure up the faces of Manfred and Rhea cu Llwyr. Had the stranger known them? No matter how hard she concentrated, though, no images would come from her memory. It was as if a stone wall existed in her mind, thick and impenetrable, keeping the secrets of her past hidden from view.

The rustling of leaves outside told her someone was coming. The moment she'd been agonizing over all day had finally arrived. It was time for the public admittance of her sins and the beating that would follow. Why had she said anything? She had known what she was inviting but had spoken out just the same. What was wrong with her that she couldn't keep her mouth closed? Surely, the abbess had told her many a time her tongue was much too loose.

Had she really been so foolish as to believe Father John would treat her any differently than he treated the other novitiates? Had she really been silly enough to think he was a messenger from God, sent to her as she prayed for guidance? Why, after all, would she expect Him to send someone to look after her and her needs, lowly maiden that she was?

"Maere?"

Surprised, Maere turned her head in the direction of the voice. "Seelie?"

"Aye." Seelie reached a hand through the opening. "Grab hold. I'll help you."

Maere flattened herself against the dirt floor, extended her hand, and allowed the other woman to pull her through. When she emerged, she pushed herself to her feet and immediately shaded her eyes from the sun. Though it was fast approaching dusk, the orb still glowed with rich spring brilliance against the azure sky. Maere looked away and patted and tugged her habit into place. A cloud of dust she'd gathered in leaving the anchorage flew up around her. She shook as much of it away as she could, hoping the rest would blend into her clothing.

"I don't think they'll care much about how your dress looks," Seelie said.

"I suppose not." Maere bent over a patch of grass and wiped her hands on the ground covering. "You know what's happened, then?"

Seelie nodded. "The abbess told me, when she asked me to come after you." She grabbed Maere's arm and leaned toward her friend as they began to walk. "I can't believe you told the priest about your dreams." She pinched the fleshy part of the young woman's upper arm. "What could you have been thinking?"

Maere jerked to a stop, yelping and grimacing. She rubbed the bruise Seelie had inflicted. "What did you do that for?"

"To try and force some sense into you." Seelie stopped walking as well. "Don't you realize everyone has these same thoughts? But do you think they tell?" She stomped her foot, startling a squirrel. The animal turned tail and scurried up the scarred trunk of an old oak. "Of course, they don't tell! And do you know why? Because they know they'll get a beating for having them!"

"What about the ones who did tell?" Maere countered. "Were they not absolved of the sin?" She pursed her lips together. "Or are you suggesting they wanted to be beaten?"

"I have no idea either way." Seelie snorted. The young women began walking again. "As far as I'm concerned, it's plain to see they're simple-minded." She glanced at Maere. "And now I suppose I'll be putting you in the same basket."

"I—I didn't want this to happen, Seelie." Tears tumbled down Maere's cheeks. "I don't know what I was thinking. I s'pose I just needed to say the words out loud."

"Oh, I know, girl." Seelie put her arm around Maere's shoulders. "And I'm sorry to be scolding you at a time like this."

"I don't know what came over me. There I was, praying for guidance, when Father John appeared out of the air." She shrugged. "I thought he was sent by God to help me sort the thoughts in my head. I realized my mistake too late." She stopped walking and leaned against the stone wall which separated the abbey and its grounds from the monastery. A bower of green ivy spilled over the rocks and teased the back of Maere's neck. She brushed it away and continued talking. "I didn't even tell him about the *other* man."

"What *other* man?" Seelie asked, her eyes wide. "You haven't told me about him, either."

"He only just appeared since I've been ensconced. I saw him, here." She pointed to her head. "He was older, with gray hair. He said he was coming for me." Maere pushed herself away from the wall and faced Seelie. "Have I gone mad?" She searched the other woman's face. "We've known each other for a long time. Tell me honestly. Do I seem different to you? Have I changed?"

Maere shifted from foot to foot as her friend looked her over. Seelie took Maere's hands into her own. "Aye. You've changed. I can see the lines of worry etched around your mouth and across your forehead. There are dark circles under your eyes, telling me you haven't slept. I don't mind telling you, you're a fright, girl." She gripped Maere's arms. "You must overcome this. The priests'll like nothing better than if you become hysterical. They'll say the Devil himself has possessed you and give you an even worse beating."

Maere looked away and hung her head. She blinked back the new tears forming in her eyes. "I fear they'll be right," she murmured.

Seelie gave her a hard shake and Maere's hair tumbled loose down her back. "Leave that nonsense behind. Keep your head high when they question you and try not to stumble before them." She released her and Maere pushed the coppery strands out of her eyes.

Maere stared hard at Seelie for a moment, considering her words. "When did you become so wise?" she finally asked, wiping the tears away with the back of her hand. "You give good advice, my friend." She offered a weak smile. "I'll try my best to follow it."

Seelie patted Maere on the shoulder. "What you call wisdom is very new to me. The knowledge has only come upon me since that night in your room. It's only fitting that I should use it now to assist you." She nodded in the direction of the timber and dried-sod chapel. "They'll be waiting."

"Lead the way, then," Maere said, her voice strained. "I'll offer up the beating for the sinful souls of the deceased who are burning with the Devil. Surely, they need comfort more than me." She shook her head as they began to walk again. "And next time, I swear I'll be keeping my thoughts to myself."

"Maere! Seelie!" A girl with dark brown hair flying behind her came running toward them.

"What is it, Robin?" Seelie asked. It was Abbess Magrethe's young maid. "You look as if you've seen a spirit."

"Not a spirit," she panted. "A man!"

Maere smiled and ruffled the girl's hair. "It's not like you haven't seen one before. The priests and monks do live in the building on the other side of the wall, after all."

Robin sighed, exasperated. "There's something different about 'im. And, besides, he's asked for you, Maere. The abbess says you're to come right away."

Maere's stomach dropped. She pushed her hands against the soft flesh as her face grew pale. "What did he look like?" she asked, her voice barely a whisper.

Robin turned and started running toward the abbey. "I don't have time to tell you," she called over her shoulder. "Abbess'll punish me if I don't return right away." She turned and ran backwards, her long skirt whipping between her gangly legs. "Please. You have to come along now!" she shouted, then turned around again and began running in earnest.

Seelie started after the girl when Maere stepped in front of her, her eyes wild. She waved her hand in the air. "We can't go! What if it's *him*?"

Seelie planted her fists on her hips. "So what if it is? You can't be running forever." She pointed at Maere. "Get some courage, girl, and let's go face whatever the Lord has planned for you."

Maere glanced over Seelie's shoulder. The sun was almost down. The abbey—with its tall bell tower and long corridors that reached out like pointed fingers—was looming dark in the distance. She took a deep breath and let it out slowly.

Deep in thought, Maere began walking. Seelie was right. She couldn't go on running from her fears for the rest of her life. It was time she faced them, head on. She squared her shoulders and tilted her chin a notch higher. Face them she would, beginning with this moment.

CHAPTER ELEVEN

Despite her firm resolve, when Maere entered the abbey, the voice of doubt began ringing in her head. With each stone step she climbed toward the abbess's upstairs office, the words repeated themselves over and over. Step. *Run.* Step. *Away.* Step. *Run.* Step. *Away.* Each scrape of her thin leather shoes sounded out the verse like a child's song. But before she could react to the command, she was at the top of the long open stairway.

Don't do this! The words screamed inside her soul. It's going to be *him*! Panic—already living in the pit of her stomach like a hungry snake—uncoiled and shot through her chest. It choked her with its intensity. She couldn't breathe. With a sudden gasp of air, she took heed of the warning and turned to bolt back down the stairs. At that moment, a door opened behind her. She froze as Abbess Magrethe spoke.

"Maere? Where are you going, girl? I've been waiting for you."

Slowly, tentatively, Maere turned around and faced the abbess. Magrethe waved a long thin hand delicately toward her. "Come along. There's something we need to discuss."

Maere followed the older woman into her chambers, dragging her feet across the slate floor. She braced herself—ready to run if need be—as her eyes darted around the room. When she saw the abbess was alone, she let her breath out and relaxed a little. Not much, but a little. Could it be that Robin was mistaken in what she'd told her?

"Take a breath, Maere," Magrethe bade, her watery blue eyes mirroring concern. "You look frightened half to death."

"Is it true?" Maere asked, her voice barely a whisper. "Is there a man here to see me?"

"Don't mumble, girl," the abbess scolded as she took her place behind the finely carved desk.

Maere cleared her throat and asked louder this time, "Where is he?"

Magrethe frowned. "Robin has obviously told you more than she had a right to. It's a fine testimony to your obedience training you came at all, given the events of late." She leaned forward and crossed her arms in front of her. "What exactly did the child reveal to you?"

"Only that there was a man here who wanted to see me." She wrung her hands together and glanced around the room again. The sun had gone down and she could see the rising moon outside the window behind the abbess. "Is it true?"

"Yes, it's true. A man *is* here for you."

Maere's eyes grew wide and the abbess quickly added, "But he's not the evil you fear, my daughter." She shook her head and offered a small smile. "I've spoken with him. He's not the evil you have dreamed about."

Maere took a tentative step forward. "What manner of man is he then, that he should come seeking me?"

"He was sent by your kind Uncle Eugis." Magrethe watched the younger woman closely as she continued, "He is your betrothed."

Maere's mouth fell open. She quickly closed it again. "Betrothed?" She dropped into the wooden chair opposite the abbess's desk. "I have no betrothed." Her eyes widened. "Even if it *were* so, I couldn't leave. You and the sisters are the only family I have ever known."

"That's not true," a male voice replied.

Her back grew rigid and the hair on Maere's nape stood on end. She frantically searched her memory. She'd heard this voice before, but where? Was it from one of her dreams?

"Would you tell me truly you have no memory of your people?" he continued. "The Dumnonii who live in the lush green hills and thick forests of Tintagel?"

The abbess rose and walked toward the door. "Please, enter, sir. It is most unfortunate but, you see, Maere has no recollection of her life before arriving at Saint Columba's." She ushered him into her office. "In the beginning, we tried everything we could think of to bring back her memories. After a while, when they didn't return, we determined it was God's will she remain apart from them and we let it be."

"*God's* will?"

"You question the workings of our Savior? Ah, you are pagan, aren't you? I suspected as much." Magrethe sat back down at her desk and spoke directly to Maere. "Think of the joy in heaven you'll bring for converting this man." She sat back in her chair and directed her words to the man, "Maere and I were just now discussing the details of your arrival."

Maere heard the man walking toward her, but she couldn't turn around. She was frozen solid, like a stream in the dead of winter.

Oh, Sweet Virgin, where is my strength?

Get a firm hold on yourself.

She held her breath as he approached her chair.

"So I heard as I neared your office."

That voice! She remembered now! He was the pilgrim who'd left behind the strange drawing, the one who knew her kin's names. Maere finally forced herself to breathe and, gripping the arms of the chair, pushed herself to her feet. Slowly, she turned to face him, to face the nameless entity who had haunted her ever since that brief encounter.

As she turned, she found him standing close to her as if his being there, so near, was the most natural thing in the world. Her eyes met his—as dark as a winter's night, they were. She ignored his mild look of amusement as her gaze lingered on what otherwise would be a most serious face…That face! She had never seen such a man. He was handsome and dangerous-looking, with well-formed lips, high cheekbones, and wild black hair hanging to his wide shoulders.

Fear enveloped her, overwhelming in its intensity. Her head swam. Maere took a step back and bumped into the desk. She grabbed hold of the edge, squeezing so hard her fingers hurt. Dearest blessed Mother but he was the man in her dreams! He had to be! Never mind she'd never seen the face of the demon in such detail, she sensed a connection between the man from her dreams and this man here. And the thin silvery scar that ran like an easy caress down his cheek only served to make him even more striking in appearance. He was from another world, there could be no doubt about it.

She shuddered as his eyes moved over her face and down her body. The black orbs returned to meet hers and held her own in a tight embrace. Near the open window, a raven cried out and the spell was broken. Maere's gut jumped and stumbled over itself as she looked toward the sound.

With a thumping of wings, the raven settled on the window's thick stone ledge. It sat quietly, with silver eyes that seemed to take in its surroundings, though its eyes were much too shrewd for a simple bird.

Maere looked from the man who was staring at the raven with a frown, to the abbess, whose own fair face had grown even paler. She watched as the older woman made a quick sign of the cross over her breast.

"Abbess?" Maere cried out weakly. "What goes on here?" Her legs trembled and her knees threatened to give way. She forced out the words, "Surely you cannot mean for me to go with this, this devil?"

"Really, sir. Can't you see you're frightening the girl?" Magrethe said, gesturing at the bird. "Is that your bird?"

The man smiled stiffly. "I am acquainted with the raven. 'Tis but a harmless thing, seeking some attention."

The raven glared at him and ruffled its feathers.

Magrethe waited a moment, looking pointedly from man to creature and back again. She shook her head and set her mouth in a firm line. Lifting a document from the pile of precious parchment neatly stacked on one side of her desk. she looked it over, sighed, and handed it to Maere. "This is the betrothal agreement. Turn it over," she said. "It bears your family's mark and seal."

Maere glanced at the paper, but couldn't really see it. She felt eyes on her from all around. She looked up to find the strange demon of a man and the raven both staring at her, their gaze so tangible it all but pierced her flesh.

The man took a step toward Maere and she instinctively withdrew. "Can it be true that you do not remember me?" he said. "Are you certain you have no recall of the times we shared?" The words were low, somehow expectant.

Maere cleared her throat, searching for her voice. "Aye, I remember you," she finally said. But the smile that had formed on his face quickly faded when she added, "You're the man who came when I was in the anchorage."

"Of course. I should have recognized you myself," the abbess said. She clasped her hands in front of her. "Why didn't you make yourself known to us upon your arrival in Glastonbury?"

Maere interrupted before he could respond. "Tell me true, sir. Who are you?" She held her breath, waiting for the response. Legend had it if you asked a demon a direct question he couldn't lie in the answering. And if ever a demon existed, it was this man.

He smiled again, a flash of bright white against his olive skin, and bowed before her. "I would be most happy to introduce myself. It is as you have said. I am the same who visited you when you were ensconced. But I am also your betrothed, Dylan mac Connall." He watched her, his gaze hard.

She squirmed under his scrutiny. Did he expect her to respond in some way to his declaration? Oh, but this had to be one of her visions…

"You would say, in truth, my name means nothing to you?" The man leaned forward, pressing his point. "What new game are you playing, Maere?"

Maere squared her shoulders as anger began to work its way through the raw fear that had overpowered her earlier. She shook off the question. Game, indeed. "You have not answered the abbess. Why didn't you identify yourself to us?"

"I prefer to take my time with such matters. It is my way," he said. "Besides, I assumed you would know who I was."

Maere pitched the parchment to the floor. "A document from an uncle I haven't seen in ten years means nothing to me." She let her gaze wander over him. She raised her chin and tossed her loose hair behind her. Seelie was right. She desperately needed to find some courage. Her voice quavered when she spoke again. "You and your claimed betrothal mean nothing to me. I will not leave the abbey."

Dylan took a step forward. "You will leave, Maere cu Llwyr. And when you do, it will be as my wife."

The bird screeched loudly, flapped its wings, and disappeared through the window, its black form lost to the night.

Dylan turned to the abbess. "Please explain her duties to her. I'll return in an hour with one of your priests." He watched Maere for a moment. "Have your belongings gathered and be ready to leave. I'll not be kept waiting any longer." He pivoted on the ball of his foot and left the room.

Maere turned to Magrethe. "You cannot mean for me to go with this, this man." She gestured toward the door Dylan had just passed through. "You saw him with that creature of his. He is *not* Christian!"

Magrethe rose and approached the younger woman, forcing a smile on her drawn face. "Yes. And as I said, what a wonderful opportunity for you, to be handed a pagan soul for conversion." She put her palms together. "I will have a word with Father John. Given the change of events, it would be unseemly to go to your betrothed after such a penance as flagellation."

She took Maere's hands in her own and nodded toward the document where it rested on the floor. "The paper is binding and you must honor it. Your good uncle himself told me he would find you a husband by your eighteenth year."

"I remember you telling me this." Maere fell back into the chair. "So much time has passed. I'd hoped he'd forgotten all about me."

Magrethe lightly touched Maere's cheek. "If it were up to me, you'd stay." She shrugged. "But it is not my place. I'm sorry, but you really have no choice in this matter." The abbess blinked and a thin tear traveled down her lightly lined cheek. "No choice whatsoever, child."

CHAPTER TWELVE

"You will explain yourself to me, Dylan mac Connall." Morrigu paced back and forth in front of him. The sharp pine needles littering the ground caused her no obvious discomfort as her bare feet padded over them.

Dylan glanced up from where he sat on a tree stump and stretched his long, muscular legs out in front of him. The fire he'd lit cast a warm glow on the goddess' body. Normally, the sight of her in human form was enough to drive all reason from his mind. But now, he was surprised to find he actually had other thoughts. Thoughts of long copper hair and sea-green eyes. Eyes so innocent and beguiling—such a contrast to the woman before him—whose own eyes now shone with venom.

"There is nothing to explain," he said, his voice tense.

"You are greatly mistaken." She leaned over and aimed a sharp fingernail straight at his face. "There is much you must answer for."

He pushed her hand aside. "Such as?"

"What are these words of marriage of which you spoke? That was not part of the agreement we made earlier. You were to only act on the betrothal, not actually wed the girl!" She straightened and presented her slim back to him. "You test my patience, mortal. Tell me now this marriage will not take place and I may yet let you live."

Dylan pushed himself to his feet and stood directly behind Morrigu, a good head taller than she. But he knew this was part of her game, her temptation, to appear small and vulnerable. To appear as if she needed him. He shook his head. She didn't need him. He realized that now. But a question remained: Did *he* need *her*? He shifted uneasily. "Are you jealous, Goddess?" he finally asked.

Morrigu turned on him in fury, her silver eyes glowing with the reflection of her sister Nimue, the moon. "I'm not certain I heard you correctly," she said, her voice low and forbidding. "Have you accused me of possessing one of your *human* emotions?"

"You forget too easily how well I know you, Morrigu." Dylan stared hard into those glinting eyes. "Dowse the fire that burns in your breast. It's most unbecoming."

She reached out and grabbed the back of his neck with her hand, scraping her nails along the tender flesh. Dylan flinched, but his gaze never wavered. Morrigu took a deep breath and, as the air filled her lungs, her body stretched and grew. Another breath and she was two feet taller than him. A third breath and she was so large, Dylan only reached her navel. She released him and crossed her arms in front of her. She looked down, a smug smile on her lips. "You were saying?"

Dylan walked in silence to the pine tree behind him. He touched his forehead to the rough bark and immediately saw in his mind's eye an explosion of golden-yellow color, the amber lifeblood of the tree. "Bend, that I might stand tall," he whispered. The tree began to shake as he stepped away from it. It continued to tremble and quake, sending dead needles to the ground as, ever so slowly, the thick trunk bowed before him. Dylan grabbed hold near the center of the tree, settled his feet on a stout branch, and said, "Rise." Then, just as slowly, the pine righted itself until Dylan was face-to-face with Morrigu.

"I have gifted you with this power and you would challenge me with it?" The goddess' cheeks grew red with anger. "Without me, you are nothing," she hissed.

"I am Dylan, son of Fox and Dara mac Connall, same as I have always been." He lowered his voice. "With or without your assistance."

Morrigu shook her head and laughed. The loud, cold sound shook the very air itself, its vibration causing all manner of forest creature to flee their nests this dark night. "Do you think you can cast me aside so easily? Do you believe there would be no repercussions for such an action?"

Dylan leaned into the tree branches and they wrapped themselves around him, cradling and protecting him. The trees were his true friends, his instincts told him that. The smell of pine tar filled his nostrils, an aroma he knew would always remind him now of Morrigu, of this moment. "It was arranged by our families all those years ago," he said. "I'm bound by their pledge. I must marry her."

"No, Dylan, you mustn't. Take her away from the convent, if you insist on hiding her from Eugis, but deposit her with some unsuspecting farmer." She smiled. "Then you and I can move on to other things."

Dylan snorted. "I am merely a plaything to you Morrigu," Dylan touched the scar on his cheek, the scar she'd left behind the night she first made love to him. *Nay, not love,* he corrected himself.

"And what is so wrong with that?" Her silver eyes blazed at him. "You have never seemed to mind before."

"I would see the circle mended, Morrigu," he said changing the subject. "It was broken the night Eugis murdered our families and took Maere away from me. Do you think it's been easy for me, spending all these years waiting? While I learned everything I could about the nature of power?" He ran a hand through his thick black hair and his eyes met the goddess' again. "I won't wait any longer. I am going to marry the girl, with or without your permission. Our destiny will be fulfilled."

"Ah, I understand," she whispered. "You seek her power. You believe the first who beds her will share the gift she possesses, don't you?"

Dylan rubbed away the tension in his neck but pulled his hand away when he felt stickiness. It was covered with blood left from the goddess' touch. Wiping his hand on his breeches, he said, "That has nothing to do with this."

"Of course, it does. You cannot fool me." She took a step forward. "Simply take the girl's virginity and be done with her."

His eyes narrowed at the callous suggestion. "No matter how much you may desire it, Maere is my betrothed and I won't dishonor her. Manfred was my teacher and friend and I promised him I'd always care for her."

Morrigu began to laugh again and her body slowly resumed its smaller, mortal form. Dylan bade the tree to let him down to the ground. In two long strides, he was behind the goddess. He grabbed her shoulders and turned her to face him. "I would know what it is you find so amusing."

"You. And your sense of honor. Do you really think that matters? I thought you were cleverer than that." She jerked away from him. "This world exists for the strong and for those who would seize life and power, not for those who hide behind pretty words and noble promises." Morrigu reached out and ran a fingertip across and down his chest. "Now, this is the last opportunity I will grant you to change your mind. Call off the marriage."

"I will not," he insisted, standing his ground and refusing to waver before the goddess. "The circle *must* be redeemed. You know this. Balance cannot be restored until Maere and I are joined and Eugis is punished."

Morrigu spun around, presenting him with her back again. "I could kill you, you know." Her words hung in the air between them like icicles on a blustery winter night.

"I know this." Dylan took a deep breath and let it out slowly. "But, like you, I do what I must."

She held her arms out to her sides and long black feathers began to sprout from the flesh, forming thick raven wings. Morrigu turned her head and looked at him sideways. "I won't, though." She shook her long hair and a cascade of feathers grew, starting at her forehead and running the length of her back. "I will make you beg for forgiveness for your betrayal of me. And you will suffer for your stubbornness." She stood on tiptoes and took flight, half-woman, half-bird, and circled a few feet above his head. "So will Maere. It will be much more interesting than simply killing you." With an ear-splitting screech, she bolted straight into the sky, a dark outline against the stars before she blended with the night.

MAERE AND SEELIE WALKED, arms linked, down the long, sparsely-lit corridor leading from their cells to the convent chapel. Scattered candles, placed in sconces high on the stone walls, offered uneven blotches of dim yellow light and cast odd shadows as the women moved along. It would be frightening, if it weren't so familiar.

Seelie squeezed Maere's hand. "Everything will be fine," she whispered. "I feel it in my bones."

"I only wish it were so," Maere said, her voice equally hushed. "I don't want to leave, Seelie." She began to cry. The quiet sobbing bounced off the heavy walls and reverberated in her ears. "I don't want to leave."

"Hush, now." Seelie placed her arm around Maere's shoulders and hugged her as they continued to walk. "You're a strong young woman. You just don't realize it yet."

Maere sighed. She lifted the long sleeve of her dark green tunic— the only article of clothing she wore to indicate she was to be a bride— and wiped away her tears. It seemed so absurd to her that she should be wearing the wedding color, the color of fertility, considering she was about to be wed to a demon. "If only I had your faith."

"It's *your* faith, girl. You were the one who shared it with me that night Bertrand did his evil. You just need to find it again inside of yourself."

The pair grew silent as they approached the chapel doors. Built of thick oak and carved with intricate details of Christ's sufferings, they had been hand rubbed over the years to a fine golden patina. Maere had always found comfort behind their heavy embrace, but now she felt stifled as the sisters stationed outside the chapel pulled them open. In her mind's eye, the doors became the hands of a huge dragon, beckoning her into its lair.

Maere froze, her face pale, as she peered into the chapel. The eyes of all the nuns, sitting on the stone benches, were on her. Father John stood off to the side, his arms crossed tightly in front of him, giving the impression he didn't quite approve of the proceedings. Panic squeezed her throat. "I can't do this," she whispered.

Frantic, Maere began to plot her escape. She couldn't go out the way she came. Not with everyone behind her, watching. She'd have to go forward, try to make it to the side door before it was closed for the ceremony. Her eyes were steady on the portal, considering the number of steps it would require to get to there—fifteen, twenty perhaps…She considered her options as Abbess Magrethe approached, a tall candlestick in one hand, a worn leather manuscript in the other.

"Sign your name here as a record of your marriage." She handed the book of parchment to the younger woman, along with a quill. She pulled a flask of ink from her robe.

Maere's hand visibly shook as she took the record book and quill. Magrethe uncorked the ink bottle and held it out in front of her. "I'll hold this for you." As she spoke, moisture formed in her pale blue eyes and glistened in the candlelight.

Maere glanced at Seelie, who nodded at the parchment. Maere looked around the chapel. It was dark except for a few large tallow candles, their odor of fat as thick as smoke in the air, glowing brightly around the hand-hewn altar of stone. The flames illuminated the tormented figure of Jesus nailed to the cross, hanging directly above the altar. The shadows danced over the statue and seemed to highlight her own agony. She swallowed hard, forcing back the bile roiling in the back of her throat.

She glanced at the side door again, wrestling with the wild notion of escaping or the acceptance of seeing her duty through. How could she stand in the way of what she had been taught was most certainly God's will? Everyone knew fate was determined the day you were born and recorded by God's own hand in a great book in Heaven.

Maere prayed silently for strength. *If this is your desire, Lord, that I should marry this strange man, then I will abide by it. If it is not, then please send a sign before I am committed to him for life…Oh, and please be as quick as you can about it.*

Maere's gaze dropped back to the anxious faces of the sisters, their eyes fixed on her. She closed her eyes and waited as long as she dared.

After a few breaths, she sighed, realizing there would be no sign.

She must proceed with the ceremony.

With a still shaky hand, she dipped the quill into the black ink and rendered her name on the wedding record, under the fancy curved handwriting of the person who claimed to be her betrothed, Dylan mac Connall.

CHAPTER THIRTEEN

A fter signing her name, Maere silently walked up the aisle, toward the limestone altar. Carved on either side of the front legs were the letters *A* and *U*. The initials for Alpha and Omega, in Latin. The Beginning and the End. Is this how it would end for her? Married to a man she knew nothing about? Her heart skipped a beat as the subject of her thoughts entered the chapel from the same side door she had considered escaping through.

He had changed from his traveling clothes into a linen tunic and hose. A mantel of blue lined with emerald green was tossed over his shoulders, held in place with an intricately-wrought gold-and-garnet pin. His black hair was neatly combed and hung loosely to his shoulders. His expression was calm but expectant, not at all like the horrible anxiety Maere was certain showed on her own face.

As Dylan took another step, he entered the candlelight fully and Maere's breath caught. Oh, but he was handsome, with that dark mane of hair, those full lips, and luminous black eyes that made her want to lose herself in their depths…

Sweet Jesus, what am I thinking?

The man was evil. He had to be! He invaded her thoughts and made her think things she should never be thinking!

A warm blush crept over her face and just as quickly receded as another man walked into the candle's glow.

Maere sucked in her breath. It couldn't be! Oh, but it was, she realized with dread. The monk Bertrand, the same who had molested Seelie and nearly killed her! Why was he here?

Maere spun around. Seelie was moving quickly toward her. The sisters began to chatter in hushed tones and a few leaned forward, eager to hear what the problem was. As her friend reached her side, Maere had the sinking feeling they should have revealed Bertrand's deed to the abbess. Surely the two of them had imagination enough to come up with a plausible story so the healing wouldn't have had to be mentioned.

"Seelie," Maere called out, her voice a harsh whisper. They hadn't seen the man since his deed so they'd hoped he had moved on to another monastery. Maere glanced back at him. His face was so serene, almost beatific, not at all the face of a murderer. Never mind the fact Seelie was still alive, despite his brutality. And now he had the audacity to stand before them, looking saintly in his monk's garb? God only knew how many other women he had lured to their death.

"It doesn't matter." Seelie said into Maere's ear. "Ignore him and go on with your ceremony."

"You can't be serious."

"I am. I've forgiven him."

"Forgiven him? How in the name of God could you forgive him for what he did?" Maere gestured toward the monk and struggled to keep her voice low. "He killed you, girl."

Gently, Seelie turned Maere around and began escorting her toward the altar. "Being faced with death makes a person realize what's important in this life. Carrying grudges and past hurts isn't what matters. What matters is we do the best we can with the time God has given us."

Maere heard the words, even felt them, but they didn't make any sense. Her breathing grew shallow as she remembered holding Seelie as she lay dying. Maere leaned on Seelie and moved now as if in a dream, everything around her taking on a distorted, unnatural appearance. Why couldn't she catch her breath? The sisters' smiles were exaggerated, the chapel windows grew long and thin, even Father John looked angrier than he had earlier. As they reached the altar, she and Seelie stepped into the embrace of the candlelight. Maere took a deep breath and forced herself to focus as her eyes found the monk.

But Bertrand's stare was fixed on Seelie. He took a step back. "You!" he hissed. "What are *you* doing here?"

Seelie raised her chin and stared back at him.

"Is there something amiss, Brother?" Father John asked from his place on the altar.

Bertrand didn't respond but instead raised his arms heavenward, then dropped them in the direction of the gathered guests. "I would tell all of you. This woman," he said, pointing at Seelie, "is a sinner in the first degree against our Lord God. Against the holy men of the cloth."

The grumbling of the sisters grew louder and echoed through the small chapel. Abbess Magrethe stood and stepped forward, her gaze level with the monk. "Of what do you accuse our Seelie?"

"She is a whore. A temptress! She seeks to lure men away from God's sacred calling!" Bertrand looked around, his expression growing wild. Perspiration glistened on his forehead. He reached a hand toward Seelie, grasping for her.

Maere stepped between them and pushed his arm out of the way. "How dare you accuse her? How dare you blame *her* for what *you* did!"

Bertrand shoved Maere out of the way and grabbed for Seelie again. Maere stumbled on the altar step and Dylan quickly moved to her side as she regained her balance. He eyed the monk. "Do not touch the lady again," he said.

"What happened? Of what is Bertrand speaking?" the abbess demanded. She laid a gentle hand on Seelie's shoulder. "I can't help if you don't tell me."

Seelie glanced from the abbess to Maere. She chewed on her bottom lip, then dropped her head in resigned silence.

Magrethe sighed. "Nothing, eh?" She looked at Maere. "Would you speak here this night?" She nodded toward Bertrand. "I have a notion of what has happened, have seen it before, but one of you must speak out on the matter." Magrethe glanced at Father John. "I am bound by a vow to keep silent."

Maere shook her head. She had promised Seelie she wouldn't tell. If her friend wanted the abbess to know, that was one matter, but she couldn't betray the confidence placed in her, though the man deserved to be punished mightily.

Father John plowed past Magrethe, Dylan, Maere, and Seelie, stopping when he reached the other side of the altar where the young monk was standing. "What is this about, son? What did the novice do to you?"

Angered washed over Maere at the priest's words—*What did the novice do to you?*

She glanced at the abbess whose eyes flashed with a fire Maere had never seen before. Then the abbess did something Maere had never seen her do—she scowled at the priest and stepped in front of him. Turning to Bertrand, the abbess declared in a strong voice. "I will have answers and I will have them now. What have *you* done to *her?*"

Outside the window, a raven beat its wings against the leaded glass and cawed, its voice loud and raucous. Bertrand grabbed his head. "Pain!" he gasped. He began sweating profusely and dropped to his knees, his once-handsome face contorted. "She tempted me!" he shouted. He waved his arm at Seelie. "Don't you understand?"

Magrethe glanced at Seelie and Maere, but both maintained their silence. She leaned forward, her eyes as cold as a winter's night. "I understand all too well. The pain is your penance!"

"This is obviously not a matter for you to be questioning, Abbess," Father John said. "You have no place here with this man."

"I am responsible for these two young women." She nodded at Maere and Seelie. "It is up to me to protect them and if it means questioning this monk, I'll do it. This is my vow."

Bertrand dropped his head and sobbed. "She cannot tempt a man of God without facing the consequences. She's a whore. Whores must die."

The raven screeched again and Dylan turned toward the sound. "Morrigu," he whispered. He took in the hectic scene before him. He should have recognized her touch. This was the goddess' doing, all of it!

"You women do not understand. The Devil himself lives in your bodies and causes you to flaunt them." Bertrand rose to face Magrethe. His voice grew quieter. "She came to me and I took her, pounding God's love into her." He stared at Seelie. "Not that she deserves God's love!"

"By the Virgin!" Magrethe's hand flew to her mouth. "You are perverted, *brother*, to believe such a thing."

"No. I am God's messenger. He wanted me to right this wrong, to destroy the temptress. And that girl there," he nodded toward Maere. "She is the Devil's offspring, she is. She brought the whore back to life."

Magrethe's face paled and her lips drew tightly together. She took a step back and crossed her arms. Her fingers found the cross hanging from her neck.

"Ask her!" Bertrand sobbed. Dylan stepped forward, standing between the monk and Maere. Bertrand fell prostrate on the altar and began praying out loud, his words a jumble. The raven found an open window and flew into the chapel, circling and cawing, its song a taunting melody.

The abbess turned from the sight of the tortured man. She and the other sisters surrounded Maere and Seelie. "You healed her, didn't you?" Magrethe asked quietly, nodding her head as if she now understood. "The night we found her in your room. You said she'd fallen. It was magic, wasn't it?"

Father John entered the circle of nuns and novices and gripped Maere's shoulders. "Did you raise this one from the dead?" he nodded toward Seelie. "As this most blessed man of God has claimed?"

"He's no man of God." Maere pulled away from the priest. "He is a defiler of women and deserves to be punished for his actions."

"He took me against my will, Father, and then tried to kill me to cover his deed," Seelie said. "Don't you understand? Maere tended to my injuries. That's all. If it weren't for her, I wouldn't be alive now."

"So, it is true," the abbess said, more to herself than out loud.

Sweet Mother, the deed was out in the open! Maere glanced around, frantic. All eyes were on her. In desperation, she explained, "Bertrand broke his vow of celibacy. He hurt her. He's the one who broke the law of God. Not Seelie. Not me."

Father John's face remained solemn as he spoke. "I always knew there was something very wrong with you, girl." He looked at the faces around him. "Go about your business, all of you. This wedding will not take place until we have been able to discern the facts surrounding this incident."

"You are wrong, old man." Dylan stepped forward, his eyes intent on the priest. "None of this concerns Maere." He nodded toward the prone, broken figure of Bertrand. "It's more than obvious the problem lies within him, not these women. I will see us wed tonight if I have to rouse every priest in the monastery 'til I find one to perform the ceremony."

"That will not be possible, sir. None of them would do such a thing without my permission." Father John's stare remained fixed on Maere. "We must find out what demon has possessed her, in order that it may be exorcised from her soul. I am determined to discover the nature of her magic that we might break the spell she has so obviously cast on our dear brother Bertrand." He set his mouth in a firm line. "Even if we must beat it out of her." He tore his gaze from Maere and looked at Dylan. "You certainly should consider yourself lucky all of this was revealed before the marriage took place."

Maere gasped and took a step back. It was as if everyone was reaching for her now, trying to push her along down the aisle and back toward the convent corridor. A few moments ago, she would have gladly welcomed the opportunity to avoid the strange man with the wild hair and burning eyes that looked into her very soul. But everything was different now. Dear Jesus, they knew about her! The priests would whip her until she confessed to performing black acts. She knew this in her heart, had witnessed it before. And in the end, they would just as surely murder her as they'd tried to murder Seelie.

The sisters closed in tighter and Maere could no longer see Dylan. In the ruckus, a candle was knocked over. It fell against the heavy homespun drapes, immediately igniting the fabric like dried tinder. Sister Jane screamed as Dylan shoved her out of the way to reach Maere.

He made his way through the crowd, and for a brief instant, Maere thought she saw something in those hard black eyes, something akin to a mixture of pain and longing. "Come," he shouted over the din.

Maere knew there was no choice but to go with him, but she was rooted to the spot, as if her legs were cast of heavy lead. Flames shot up behind the altar and licked at the crucifix. Maere's gaze followed the line of the statue. Near the top, right above the crossbeam, black wings were spread wide and silver eyes stared back at her. "Oh, dear God."

Dylan turned his head and saw it too. "Be gone from here!" he shouted at the raven. He grabbed Maere's arm and gave her a hard shake. "We have to go. Now."

She looked at him. Didn't he understand? In the course of a single evening, the abbey she had loved and felt secure in had been transformed into a hateful place of accusations and mistrust. Maere began to cry, desperate to be away from the maddening noise and the sight of the sisters, frantically trying to douse the fire and save the chapel. But Maere was still unable to take a single step.

Seelie touched Maere's shoulder, making her jump. She looked at her friend through tears. "You must go with him," Seelie said. "You know what awaits you here. You cannot stay."

"But what of you? You're in danger as well, now that they know."

"I'm not afraid." Seelie smiled, a little. "When I died that night, I saw Heaven. It's a peaceful place and I will return with joy in my heart when my time comes." A sister jostled past, a bucket of water in hand, and tossed it at a smoldering altar cloth. Shouts and screams echoed throughout the chapel. "The fire spreads quickly." Seelie hugged Maere. "Now, off with you. He's a good man. I can feel it. He'll keep you safe." Seelie gave her a shove and Maere's legs finally began to move.

"Thank you, Seelie," Dylan said. He grabbed Maere around the waist as she stepped forward. Dragging her beside him, he shoved his way past the sisters and Father John, stopping only when Abbess Magrethe blocked their way. In her hand was the iron processional pole, the banner hanging from it was stained and bloodied. On the steps of the altar, at her feet, lay the monk. His head was bashed on one side and his eyes stared sightlessly at the simple vaulted ceiling.

"I've loved her like my own and would protect her with my life," the abbess said, looking at Maere. "There is no evil in you, my child. This I believe." She nodded toward Bertrand's lifeless body. "I have fulfilled my vow to protect you and dealt with that evil man. He can no longer hurl vile accusations at you. Seelie was not the first girl he attacked. And he will never be able to harm another girl again."

"What about Seelie?" Maere asked. "Will you watch over her?"

"I promise no harm will come to her."

Tears ran down Magrethe's cheeks as she reached for Maere and held her in a tight embrace.

The abbess looked up at Dylan. "Take her far from this place and keep her safe for me."

Dylan nodded, and pulled Maere away from the abbess and toward the side door. As he pushed it open and directed Maere outside, she turned for one last look at the people who had been her family for ten years. Sisters were scrambling back and forth, hauling pans of water and tossing them at the burning drapery and wood statues while Father John waved his arms and shouted. Magrethe stood serenely where they had left her.

CHAPTER FOURTEEN

On the distant horizon, with the setting moon behind them, a band of men on horseback approached Saint Columba's Abbey. It was still cool this late May morning and a fine mist rose from the land. The horses' and riders' breath mixed together, billowing out and blending with the fog. At times the animals were concealed as they made their way east, appearing as if the riders floated on the very air itself. And so it seemed to the occupants of the abbey when they first spied the men emerging from the surrounding forest.

An alarm sounded from behind the fortified stone walls as the riders came closer to the grounds. Vikings! The loud iron bell pealed unceasingly, mixing with the shouts of women and men barking orders.

"Damn," Eugis cursed under his breath. He supposed he should have expected as much, surrounded as he was by the fair-haired men of the north. He had hoped that Glastonbury was far enough inland to be unaware of the tales of the savage acts performed by the Viking raiders. And in this hope, he had allowed his driving urge to retrieve Maere to cloud his judgment. He sighed. It was too late for regrets now. He'd have to make the best of this situation.

Eugis drew in the reins, slowing his mount as he and his companions neared the large iron and oak gate. He motioned with his hand and the escort hung back while Eugis rode forward. "Greetings," he called.

"Go away, Northmen!" came a man's voice from within. "This is a place of God. Take your heathen ways from here. We want no trouble from you." Despite the commanding words, the voice was shaky.

"We're not here as raiders. If you know of the Vikings, then you know they prefer the easy prey of monasteries along the coastline," Eugis said with a smile, in case someone was watching. He wasn't given to easy friendliness, though there were times, such as this, where he tried to affect a gentle nature. "These men here are in my employ. We mean no harm to any of you."

"What could possibly bring you to Saint Columba's if not looting and murder? We know the tales of those men you ride with. You might be a Briton, but you will not take us for fools!" Behind the wall, several men joined in shouting their agreement.

Eugis shifted on his saddle, renewed urgency threatening his careful composure. "I have come to visit with Abbess Magrethe."

There was a long silence before a man answered. "She is no longer with us."

Eugis looked sharply at the gate. "No longer with you? Has she been transferred to another position?" The forced smile quickly disappeared. "Tell me, where might I find her?"

Voices rose from beyond the walls of the abbey as the residents argued among themselves. Finally, an older man replied, "You'll find her nowhere on this earth. Magrethe is with the Lord our God. She died just last evening in the chapel fire. May God have mercy on her soul."

Dead? Eugis leaned back in his saddle and thought of the proper-born abbess with her commanding presence. He hadn't seen her since bringing Maere to the abbey. Images of that night, so long ago, filled his thoughts. After he'd killed Manfred, Rhea, and Fox, he'd carried the young girl off and hidden her away with Magrethe, filling the nun's head with notions of Northmen and murder and pagan rituals in order to entice her to take on the child. He remembered that day clearly and the story he'd concocted to convince the abbess...

"Poor Maere's family was lost at sea during a Viking raid," Euris said to Magrethe. He looked heavenward and dabbed at the corners of his eyes delicately with his little finger. He leaned forward and rested his elbows on the woman's finely carved golden oak desk. "She is the sole survivor of the attack."

Magrethe raised her thin, ethereal form out of the tapestry-covered chair. Holding the skirt of her bark brown habit in one hand, her worn prayer beads in the other, she approached the girl. She walked slowly all around her as Maere stood perfectly still, her eyes focused straight ahead. Magrethe slipped the beads around her own neck, arranging them neatly beneath the long black cowl, then lifted a lock of Maere's dark red hair. She let it sift through her fingers. She touched the girl's shoulder. The child never moved.

The woman crouched and looked into the girl's expressionless eyes. "Would you like to tell me what happened?" she asked, a warm, encouraging smile on her faintly lined face.

Maere continued to stare, blinking only once or twice, while the nun waited for a reply.

"Does she not speak?" Magrethe finally asked Eugis as she straightened.

Eugis stood and motioned for the abbess to follow him to the other side of the room. His boots scuffed against the polished stone floor as he walked, the only sound to be heard in the abbess's chamber. When they were out of earshot of the girl, Eugis answered. "Not since the attack." He tugged at his dark blue tunic, then tucked a strand of brown hair behind a long ear. "As her only living relative, the responsibility of her welfare has fallen to me. I am not married so, naturally, the first thought that came to mind was to have her placed in your fine convent here in Glastonbury. The piety and devotion of your sisters is known throughout southern Britain."

Magrethe smiled and nodded. She folded her hands beneath her mantle as she continued to listen.

"Though there are a few things of which I must warn you." He took a step nearer the abbess. "She is given to the telling of fanciful stories." He glanced at Maere. "Of course, that was before the accident. But once she finds her voice again, I imagine she'll bend your ear with many a tale. It's nothing you need to be concerned with and she'll no doubt outgrow the inclination." While he spoke, Eugis stroked his beard. "And I think it best you are aware that my brother's family had lived in the wild region of Tintagel."

"The land of pagans and Devil worshippers," Magrethe said, then set her mouth in a firm line.

"There are a growing number of Christians in the area, but," Eugis said, "unfortunately, Maere's mother and father—Rhea and Manfred—were not among them. They practiced the pagan ways."

Aghast, Magrethe's hand flew to her mouth. She looked at the child again and shook her head. *"You're telling me she knows nothing of the Lord our God?"*

"I fear not. I cannot tell you how many times I tried to get my brother to accept the sacrament of baptism." He shrugged and tossed his hands in the air. *"But, alas, he'd have none of it. Now, he has died with nary a chance of seeing Heaven."*

"It seems to me our Lord has guided you wisely, sir." The abbess turned and walked back to her desk. Perching lightly on the edge of the chair, she said, *"We at St. Columba's are always eager to accept potential novices. There can never be enough serving in His name."* She made a short sign of the cross over her breast. *"Of course, there is the matter of a dowry."*

"Say no more." Eugis reached into the purple sash tied neatly around his waist and extracted a bulging leather pouch. The coins clinked as he set it on the desk. *"Are there any other requirements for admission?"*

"No. The dowry will cover whatever the girl will need," Magrethe said, reaching for the money as she spoke. Eugis immediately placed his hand down over it.

"However, I have one special requirement of my own," he said.

The nun raised an eyebrow. *"What is this requirement?"*

"Maere is very dear to me," he said. *"I want you personally to make certain no man touches her. When she is eighteen, I will return to claim her."*

"Claim her?" Her eyes narrowed.

"What I meant to say is: I'm certain that by then I will have arranged a marriage for the girl. No doubt her betrothed won't want to wait any longer past the age of maturity than that." Eugis buffed his nails on his sleeve and looked at the abbess.

"I understand." She shifted again. *"Now, you say there is no other family?"*

Eugis shook his head. *"None."*

"And no betrothed at this time?"

He leaned forward. *"There was, but he's been killed as well. Most unfortunate."* He sighed and leaned back. *"I don't mind telling you, finding a betrothed is the least of my concerns at the moment. For now, I wish only to see the child safe and protected."*

Magrethe folded her hands in front of her and nodded *"Considering the circumstances you have described, I will admit her." Her eyes met his. "And await your instructions concerning her future…"*

Eugis had left that night with a smile on his face, knowing Maere would be kept safe for him, untouched. And now that he was here, he'd not let something as minor as Magrethe's death stand in his way. "What of Maere cu Llwyr? I am her uncle, Eugis cu Llwyr, and I would have a word with her."

Another argument from behind the walls. This was growing tiresome, indeed. "Is there no one in charge of this blasted place?" Eugis interrupted.

"That girl has gone as well," came the solemn reply.

"Gone? Did you say gone? Where did she go?" Eugis barked. When no answer came, he sidled his horse, reached across the large animal, and pounded on the heavy gate. "I've had enough of talking through wood and iron! Let me in!"

A small portal opened, just large enough to reveal an old man's face, blackened with soot. "Not likely, considering your escort." The man snorted as he looked past Eugis, to the Vikings lined up neatly behind him. "I am Father John, the head of this monastery. Not one of you will be allowed in here. Unlike some of our brothers, we are not averse to defending ourselves." He glanced up and Eugis followed his gaze. Several priests were assembled at the top of the wall, bows in hand, arrows pointed and ready to fly.

"Consider yourself lucky, man," John continued. "The young woman you call your niece was tainted with the Devil's blood. We're glad to be rid of her."

"I beg your pardon?" A shiver ran the length of Eugis's spine and the hair on his arms prickled. "Did you say 'tainted'?"

"Raised a girl from the dead, she did. I saw the results of her mischief with my own eyes," the priest said. "Now, I'll say nothing more to you. Take the Northmen and leave." With these words, Father John slammed the small portal shut.

Raised a girl from the dead? Is the priest certain? Even in his strangest imaginings, Eugis hadn't dreamt that such a power could be granted.

He spun the horse around to face the men behind him. One of the northerners rode forward.

"What is wrong?" the rider asked.

Eugis spat on the ground. "They say Abbess Magrethe is dead, Jorvik. And that my niece Maere is gone as well."

Eugis called back, over his shoulder to Father John. "One last question, then we'll be on our way, kind priest."

"You test my patience, man. I'll allow it only if it means you will truly leave this time."

"I swear," Eugis said. *On my dead brother's body.* "Do you know where the girl might have gone?"

"All I can tell you is that she left with her betrothed. Which you would well know if you are whom you say you are, since he bore a document with your family's mark on it. I saw it myself."

Betrothed?! The word screamed inside Eugis' head. *What mischief is this?* "Please, sir." He gritted his teeth together. "You must tell me. Did this man have a name?"

"So you don't know, do you?" Father John laughed sharply. "I'm done with your questions. I have dead to tend to."

Eugis turned the horse and approached the gate again. Ten years of waiting for this day had worn his patience thin. "You will tell me, old man, or I will order my men to knock this gate down and kill all of you," he roared. "You have my word on this."

The small door swung open again. Father John eyed him, and then said, "It was a strange young man. Said his name was Dylan mac Connall. And like I've already told you, he bore betrothal papers, with your family mark on them."

Eugis's head reeled. He doubled over, sending his gray hair spilling over his blue eyes as he struggled to catch his breath. *Impossible! My own men killed the boy all those years ago. Could it be an imposter?* He searched his mind for some explanation, but could find none. *No, it had to be Fox's son.* He knew this in his gut, knew it with his entire being. *Somehow, the boy had survived the attack.*

CHAPTER FIFTEEN

Eugis and his men made their way carefully through the thick brambles and back to the clearing where they had spent the previous night. The riders dismounted and left the horses, loosely tied, to forage in a patch of tall grass.

One of the men began working a stick against a rock beside the pile of ashes left from their dinner fire the night before. As the wood began to smoke his comrade sprinkled dried bits of grass on the stone. In a few moments, a small fire was started. They placed more grass and twigs on the flames, feeding it until it was burning well enough to accept larger logs.

The remaining riders sat in a circle on the dew-covered ground and began to remove bits of dried meat and hard bread from the skin pouches slung over their shoulders. Eugis rubbed his hands together, trying to warm them from the chill that had overtaken his body since leaving Columba's. When he finally felt consoled against the damp air, he waved his hand, motioning for Jorvik to follow him as he walked away from the others.

The Viking acknowledged the gesture with a slight nod. He stuffed the last bit of meat into his mouth and—with surprising ease for one as large as he—unfolded his war-hardened body from the ground and approached Eugis. He pulled his dark blonde hair away from his steely eyes and tied it with a leather thong. He didn't speak, but only watched the older man.

"We have to find her," Eugis said, his back to the other man. "I've waited too long for this. I tell you, I won't have her taken by another." His voice grew louder. "She *will* be mine. Her powers *will* be mine." He turned to face Jorvik. Eugis's blue eyes were blazing, his face contorted in anger.

"What will you do?" Jorvik asked, his voice steady, his expression blank.

Eugis laughed and some of his stress disappeared. "You Northmen do have a talent for getting to the point, don't you? No mincing of words, just pure action."

"Our companion, Skuld, is a *rynstr*. We can ask him to cast the runes. If the *landvaettir* in this area are friendly, they will position the stones just so and tell us the path the pair you seek are traveling." Jorvik shrugged. "Of course, you can't always trust the land spirits. If they've become offended for some reason, they could send us in circles." He rested his hand on the carved bone hilt of a dagger tucked in his leather waistband. "What say you to this?"

"I have no need of Skuld." Eugis rubbed his lightly bearded chin. "I know Dylan. If indeed it's him, I would venture he would take Maere back to their village." Eugis's voice trailed off as a raven shrieked in the distance, its loud discordant song filling the forest air. The trees leaned forward as the wind increased and their light green leaves brushed against the ground. A flurry of birds rose overhead, fleeing the safety of their perches. The raven screamed again, this time much closer, before landing on a boulder several feet away from the two men.

"It is Hugginn, Odhinn's messenger to the nine worlds!" Jorvik said. He fell to one knee and dropped his head, clasping his hands before him. "You have angered the gods with this talk of taking power which is not yours."

"Nay, my friend." Eugis lightly touched the other man's shoulder and he looked up. "I believe it is someone even greater than your Odhinn," he whispered, his eyes glistening. "It is the goddess Morrigu."

The raven blinked at the pair and turned its head sideways. Eugis took a cautious step toward the animal. It spread its wings. The feathers slowly dropped to the ground and melted away as its body began to transform. In the span of a few breaths, a nude woman stood before them. Jorvik jumped to his feet, his hand once again on the dagger.

Eugis opened his arms wide and bowed low. "Welcome, my Lady. It's been many years since you have blessed me with your presence."

Without speaking, the goddess reached out her hand and ran a sharp fingernail across Eugis's cheek, leaving a trail of blood on his skin. He licked his lips as the warm liquid trickled into the corner of his mouth.

Morrigu leaned forward and pressed her bare breasts against Eugis's leather tunic. "You have found favor with me, Eugis cu Llwyr," she whispered. "I understand you seek power, that you seek two people."

"Yes, my Lady, 'tis true," he said, breathless, his eyes half-closed with desire as the goddess continued to rub against him.

"I will tell you where they have gone, for I would see them receive their proper reward." She smiled, her red lips full and smooth against her white teeth. "But first you must promise to worship me. As I deserve to be worshipped."

Eugis ran his splayed fingers down the sides of her body. He caught his breath as he stared into the depths of her silver eyes. *She was so beautiful. And so deadly.* Jorvik cleared his throat and took a step forward. His foot came down on a branch and it cracked loudly, breaking the spell.

"Leave us, Jorvik," Eugis said, his eyes still on the goddess's face. "We will finish our discussion later."

"There is no good in playing with her kind," Jorvik said. He nodded toward Morrigu. "Especially those that reek evil such as this one."

Eugis glanced at him. "I will hear none of this talk. Leave us now."

Morrigu smiled and entwined her fingers in Eugis's hair. "Know this, Dylan is as aware of Maere's power as you are. He seeks it as well." She touched her lips to his. The blood on his cheek flowed and mixed between them.

"Know your assumption about them is also true. They travel north," Morrigu whispered between hard kisses. She pushed him to the ground, straddling his tall thin body. As she lowered herself, Morrigu whispered again, "North to Tintagel."

CHAPTER SIXTEEN

Dylan sat on his haunches, near the waning embers of the evening fire, and stared at the crescent moon. A long, willowy cloud passed in front of its waning face, paused for a moment, then continued on its journey with the help of the night breeze. Strands of Dylan's black hair lifted lightly from his shoulders, then settled in place again.

He picked up a stick and poked at the glowing bits of wood. It flamed slightly at its tip for a moment, then smoldered and the aromatic scent of pine wafted toward Dylan. The scent filled him, made him alert, strong with the life force of the very tree itself. His cheeks burned, despite the coolness of the night. His muscles grew taut beneath the leather tunic he now wore.

A woman's muffled cry rose from his left. Dylan dropped the stick as he turned his head in the direction of the sound. Maere rolled onto her side and faced him now, her eyes closed in slumber. He'd covered her with the quilt Kate had made, in the hopes its magic would give her comfort as well as warmth. She made a small sound again. Her hands balled into fists, then relaxed. Just as it had been the last three nights, ever since their escape from the abbey. Whatever demons haunted her—and he was certain there were many, with all she'd been through—preferred the dark cover of dreams.

In the few days they had been together, she hadn't offered any hint of recognition, any indication that she knew who he was. He had allowed himself to believe, in the beginning, she'd only pretended not to know. Perhaps she'd learned to hide her secrets from the nuns, play along with them so as not to be punished. That would have been much like the Maere he remembered. But if it were so, surely she would have revealed this to him by now.

He shook his head. *No.* The more time he spent with Maere, the more he realized the truth—she had wedged a boulder so large between her memories and her waking mind he wondered if it would ever be possible to loosen it. Dylan was reminded of a time when they were small and Maere had sought to move a sacred stone out of her path. Back then she was as stubborn as they came. He could see her even now, seven winters old, full of herself, and in charge of the world. He chuckled at the memory...

Maere was walking home from the forest, after one of their explorations. She was mad at him—as she was a good part of the time—so he kept his distance behind her. She suddenly stopped in her tracks when she came to a round rock stuck in the center of the path. She apparently decided to take her anger out on the poor unsuspecting stone, because she kicked it. She yelped in pain and then kicked it again, grunting with frustration when it wouldn't budge for her.

"Cursed stone!" she said, rubbing her bare toes. "I'll see to it you don't hurt anyone else. I will!" She bent over and dug her fingers in under its edges. She tugged and tugged until it began to loosen. Maere stood upright and smiled. "See? I told you, didn't I?" She bent back down and pulled it from its resting place.

"Stop that, girl!"

Maere spun around, dropping the stone. With a thud, it rolled and settled back into its hole. "I didn't do anything, Uncle Eugis." She hid her dirt-covered hands behind her back. She looked away, hoping he wouldn't see her eyes when she spoke. "To tell the truth, I didn't."

"You're a lying child, aren't you Maere?" Eugis sighed and shook his head. His brown hair, bobbed at the ears, jumped with the motion. "Your mother and father protect you too much." He studied her, hard, his eyes squinting so they looked like dark slits in his thin gray face. "A spoiled girl deserving of a whipping, if you ask me. You know better than to disturb the sacred rocks." He grabbed her by the shoulders and she cringed.

Maere stared at her father's brother as fat tears began to roll down her cheeks. "It was in my way."

"In your way?" he thundered. "In your way?" He pointed at the rock. "You would move something that has been in place since the beginning of time simply because it was in your way?"

Maere sniffled and wiped at the tears, leaving streaks of mud on her cheeks. "What else was I supposed to do?"

Eugis threw her down, disgusted. "You could have gone around it, ungrateful child!"

Having witnessed Eugis's brutal treatment of Maere, Dylan ran at break-neck speed. "H – a – l – l – o – o! H – a – l – l – o – o," Dylan shrieked.

Eugis spun around, just as Dylan whipped by him, a cloud of dust following. Eugis sputtered and spat as it whirled around his head.

Dylan grabbed Maere's hand and dragged her along with him. Laughing and screaming, they left Uncle Eugis behind to shake the dirt from his robe.

Once they were clear, they fell to the ground, landing in a soft bed of moss. Maere rolled and giggled so hard, her side hurt. "Why'd you do that? We'll both be in trouble now." She smiled despite the punishment she knew would be coming. "Did you see how he looked at you when you were running? He must've thought you were a phouka coming to claim him as your own." Maere rolled over onto her stomach. "Why'd you save me like that, Dylan?" she asked, growing serious. "It seems like you're always saving me…"

Dylan let go of the memories, pushing them aside as they threatened to overwhelm him. Maere had been right. He had always saved her. *Except on that long ago night of our betrothal.*

I couldn't save Maere, nor our parents, from Eugis's murderous betrayal.

So many years had passed before he'd been able to rescue Maere once again. Maybe too many.

But have I truly rescued her?

He'd used the betrothal as a ploy to get what he wanted, which was to keep Eugis away from her. While he did believe in honoring the vows their families had made when they were betrothed, it had become secondary to his need for revenge.

It doesn't matter. You did the right thing. You kept Maere from Eugis's clutches, and the gods only knew what those priests had been bent on doing at the abbey.

Dylan shook his head. There was no time for dissecting his motives right now. Maere needed to get her mind back and he feared it would take more than her stubbornness this time. It would take determination on both their parts, and a little luck couldn't hurt either.

He shifted on the hard ground. He couldn't deny there was a part of him that longed to hold her and take away her pain, push away the demons stirring her even in sleep. She had grown into a beauty. Even so, he knew the impish child he saw in his mind's eye was sleeping there, waiting to be rediscovered. But how? She was so frightened of him. What was it she had said? "You're the son of the Devil and I can see it in your eyes."

Dylan set his mouth in a straight line and picked up the stick he'd dropped earlier. Whether she remembered him or not made no difference now. It would be nice, perhaps, but it didn't change anything. There would be time enough later for the pleasantries of betrothal. Eugis was undoubtedly pursuing them by now. He knew the bid for Maere's power was coming. And Dylan vowed to win.

MAERE WAS SLIPPING into another dream. She felt her eyes flutter and a sigh escape her lips. It was so strange, the clear state of mind she experienced while sleeping. It made it harder and harder these days to tell where the dreams—nay, nightmares—ended and wakefulness began. Her entire life had become an event from which she wished she could awake. If only she could. If only...

A man appeared, bathed in the indigo light of the night. He stood in front of her, his hands on his hips, a beautiful black steed behind him. The long white robe he wore billowed around his lean form, though Maere felt no breeze. Dark hair hung loosely about his shoulders.

He turned and grabbed a fistful of the horse's mane, pulling himself onto its unsaddled back. Sitting astride the animal, he reached down and smiled. "Maere," he called in a lilting voice, gesturing her to come forward. "Come to me, Maere."

She felt certain he must be an angel of the Lord, sent to offer comfort in her time of distress. She began to move toward him, smiling, happiness bubbling up inside her. But when she got within his reach, her smile faded and her eyes widened in alarm.

The wind began to swirl around them. The man's sleek black hair changed to gray and his white robes were covered in blood.

Maere screamed and tried to pull away from his grasp. "No! No!"

He began to laugh. "You're mine now, just as she intended." He hauled her up in front of him on the horse and flew into the sky over the tree-tops, and toward St. Columba. She looked down and gasped at the burning chapel, the flames reaching up so high they almost touched her feet.

The gray-haired man laughed. "It's time, Maere."

"Time for what?"

"Soon, you'll know, Maere." He pushed her off the horse and she fell down, down, down into the flames.

"No!"she screamed as she was engulfed by the fire.

"Maere!"

Hands gripped her shoulders and shook her.

"Maere, you must wake up."

She gasped and her eyes flew open. "You," she whispered.

The young man—the one who called himself her betrothed—Dylan mac Connall was hovering above her. His handsome face was so close she could see the reflection of her own image in the midnight depths of his eyes.

He held tight to her. "Tell me what you were dreaming," he demanded. "What did you see?"

Maere twisted sideways, rolling away from him. In a quick movement, she was on her feet and ready to run.

Dylan dove and grabbed her by the ankle, pulling her down to the ground. Maere gasped, the wind knocked out of her. Dylan forced her onto her back and pinned her down with his hands, bracing himself over her.

"Let go of me!" she said, grinding the words out through the pain in her chest. "You have no right to treat me so!"

"I have every right, as your betrothed." He leaned forward and stared hard into her eyes. "What did you see?"

Maere struggled against him, but it was no use. He was so much stronger. And it was this very strength she found so infuriating. Oh, to be a man for a brief moment. *I'd teach him a lesson or two!*

"Tell me and I'll let you go," he said in a softer tone.

Resigned, she closed her eyes, and began to speak. "There was a man, it was you. At least I thought it was you. The man had long dark hair and he was wearing a beautiful white robe and he was sitting on a white horse. He beckoned to me and when I got close enough to him, close enough where he could touch me, he suddenly changed. He wasn't you anymore. He had gray hair and the white robe was stained with blood." Maere frowned as she struggled with the memory.

"He hauled me up in front of him and flew over St. Columba's. The chapel was on fire, the flames were so high they reached the sky. And then he pushed me off the horse and I dropped down into the flames." Maere shivered as tears streamed down her cheeks.

Dylan gently wiped her tears away. "In dreams, fire is cleansing. Being dropped into it means you'll face a rebirth."

Maere opened her eyes, at his gentle touch.

"I believe the Christians call this baptism by fire," he went on. "You will go into the flames as one person and emerge as another. Based on the description of the man and horse, I believe your Uncle Eugis will be involved. He might even instigate these events."

"Uncle Eugis? How can you be so certain?" She shook her head. "He treated me with kindness. The abbess told me everything he did." Maere's words tumbled out as she recalled what Magrethe had told her time and again over the years. "He took care of me after my mother and father were killed by the Northmen. He took me to St. Columba's so I would be safe."

Dylan's face darkened. "Not killed, Maere. Murdered. And not by Vikings, but by Eugis's own hand."

"You lie." Maere turned her face away. "I won't listen to you."

"This is not a lie, Maere, but a forgotten truth." Dylan cupped her chin, forcing her to look at him. He was so close, their lips were almost touching. "Do you know what it means to be betrothed?" he asked, his voice barely a whisper. "It means you must obey me and honor my wishes. It means you are bound to believe all I tell you as the God's own truth. We're as good as married already, with all the rights contained therein." As he spoke, his breath caressed her mouth.

Maere's body tensed as she stared at his lips. Her stomach quivered. Her heartbeat pounded out an ancient rhythm in her ears. Her blood burned as it ran through her veins. She licked her lips, unintentionally drawing Dylan's focus, and she immediately wished she hadn't.

Dylan brushed his mouth lightly against hers. She trembled beneath the caress and a pleasant tingle filled her belly. She searched his lips with her own. He pulled back a few inches, studied her face for a moment, then slowly pushed himself to his feet. "Perhaps a thought to ponder?"

As she watched him walk away, Maere fought back the empty ache which filled her the moment he stood up. She wiped at her mouth as if to cleanse the memory of his touch. *Blast him to the devil, anyway.* As far as she was concerned, there was no betrothal. She was sworn only to Christ.

Maere sat up, fingering her stone necklace through the cloth of her gown. On impulse, she yanked it out and off and threw it at Dylan with all her might. It hit him squarely in the back of the head before bouncing to the ground.

Dylan spun around and spotted the offending object. With a scowl, he bent over and scooped it up. "What is—"

Maere scrambled to her feet.

"You still have this?" he asked looking at the stone.

Maere hurried toward him, her hair flying wildly about her. "Give it back," she snapped, her fingers grasping for the disk.

He held the citrine high, dangling it just out of Maere's reach, a smile playing about his lips. "Have you seen them lately?"

"Seen who?" she asked, leaning into him as she stretched on tiptoes. Why wouldn't he just give it back to her?

"The fays, girl. Who else?"

Maere blanched. She took a step back and crossed herself. "I don't know what you're talking about."

"No?" Dylan smiled. He held the stone between his thumb and forefinger, level with Maere's eyes, the hole pointed toward the deep green of the forest. "Look through the opening."

She took another step back. This seemed so familiar. What did it mean? She felt a pain in her head, a clear warning. There would be more pain, in the remembering. "I won't!"

"You must look, Maere." He closed his eyes. "Please." He opened his eyes and stared at her. Sadness flickered in those dark depths.

What could it hurt to humor him? She leaned forward and focused one eye through the hole. "So much for your little game. I don't see a thing." She took a step back.

Dylan sighed. He pulled her forward. "One more time."

She hesitated, then looked again. After a moment, the citrine began to glow, concentrating her attention more directly on what lay beyond, in the forest. At first, she detected only a small movement, a rustle of ground cover. And then it appeared. *Sweet Mother of God.* A small thing —nearly a person—with long blonde hair and a dress fashioned from moss. Maere watched, transfixed, as it stepped forward. The miniature woman smiled and waved.

"Oh, Maere, I've missed ye." She jumped up and down in delight and clapped her hands together. "It's so good to be seen by ye again, child."

Maere's mouth fell open. She jerked her head back. "It can't be!" she exclaimed. She grabbed the stone away from Dylan and held it out in front of her, horrified. "All these years, I had no idea. I've carried a tool of the Devil with me." Another sharp pain shot through her head. *Don't remember.* Maere looked at Dylan, her eyes wild. "I'll be having no part of it, I tell you. No part!"

Before Dylan could intervene, Maere turned and slammed the disk against a rock. The citrine split in two. Dylan bent to pick up the pieces. "What have you done?" he thundered. "This was a gift, woman! Given to you by the fays themselves." He threw up his hands. "You've seen them yourself, just now. How can you not remember?"

Maere covered her ears as tightly as she could. "I won't listen to you, Dylan mac Connall." The earth began spinning under her feet. "I won't remember." She felt her feet slipping out from beneath her as her sight narrowed and grew black. Her head hurt so badly. Why hadn't she heeded the warning? "I won't remember," Maere whispered once more before the darkness completely enveloped her and she crumpled to the ground.

CHAPTER SEVENTEEN

A slow, steady rhythm resounded in Maere's ears. Thump-thump. Thump-thump. Thump-thump. Like heavy raindrops beating against a hollow log, it was continuous and reassuring. She prayed it would never stop as she nestled her head tighter against the pillow.

Wait. Something was wrong here. The pillow wasn't plump and soft. Rather, it was hard and tense. Her eyes still closed, she reached up and punched at the cushion, hoping to loosen the down.

"What was that for?" a man's voice asked with a laugh.

Maere's eyes flew open. Sweet Jesus, she wasn't in bed! Horror filled her as she realized she was being carried by that man, that spawn of Satan who encouraged the practice of black magic. The evil one who had turned her world upside down the moment he appeared. The steady, soothing sound wasn't rain, but his heartbeat echoing in her ears. She jerked her head away from the crook of his arm.

"Put me down," she demanded, trying to wriggle free from his hold.

"I think I like you better right here. You can do no damage to me or yourself if I hold onto you." He chuckled and Maere felt the vibration of it rise from the depths of his chest.

Maere pushed against him harder this time. Oh, but this wasn't good at all. What would the monster do with her now that he had her in his grasp? With a free hand, she made a quick sign of the cross over her breast. Then, with all her might, Maere gave him one good shove and almost succeeded in tumbling out of his arms.

Dylan stopped walking. "You're as hard to hold onto as a fish, girl." He shook his head. "Nay. I'd say a fish is easier to hold."

As he let Maere's legs slide free, Dylan pulled her close. With the motion, her arms went up and her chest flattened against him. To her dismay, Maere's heartbeat fell into rhythm with his. *Judas*, she hissed to the offending organ. Its pace quickened and so did his. This was too much! To be betrayed by one's own body was beyond forgiveness.

With his left arm wrapped around Maere's back, Dylan reached out his free hand and pushed back the wild mane of copper hair spilling over her eyes. Without speaking, he gazed at her, as if looking into her eyes for whatever information they might offer.

Maere pushed against him with all her might. "Let me go, man." She ground out the words, but Dylan held fast to her. "I demand you tell me where we are." When he didn't answer, she looked up and found his eyes steadily fixed on hers. Maere felt her body begin to relax under that gaze. What magic was he working on her now? What magic did his eyes speak as they held hers in their grasp?

"Please. I'd like to sit," she whispered.

Dylan didn't release her. Instead, he squeezed her even tighter against him. Maere's lips parted. She watched in quiet fascination as his gaze shifted from her eyes to her mouth.

"We're still moving north," he replied, his voice smooth and even. "You've been asleep only a short time."

"Why didn't you wake me?"

Dylan smiled. "I tried, to be certain. After you fainted, there was no stirring you, so I left you to rest." He shrugged. "There seemed no reason to not continue on. You're easy enough to carry."

A faint blush stained Maere's cheeks. "You take much for granted, don't you, Dylan mac Connall?"

A flash of lightning in the distance warned of a turn of the weather and lit up Dylan's face. "I take what is mine. Nothing more. Absolutely nothing less."

For the first time since he'd appeared, Maere looked at him, really looked at him. Until this moment, she hadn't allowed herself to do so. It was much easier to look away and carry the image in her mind of this man as a monster.

His presence was strong but there was pain in his eyes and on his face. She could read it in the lines around his mouth, in the faint circles under his eyes. And strangest of all, Maere could feel it herself, in the pit of her stomach. It was if she had experienced the same pain he had. Felt the same anger. Dylan must have felt it too, for in that moment of Maere's realization, a single tear fell from the corner of his eye. Without thinking, she reached up and traced its path down his cheek, as it followed the light scar he bore, along the strong line of his chin, to where it rested in the hollow of his neck. He sucked in his breath as she touched him, as if the simple act pained him even more.

He closed his eyes for a moment, as lightning illuminated the sky again. Large drops of rain began to fall. They washed over his face, cleansing away the line of the tear. When Dylan opened his eyes again, Maere saw the sense of purpose in his soul. And she now realized his struggle with that purpose.

"What is it? What pains you so?"

Dylan blinked away the new moisture forming in his eyes. "It'll do me no good to try to explain it to you. You need to remember for yourself."

Maere touched his arm. "What is it I should remember?" He didn't need to explain, though, for as she finished speaking, a shiver came over her. It started in the center of her gut, feeling like the rush of a hundred birds flapping their wings. She saw them in her mind's eye: Blackbirds. Crows. Ravens. Evil birds with silver eyes, unleashed and running rampant. More images floated into the scene. A man in a white robe. A cup of poison offered in false friendship. Maere pulled her hand away from Dylan. *Sweet Jesus, what had happened to this man? What had tainted him so? And how was it she could see it all as if it had only just happened?*

She searched his eyes, struggling to explore the images further, but they vanished as surely as if an iron door had dropped over them. Maere knew Dylan had seen the same images. She knew it by the expression on his face. The pain was still there, but it was softened, now that it was shared between them.

Dylan leaned forward, tilting his head slightly, and Maere knew he meant to claim her mouth with his own. Truth be told, she suddenly realized she welcomed it and would be disappointed if he didn't kiss her right now. There would be solace in his touch.

She reached her hand toward his face as their lips met. The kiss was slow and sweet. As their forms mingled, Maere inhaled deeply of his scent. He smelled of wild pine groves, of the moon at night, of morning dew. Maere's senses filled and she pushed her mouth against his, savoring the taste of him as their tongues met.

Dylan's arms encircled her in a warm embrace, one around her waist, the other cradling her head. His hand played with the back of her neck, sending delicious tingles down her spine, as they continued to explore each other's mouths. *So, this is what Seelie had found so appealing.*

The rain began to fall harder and Maere was dimly aware of the pine boughs on either side of the clearing where they stood, as the branches seemed to bend and shelter the two of them from the coming storm. Lightning bolted across the sky and then struck the ground not twenty feet away. Dylan jerked his head away from Maere, releasing her and pushing her behind him. The forest floor, still dry under the heavy foliage, burst into flames. Aided by the burgeoning wind, it began to travel in their direction.

"Come," Dylan urged as he turned around to face her. "The fire will consume us if we tarry any longer."

But Maere found she couldn't move. She was rooted dead to the spot as she stared in awe at the flames. She wanted to move, really she did. But there was something so familiar about a fire in the forest. The cup of poison passed before her mind's eye again. The rest of the memory hung at the dark edges of her mind but refused to become visible. She shook her head, trying to clear it.

Maere looked at Dylan. The pain she was feeling reflected in his eyes.

Dylan grabbed her arm. "I know of some caves near here, where we can wait out the storm."

They left the trail and moved deeper into the forest. Again, it seemed to Maere the trees were either moving intentionally out of their way or covering them as they hurried through the rain. How could that be?

"Are the trees—are they—helping us?" she shouted over the wind. Another branch shifted before her, moving away, and Maere realized she needed no reply. It was obvious they were, as the trees intervened to offer some measure of shelter. Given everything she'd seen and lived the past few days, why did she even bother to wonder over it?

Dylan called out an answer, but it was lost to the storm. The water was coming down harder now. The cold drops stung as they hit the tender flesh of Maere's face. She ran along behind Dylan, shielding her head with her arms.

There was something else odd happening, even odder than the recent turns of events. Maere couldn't quite put her finger on what it was, but the quiver in her stomach was growing again. Then she realized every time Dylan changed direction—and Maere did as well, following him—the wind changed. It forced them to turn away, to seek another direction, as if the storm were pushing them toward a specific place.

"There." Dylan stopped and pointed ahead. "It's not the cave I had in mind, but it'll do for now."

Maere stopped beside him, training her eyes on the black opening he indicated. Bushes covered with white linen knots all but concealed it. She couldn't go in there. This was a holy shrine, each tied rag symbolizing a petition offered to the patron saint of the region.

"We can't use this cave. It belongs to a saint. It's sacred ground."

Dylan looked at her curiously as he gave her a little shove forward. "We haven't time to discuss this. It's the only dry place around." He laughed as she made the sign of the cross once again. Dylan leaned forward and spoke in her ear. "Besides, this was a pagan shrine long before the Christians took it over."

Maere glanced over her shoulder at him, a reply on her lips, when lightning split the night sky. The wind lashed out, its empty howl mixing with a raven's caw, and she hurried through the entrance of the cave.

CHAPTER EIGHTEEN

F lashes of lightning lit the cave just enough to illuminate the interior. The back wall wasn't quite ten feet away, creating more of a grotto than an actual cave.

The wind howled as another bolt ripped the sky. Dylan looked around. No nests or piles of bones, sure signs of wild animals. Good. And there, off to the left, was a hoard of wood and tinder.

"Here, Maere. A place to rest." He indicated a large stone, near the opening, but well enough away from the rain pummeling through the brush just outside.

Dylan took a deep breath, closed his eyes, and focused inward. When he opened his eyes again, he didn't need the lightning to show him the woodpile. It glowed for him with the tree life still left within it. As Dylan gathered an armload and placed it in the center of the grotto, where the floor was already charred from many fires, he softly offered up a prayer to the woodland god Hu Gadarn, thanking him for the shelter and the abundance of wood.

"Did you say something?" Maere asked as she twisted her hair to squeeze the moisture from it.

Dylan glanced up, his concentration broken. He looked at her for a moment, then smiled. "Only a simple prayer of thanks."

Maere stood and went to his side, sitting easily on the dirt floor. She watched his profile as he returned to the task of assembling the wood for a fire. "To which god do you pray?" she asked quietly.

He laughed. "Do you truly wish to know?"

She drew herself up. "I wouldn't have asked if I didn't want to know."

"Hu Gadarn, the god of the woodlands and forests." He looked at her from the corner of his eyes and added, "The horned one."

Maere's hand flew to her mouth and she quickly made a sign of the cross with the other. "You pray to the Devil!"

"Not the devil, girl." He turned to fully face her. "This Christian faith running over our land has turned him into such. He is naught but the keeper of nature, consort to the great lady, our mother goddess." Dylan reached for the tinder and tucked it around the base of the wood. "He is not evil, but nor is he good. He is what he is."

A loud crash of thunder shook the walls of the grotto. Maere jumped, her eyes wide, and she shifted closer to Dylan, their shoulders nearly touching. "He is what he is," she repeated, realizing she could say the same of this man beside her. She should probably feel some outrage over talk of how this pagan god wasn't evil, but the fight within her was waning. She rubbed her eyes in exhaustion.

With the flash of lightning that followed, she saw Dylan passing his hand over the pile, his mouth moving but the words were silent. Suddenly, blue flames burst from the tinder and ignited the wood.

"Sweet Mother!" Maere scrambled to her feet and bolted for the entry, ready to run out into the storm. In an instant, Dylan was at her side, holding her tightly.

"Where would you be going on such a night?" he gently teased. Gesturing toward the fire, he added, "I've created this for you. Come. Warm your bones."

"I won't!" Maere shook her head wildly, sending curls tumbling over her face. "All this talk about how the Devil isn't the Devil. I'm not believing it, Dylan mac Connall." She pointed a shaky finger at the fire. "Those are the very flames of Hell, they are!"

Dylan laughed and the deep sound filled the cave, echoing off the walls. Maere fought the urge to cover her ears as it vibrated in her head. "Nay. 'Tis but a trick of magic." He extended his hand. "Come. Please."

Taking tiny steps, Maere allowed herself to be guided to the warmth. As she sat, she peered into the dancing brightness and discovered the small fire stirred memories of larger fires. She stared, mesmerized by the play of colors, entranced by the dance of the red, yellow, blue, and orange flames.

Leaning against the stone wall, half-hidden in the shadows, Maere could feel Dylan watching closely, even as she was deep in thought. She absently dried her hair before the fire, fanning it out over her hands.

Finally, he spoke. "What are you thinking?"

Maere tugged her eyes away from the flames and raised them to meet Dylan's. His eyes glowed with the light of the fire. Her stomach quivered. Why did he have to look at her like that? Like he was ready to devour her very soul, given the chance? Even his shadow jumped and floated above him, as though it were ready to pounce on her as well. She hugged her knees and looked away. How could his presence be so frightening yet so reassuring at the same time?

"What makes you believe I'm thinking anything at all?" she murmured. She glanced up at him again. "Perhaps I'm just sitting here enjoying the heat."

Dylan smiled and those blasted eyes went right through her. *Sweet Mother!* She sucked in her breath.

"Aye, it is hot in here now." He slid down against the wall and crouched, looking at her pointedly. She was a beautiful, wild creature of the night sitting there. Her hair in disarray from the storm, her face flushed, and her eyes shining. "And growing hotter still."

Maere considered his words for a moment. Her cheeks burned as the double meaning came to her. She hugged her knees even tighter and leaned away a bit.

Dylan laughed. Laughed at her, for heaven's sake. This man possessed more nerve than anyone she had ever met. Oh, but she would like to knock him right to the ground. Then she would be the one to laugh. Why, he must have been raised in a forest by animals, blind to the world around him, to behave so! She glared at him.

"I've been knowing you a long time, Maere cu Llwyr. I know your mind is constantly searching. I know you're always exploring the nature of things."

He smiled and this time she found the gesture not to be condescending. She found it warmed her like no fire could. She rubbed her eyes. What was the matter with her? "You know nothing of me."

Dylan smiled, a tinge of sadness playing at the corners of his mouth. "That's where you are truly wrong. I know much of you, which is why I know you must have thoughts running through your head."

She raised her hand to him, as if to block his scrutiny. Or perhaps to block the mix of emotions she was afraid she might be showing.

Dylan moved next to her and sat down. He touched her cheek and she stiffened. "I remember the night you were born, and your father held you high for the gods and goddesses to see, the triple signs appearing, marking you as one destined for greatness." He gently turned her face to his and their eyes met. "I remember the magic of your girlish laugh and your healing touch." He took her hand in his and turned it over, caressing the open palm with his thumb. "How can you say I know nothing of you?"

Maere hesitantly raised her free hand, suddenly overwhelmed with an urge to erase his sadness. His face was so beautiful when he smiled, if a man could be called beautiful. She wished him to smile again. Smile for her. Mother of God, why was she having such thoughts about this devil? She shook off the emotion and yanked back her hands. She looked away and rubbed her palms together.

Undaunted, Dylan continued, "I once knew a brave girl who stood up for herself when she was wronged. Where has that girl gone?" He touched her chin again and gently guided her eyes back to his. "I beg you, Maere. Set her free that I might enjoy her company once again."

Maere stared at him for a moment, then stood and walked to the opening of the cave, crossing her arms about her. Dylan's words spun around in her head, threatening to wipe the earth out from beneath her feet. What if his words were true? What if he did truly know her? But how could he? Her family was killed by the Vikings—that's what she had always been told by Abbess Magrethe. They weren't murdered by her uncle, as this man claimed. And she was no healer even if she did help Seelie. She was just a young woman content to join the order of sisters at St. Columba's. Why wouldn't he just let her be? Dear Lord, her head hurt. Thunder rumbled and lightning surged again. She took a step back and turned to face Dylan.

"I repeat: You know nothing of me. I am not who you described. If my father—pagan in his beliefs—ever held me for these gods and goddesses of yours to see, how would I know? If it happened as you described, I was just a newborn babe. It means nothing to me." She sighed, every last bit of energy leaving her body. "My soul belongs to Jesus Christ and His church. That's all that matters now, not the past. It's to His service I wish to return." She was so tired. "Why did you come, Dylan mac Connall? Why did you make me leave my home?"

"I would see a promise fulfilled," he whispered.

Maere snapped her head up, her eyes wary. "What promise would that be?"

"Ah, Maere," he said, sighing. "The promise I made to your father on that same night you were born. I swore to Manfred I would always care for you."

Maere stepped closer to the fire and sat down, pulling her knees to her chest again. She stared hard at Dylan, measuring his words. Light flashed in her mind, brighter than the lightning still burning the sky, and in that moment she saw into his thoughts. But the visit was so brief she couldn't make sense of it. "There's a darker reason for your coming. I would know what it is."

"You think you saw something just now, don't you?" Guilt tugged at Dylan's heart and he turned his face away. "'Tis as I said." He clenched his jaw and the muscle ticked ever so slightly. "There's nothing more."

"You lie, Dylan mac Connall."

"You truly wish to know?" He grasped her upper arms, forcing her to look at him, and their eyes locked. "See it all, then." Through his gaze he unleashed the years of hatred and sorrow and pain. He watched intently as his feelings entered Maere. He knew the moment she saw it all, the raw emotion striking out with the intensity of the storm raging outside. Maere gasped as if she had been struck. Dylan released his hold and turned his face away once more.

"Do you understand now?" he asked, his voice a rough whisper. "Is it evil you see in my heart? Or just the longing for retribution for so many years lost?"

"Sweet Mary, I don't know how, but I see the pain of old wounds—

not of the flesh, but of the soul." Her heart broke for him and she reached out in his direction, her hand tingling with power as it had that night Seelie came to her. "I can help you. Let me help you." For once, the offering to heal didn't frighten her. It seemed so natural, as if she were born to it. A wave of familiarity swept over her like she had offered this service many times before.

"I seek no healing of this wound, Maere." He pulled away from her. "At least not from you."

She dropped her hand to her lap. His words stung her like no slap could. She took a deep breath and pushed away the hurt, allowing anger to replace it. "Would you refuse healing to give your life for vengeance, then?" she demanded. "Is that all that exists for you?"

"Aye. I would. And it is."

Maere searched his eyes, seeing he would have none of her charity, that he regretted letting her inside his mind. An uncomfortable mixture of sadness and dread welled inside her. "Then tell me true, sir. Do you mean to give my life as well?"

CHAPTER NINETEEN

The wildness of the storm subsided, the rumble of thunder and flashes of lightning died away. The night was quiet now, except for the subtle pinging of leftover raindrops outside the grotto.

Maere rested near the fire, in that delicate place between wakefulness and slumber, considering Dylan's words. Yes. He would sacrifice her, so great was his need for vengeance. She had seen and felt his pain and anger, but had also felt his resistance to healing.

Perhaps it was her refusal to believe his words about her past that angered him. But the notion of pagans, gods, and goddesses were just too foreign to her mind for easy acceptance. Dear Lord, but her life had taken so many twists and turns in the last few days she doubted it would ever be right again. And how could it be? She had been wrenched from the only home she'd ever known by this complicated man who could be gentle and teasing one moment and then dark and brooding the next.

She sighed and her eyes eased open. Dylan slept opposite her, huddled near the smoldering embers of the fire. He looked so peaceful in sleep. How ironic that her pain haunted her in her dreams while his was with him when he was awake. She grew groggy again, then the soft caress of sleep brushed Maere's eyelids and they fluttered closed.

While she and Dylan rode on the wings of their dreams, a mist formed at the mouth of the grotto, its nebulous form shimmering with the moonlight. It drifted in through the opening, weaving its way to and fro, circling the sleeping pair. The vapor wafted over and around them in undulating currents. When Dylan shifted the mist halted. When his breath grew even, it moved again, spinning in a sparkling whirl. It rose to the ceiling, and dropped long tendrils to the earth, touching Maere and Dylan where they lay. As the two fell into a deeper, dreamless sleep, the vapor receded and left the cave, a soft feminine laugh echoing from its depths.

"Tell me what I desire to hear, Eugis," Morrigu whispered from behind him.

Eugis turned his head ever so slightly, covering his surprise at the arrival of the goddess, and continued to warm his hands over the fire. Let her think he was not anxious, he reasoned to himself, she would then have less power over him.

Jorvik slowly rose from where he was crouched opposite Eugis, his hand on the hilt of his dagger. Morrigu smiled at the Northman, her eyes moving over his muscled, battle-hardened body in a long caress. They came to rest on his face, her silver eyes locking with his clear blue ones. Jorvik shivered with the intensity of her gaze.

"I see even you can feel desire, Viking," she said with a smile.

Jorvik pulled his eyes away from the goddess's and turned to Eugis. "I will seek the *rynstr* to cast her from our presence." He turned on the ball of his foot to leave the camp.

Morrigu stepped in front of Eugis. The older man stood and faced her. "That is not the way I expect to be greeted," she said, her full red lips drawn into a pout.

Panic quaked in the pit of Eugis's stomach. Who knew what Morrigu was capable of if angered? "Wait, Jorvik," he called out. "You do the goddess a disservice."

"No Eugis, it is she who disservices me." Jorvik spun back around. "We have our deities in the Northland and she is but one of their evil sisters. I know her kind."

Morrigu approached the tall Viking, her eyes narrowed. "And what do you think you know of my kind?"

Jorvik snorted. "I know if I cut one of you, you will not bleed." He pulled the dagger from its leather sheath and held it in front of him. "But I would take pleasure in it, just the same." He lowered his knife and looked from the amused eyes of the goddess to the shocked eyes of Eugis.

"My father is a great warrior. My mother is a Valkyrie," Jorvik said. "The gods and goddesses of Asgard looked with disfavor on their love. When I was born, I was left with my father and they were forever separated. All I carry as a remembrance of Aislinn is the ability to draw on the power of the Valkyries before going into battle."

He leveled his gaze at Morrigu. "It is because of you and your kind that my father knows no happiness in this life. It is because of you and your kind that I was robbed of a mother. You have no honor in my eyes." He turned away from them. "I follow my own path, away from the gods," he said over his shoulder as he walked away.

Morrigu smirked. "Wherever did you find him?"

"Raiding monasteries along the coast. Plundering villages. Living an aimless existence." Eugis shrugged. "Trying to escape his past, from the sound of it."

"Sounds most interesting." Morrigu laughed and touched the scar she had left on Eugis's cheek.

"I suppose. Sad though, to live such an empty life." Eugis rubbed his chin. "Enough of that. He doesn't usually talk so much. I think I like him better when you don't have him so vexed."

Morrigu laughed and brushed her body against his. "Now, tell me what I long to hear."

Eugis wrapped his long arms around her, twining his fingers through her blue-black hair. "You are so beautiful, my goddess." He dropped to his knees and, with a light touch, his finger traced a circle around her navel. "I would worship you, if you'd allow me." He gently kissed her stomach.

Morrigu cupped his chin and raised it so their eyes met. "First, I have news for you," she whispered. "News of Maere."

Eugis slowly rose, letting his tongue run the length of her torso as he did so. "Where is she?"

"In a grotto, a Christian shrine. A place that once belonged to my sister, Macha." She all but spat the words. "In the old days, warriors would ride there to seek her blessing before going to battle. Now, these same people tie petitions to the bushes and pray to their saints at Macha's sacred keep." She looked at Eugis and the rage on her face began to fade. "She's one of them. Maere has no ken of who or what she is. You left her at the convent too long. She wants to join those nuns at St. Columba's."

"A nun?" A low laugh rose from Eugis and rumbled past his lips. "Manfred and Rhea must be restless in their graves over this." He shook his head. "I suppose 'tis sad she recalls naught of the old ways." His hand swept up the goddess's well-curved side. "But it matters not." His expression grew hard. "I'll have her anyway. And her power."

Morrigu's pink tongue flicked over her lips and she smiled. Eugis pulled her roughly to him and his mouth claimed hers, then moved down her neck. "Tell me," he whispered against her throat. "Where is Maere?"

"Not far." Morrigu chuckled, a low throaty sound. She shoved Eugis to the ground. "A little over a day's ride from here, still to the north." She watched him closely. "Dylan mac Connall is with her."

Eugis sucked in his breath. *So, it was Fox's son who had stolen the girl away from him.* "I suspected as much." He shrugged. "No matter. It will be my pleasure to let him watch me take Maere away from him once again. Then I'll kill him. Perhaps I'll kill Maere too. Or leave her for the nuns."

"You have said what I wanted to hear, Eugis." The goddess smiled.

Eugis rose up slightly from where he lay on the earth, pulled his woolen tunic over his head, and tossed it aside. He held out his hand and Morrigu slipped hers into his. "Come, Goddess. You bring me great news and I would worship you, just as you deserve."

"And so you shall." Morrigu lowered herself onto him until their naked forms merged. "You should know I've insured against them leaving the grotto with a sleeping spell." She smiled and began to move against him. "And I've sealed the cave against intruders. Anyone looking in will think it empty and be compelled to leave. Send that tall Northman in the morning to retrieve the girl." She groaned with the thought of the Viking. "He dislikes my brothers and sisters so much that I've decided to set a test for him."

"Should I be jealous?" Eugis whispered against her throat before nibbling the tender flesh.

Morrigu kissed him roughly, biting his upper lip and drawing blood. "That would be your choice, wouldn't it?"

CHAPTER TWENTY

Jorvik and his men rode hard along the worn paths that led to the northern part of the isle. Eugis had roused them early, his words urgent, as he instructed them as to the task at hand. Only a day away, he'd said, was the young woman he sought. Asleep in a cave in the north region, she'd be easy to take.

Morrigu had been nowhere about, which was good as far as Jorvik was concerned, cursed goddess that she was. If he'd known one of them was involved, he'd never have accepted the work Eugis offered. Jorvik and his men had plenty to do raiding along the coast, storming the monasteries. Eugis lured them inland with the promise of something different, a diversion for Jorvik's weary men, but now he was regretting the decision.

In spite of his misgivings, Jorvik was compelled to stay true to his word and finish the task. Though a man's oath might not mean much to these southerners, where he came from it was binding. The gold was easy, too. Perhaps easier than taking the coastal Christian compounds, now that the monks were learning how to fight. Actually, it was the easiest payment they had ever come by—four pouches of gold just for the retrieval of a simple girl. Jorvik chided himself. He should know by now that nothing is as easy as it seems.

He shifted in the worn leather saddle as he pondered this deed. Jorvik knew little of Eugis's plan, only that the girl had some sort of special ability Eugis hoped to gain. And she had to be kept virginal. Jorvik smiled to himself. Perhaps. It would, of course, depend on how comely she might be. He shrugged his cloak into place and put his hand over the gold and silver medallion which held it around him, a gift from his father in celebration of his entry to manhood. It'd been many months since he'd last seen Otto and he'd be happy when this task was complete and he could return to his base camp, to his father and his people.

As they rode, Jorvik's thoughts drifted back to Morrigu. He knew nothing of these gods and goddesses in the southern worlds, but they all seemed to possess the same traits of his land. And they all seemed amused with playing their selfish games in the world of man. What cared Morrigu whether or not Eugis succeeded in his plan? She must have her own motives. He knew this in his bones.

But then, it could be Eugis only lusted for the goddess and hoped to gain nothing more than their sensual encounters. After all, a man would have to be dead not to notice her shapely body and welcoming mouth. Eugis likely considered himself blessed by Morrigu's attentions. Jorvik snorted. The man was indeed a fool if he did.

THE SUN HAD RISEN and set over the cave where Dylan and Maere slept. Pilgrims came and went, unaware of the sleeping inhabitants. The pilgrims quietly left their simple offerings of bread or cider in the hope the patron saint, Cedric, would intercede on their behalf with the Christian God and they'd see their prayers answered.

One such pilgrim was lingering near the outside of the cave when the sound of horse hooves and men's voices reached out from the dense forest and touched her ears. She quickly gathered her things and disappeared into the thicket.

As the Northmen neared their destination, they found their way blocked more than once by tree branches. One, long and thin, suddenly slapped Jorvik across the chest. Another grabbed at his horse.

"What goes on here?" he muttered as Asa rode up alongside him.

"This place is enchanted," the *rynstyr* answered. He gestured at the path ahead of them. "Look at the trees. It's as if they would prevent us from the task at hand."

"Morrigu. She's behind this."

"I think not." Asa looked around. "This reeks of magic, but not of that one. We should stop. I should cast the stones and find out what goes on here."

Jorvik cursed as another branch bent down in front of him. "We will not stop." He raised his sword high and swung it in a wide arc. The offending limb, severed, fell to the ground with a muffled thud, the scent of sap filling the air. He held his sword in front of him as he made his way forward. "I do not fear your tricks," he shouted. "I will cut all of you if I must." The trees slowly withdrew their branches and the Northmen continued unimpeded toward their destination.

Once at the edge of the woods, Jorvik spied the grotto. It was just as Morrigu had described it. The men dismounted and the group of five approached. An old man who had been resting near the petition bush took one look at the raiders and pushed himself to his feet. He hurried away, calling ancient curses behind him. Jorvik laughed. So much for the Christian conversion of these people: When faced with real trouble, they reverted to the old ways, calling on their so-called pagan gods for protection.

"Are you certain this is the right place?" asked Vala, one of the men, as he craned his neck to see into the cave from his mount. "I see no one in there."

"This is the place." Jorvik dismounted and walked toward the shrine. "I would bet that goddess of Eugis's cast a spell so none could see the girl as she slept." He approached the opening as he would an animal. Slowly, he extended his hand in front of him. It was like touching stone with a picture painted on it. Jorvik picked up a rock and tossed it at the scene. It bounced back at him. He shook his head. Blast Morrigu to *Hel*. Her goddess-hide was in need of some time in that underworld.

"Now what?" Asa asked.

"Yes, Jorvik, how are we getting in there?" another asked.

Jorvik drew himself up and threw his entire body against the wall. The full force of his weight struck it and the momentum sent him sprawling backward. He stumbled as he found his footing again.

"Maybe we need to call for Thor?" Asa said. "We could use some help and his hammer might break the spell."

"Not Thor!" Vala said. "Loki is who we need. The Trickster is just the one to know how to get in there."

"Enough of this talk!" Jorvik thundered. "I'll not call on any of *them* to help us." He began pacing. Of course, Morrigu did this on purpose. She wanted him to have to ask for help because she knew he despised her and her "family" of gods and goddesses. But she'd miscalculated: He'd give up the gold before he'd give her the satisfaction.

Jorvik stomped off until he was about fifteen feet away from the opening. "Out of the way! All of you!" he shouted, waving his arm sideways. In a rage, he reached behind his head and unsheathed his battle sword. A shimmer of light ran along its length and coursed through Jorvik's body as he drew on his birthright, the power of the Valkyrie. A roar escaped his mouth as he flung the steel shaft forward, straight at the opening. On impact, the magical shield shattered into a thousand pieces, revealing the contents of the cave.

Jorvik strode forward and retrieved his sword, stopping just short of the entrance. Behind him, his fellow Vikings peered inside. There, just as described to them by Eugis, slept a man and woman. Two of the men started to rush past Jorvik, hands on the hilt of their swords. Jorvik held his arms out and stopped them.

"No. This one is mine."

Carefully, he entered the grotto and took in the scene before him. Cold embers were piled between the sleeping pair. The man's hand rested lightly on the young woman's shoulder. Jorvik wondered at the intimate scene before him. Perhaps she was no longer a virgin after all? He crouched down and turned the girl over onto her back. Her head rolled to the side, her hair covering her face. Jorvik pushed back her hair, revealing her features. She was comely indeed and delicate, like a woodland *huldra*.

"What do you see in there that you stay so long?" Asa called.

Jorvik shook himself out of his reverie. He shoved his own hair out of his eyes and scooped up the woman called Maere. He righted himself and strode out of the cave.

"Do we kill him?" Vala asked, nodding toward the interior of the grotto.

"He has black hair." Jorvik shook his head as he walked. "He could be Morrigu's kin, for all we know. This might be another game arranged by the evil one. If Eugis wants him, he can get him himself or send that cursed goddess for him. Our bargain was for the woman only."

Jorvik handed Maere to Asa, then swung himself onto the back of his horse. Once settled, Asa handed Maere up and Jorvik settled her in front of him, a strong arm across her chest. Her head bobbed forward as she still slept the charmed sleep. Jorvik spun his horse around and reentered the forest as his men followed close behind.

As he rode, Jorvik thought of the man they left behind, asleep in grotto. *If he's lucky, the wolves will have him—a better fate than being taken by Morrigu, to be certain.*

CHAPTER TWENTY-ONE

The Vikings stopped in a forest clearing about two hours ride away from the grotto and prepared to make camp for the night. Some of the men busied themselves putting together makeshift snares from bits of leather and fallen branches, while others tended to the horses. Jorvik carried Maere, still asleep, looking around him for a place to lay her. He found a great fir in their midst, and laid Maere on a bed of boughs and needles near its base.

Jorvik stood back and considered the huge tree before him. Surely it is a grandmother, he thought, recalling the teachings of his native land. *Yggdrasil*, the great tree of life with roots deep to the center of the earth and branches that reached to the sun, must look the same. He inhaled the rich heady scent of pine tar, the scent of life. Or, at least, the scent of life as one who was young might imagine it to be clean, fresh, full of promise.

Behind him, Jorvik's horse snorted and whinnied. He quickly spun around, his hand immediately on his dagger. He scanned the area but saw nothing. Then, overhead, a great flapping of wings drew his attention to the raven circling in the twilight sky. "Now what?" he muttered, watching in bemused silence as the creature landed in front of him. With a few steps, it shook off its bird form in the same bizarre dance he had witnessed in Eugis's camp, revealing the goddess Morrigu herself.

"What brings you here?" Jorvik gestured toward Maere where she still slept. "Are you checking on me to see if I was up to the task?"

"Careful, Jorvik," Asa said, as he and the others came forward. "She is not one to anger."

Morrigu glanced at the band of men. "Away with all of you." She stomped her foot and they were pulled into the tree line as if by an unseen hand.

The goddess returned her attention to their leader, staring hard at the Viking before her. "Do you really believe such mundane details interest me?" She stepped forward and ran a finger down the Viking's arm. His eyes widened for a brief moment as he watched a trickling of blood follow the same course.

"What is this?" He clasped his hand over the wound. "Do you curse me?" he asked, his voice a harsh whisper.

"Is that fear I detect in your words, Northman?"

Jorvik turned away from the goddess. "Any man—mortal or god— would be foolish *not* to fear you."

"What you say is true," Morrigu said. "But I do not curse you this evening." The goddess smiled, her full red lips glistening. "Could it be that I only wished to see you again?"

Jorvik grunted. "Save your pretty words. They mean nothing to me." He crossed his arms over his chest. "Why did Eugis send us to the cave with no direction as to how to unlock its secrets? Or did you not tell him of your spell?"

"I told him. But I have no control over what he tells you."

"That I do not believe," Jorvik said

She looked past him to the sleeping girl. "It would seem to me you did fine." Her silver eyes met his and she smiled again. "So, tell me fair Viking: When you found your way blocked, did your gods come to your aid? Given your scorn of all that is holy, I would imagine they were most amused to hear your entreaties for help."

"So that *was* the game, eh?" Jorvik stepped forward. Towering over the goddess by a head, he looked down at her. "I promise you no words of pleading ever passed these lips. No prayers were needed to help break your spell."

Morrigu frowned. "How then?" She crossed her arms in front of her and pouted. "How did you gain entry without the help of the gods? It was not to be so!"

He squared his shoulders and drew himself up. "I defeated your spell with the faith I put in myself." He rested a hand on the hilt of his sword. "And the faith I put in my skill with this."

Morrigu slowly nodded. "Clever man, aren't you?"

Jorvik grunted and turned away. He was stopped mid-stride. With a twirl of her finger, she lifted him into the air and spun him around until he faced her once more.

"You will not turn from me so easily," Morrigu said flatly, as she lowered him to the forest floor. "I am not through with you." She looked at Maere. "I would have you know the girl will awaken soon. Your course of action must be decided before then."

"You know what I am about. It was you who instructed Eugis where she could be found. And you know he has gone on to Tintagel to make camp and I am set to meet him there." He took a deep breath and let it out slowly, a sudden weariness filling him. "What game will you play with us now, Morrigu, soulless creature that you are?"

Morrigu laughed and shook her head, sending her black hair dancing around her naked form. "Cast your runes. A new direction must be planned."

Jorvik grabbed her arm. Her laughter faded as her eyes went from his hand on her to arm to his face. "I asked you a question. What game, Goddess? Would you betray Eugis?"

"What is he but a passing amusement? Whether or not he gains his heart's desire means nothing to me." She pulled free of his grasp and presented him with her slim back. "You, on the other hand, know of true power. You know the power of my kind." She glanced over her shoulder. "You are, at least in part, one of my kind." In one slow seductive movement, Morrigu faced Jorvik and motioned for him to come closer. Through no will of his own he moved to stand before her. She pressed her bare breasts against his chest.

Morrigu looked up at him, lips moist and parted. In an instant, his mouth covered hers in a fierce, deep kiss. Their breath mingled and Jorvik caught a glimpse into the goddess's true nature. He now understood she was neither good nor evil. But what he had only guessed at before was most certainly true. The world of mortals was only a playground for her. Well, she would find he would not be played with so easily even if she did smell of moss, wind, and smoldering embers. Using his last bit of will, Jorvik pulled free of Morrigu.

She laughed as her body began to fade with the falling of the night. "Cast your runes, Viking. And never forget." She gestured toward the thin blood-covered scar on his arm. "You are marked. You are now mine."

CHAPTER TWENTY-TWO

A large man of the northern lands rode in on a cloud of thunder, his horse black, his yellow hair flying behind him. He raised a sword high and another man appeared beside him. Tall, thin, dark: The exact opposite of the Viking. His nostrils flared and his eyes glowed with bloodlust. A fire rose and billowed behind the two men. In one slow movement they reached for her, and each grabbed an arm. They pulled in opposite directions, as if to tear her in half. Her mouth opened in a silent scream…

Maere jerked upright. Her heart racing, she opened her eyes and realized she was dreaming again.

Or was she?

As her eyes focused, she found, not fifteen feet away, a group of Northmen, with the same coloring and dress as the man in her dreams. They sat around a fire, their attention on a set of stones lying before them. Maere clutched her breast in panic, her eyes wide, until she realized they hadn't noticed she'd awakened. She glanced around her. Where was Dylan mac Connall? Briefly, she studied the night sky. Where was *she*? She had to get away, to find Dylan, and discover what had happened.

Panic seized her again. *What if he was dead?* She forced the thought away. *Time enough for worry later.* Ever so quietly, Maere slowly pushed herself to her feet and then ran into the cover of the forest.

"WHAT SAY THE RUNES, ASA?" Jorvik asked. He leaned forward to catch a closer look at the runic markings in the firelight.

Asa glanced up at his friend, his brow furrowed. He shook his head. "You won't like it."

Jorvik laughed. "Many's the time I haven't liked what you've said." He smiled warmly at the other man. "But I know of no truer *rynstr*. Now, tell us what you see."

"*Inguz* and *Ansuz* are here," Asa said, pointing to the vertical lines of small flat rectangular stones. "And here we have *Algiz* and *Vruz*." Asa closed his eyes and spoke quieter, running his index finger over the incised images. "According to this casting, there is trouble at your father's camp. I can tell you Otto has tried to communicate with you on a spirit level. You haven't heard him." He opened his eyes and looked at Jorvik. "I fear greatly for his health, friend. He needs you."

Jorvik pushed himself to his feet and cursed. This was the goddess's doing, of that he was certain. Strange, though, that he hadn't sensed his father's need, as he always had in the past. He supposed he was too intent on Eugis's work. Or perhaps Morrigu had kept him from being receptive to unspoken messages.

Morrigu had mentioned a change in course. If Jorvik headed toward his father's location, it would take him at least a day or two in a more northerly direction, away from Tintagel and his meeting with Eugis. Assuming, that is, Otto was still at the same camp where Jorvik had last left him.

He rubbed the dark blond stubble forming on his chin. Absently, he glanced over to where Maere lay sleeping. He slowly dropped his hand as his mind registered what his eyes saw—the nest of fir boughs was empty!

"Grimnir! You were supposed to watch over her!" he shouted, taking long strides to where the girl had slept.

Grimnir stood from his seat near the fire. "She was asleep. I sought only to hear Asa's words," he said, his eyes cast downward. "I am sorry."

Jorvik frowned. "Come, all of you." He waved his arm, urging them on. "The man who returns her unharmed gets an extra piece of gold when we're paid."

Murmurs of approval sounded out as the men jumped to their feet. Grabbing their weapons, they scattered into the woods in search of the girl with the red hair.

MAERE TRIED DESPERATELY to conjure up images of the last day or two, but none could be found. What in Heaven's name had she been doing in a Viking camp? And where was Dylan mac Connall?

She stopped under a tree and doubled over, struggling to catch her breath. Her hair, unbound, fell over her face as she gasped. She'd run like a woman possessed by the Devil when she awoke and saw the Northmen. And possessed she'd be if they found her. She'd heard all the stories of their plundering, of how they used the women they captured for their own pleasure and then sold them into slavery. For all she knew, the man who called himself her betrothed was either already sold off to another band or dead. And death might be the preferred of the two fates, if she were recaptured.

Maere raised her eyes to the night sky and began to pray to God for protection when the moon slipped out from behind its cloak of gray clouds. It was full and fat and glowed eerily green. She took a deep breath. *Nimue.* The name came to her, easily and unbidden. But what did it mean?

Off in the distance, an owl hooted loud and clear. Maere jumped, pulled up the hem of her dress, and began to run again.

"SHE CAN'T HAVE GONE FAR," Grimnir said as they pushed their way through the thick foliage. "We'll find her."

Jorvik grunted. He had his doubts. The goddess had hinted she wanted nothing to do with the girl, that she had not a care for Eugis and his plans. But if that were true, how was it Maere had suddenly awakened and disappeared? It was unnatural, all of it.

"Over here!" one of the men shouted. The others hurried in his direction. He pointed at the ground with his torch. Though faint, small human footprints showed in the firelight.

Jorvik clasped the man's upper arm. "If these belong to the girl, the gold is yours." The man smiled widely as his leader took a step forward, motioning for the others to remain behind. He unsheathed his dagger and walked stealthily along the hidden path. He'd gone not twenty feet when he spotted Maere darting behind a large hawthorn bush. He moved forward, carefully so as not to frighten her away. Huddled with her back to him was the young woman. Jorvik reached down and grabbed a fistful of hair, jerking her around and to her feet. Maere cried out with the sudden pain. She swung her arms and kicked but the Viking easily sidestepped her attack. "Let me go!" she screamed. "You have no right!"

Jorvik pulled her to him and wrapped his arms tightly around her, pinning hers to her sides. "You are mistaken. I have your uncle's permission."

Maere tipped her head slightly, trying to look up to see the man who held her captive. It did no good. He held her so tight she could see nothing except the bared chest in front of her. She gasped for air, the musky scent of him overpowering her senses. "You are the one mistaken, sir." She managed a whisper. "I have no uncle."

"You are not a good liar." The Viking pushed her away from him and she stumbled backward, landing hard on the ground. "Do not ever be untruthful with me again." He crouched down in front of her and ran the tip of his dagger along her breastbone. "Or I will kill you."

Maere dared not breathe. Footsteps echoed behind her and the glow of a torchlight illuminated the area, including the face of her captor. *Oh, dear God!* He was the one in her dream, the Northman who'd grabbed her. A scream froze in her throat. Who was the darker man she saw, the one who rode beside this one? Was it her uncle? Her head swam as she tried to steady her thoughts.

She'd always believed Eugis as Magrethe had painted him, a benevolent man intent on rescuing his niece after the murder of her mother and father. Could it be true that *he*—not Dylan—was the evil she had sensed so tangibly, hovering over her, chasing her down like the hunter does the stag? Was Dylan telling the truth about her uncle?

Anger stirred and Maere found her voice. "I do not honor the will of a man I haven't seen in ten years," she said. "Nor do I believe the words of a murderer!"

Jorvik raised his eyebrows. "And who is it you claim I murdered, woman?"

"My mother and father. Viking marauders killed them." Her gaze swept over him in disgust. "Evil demons from the north, the same as you."

He took a step closer and Maere instinctively inched back until she hit something hard. Looking up, her eyes met another Northman's—she glanced around and saw she was surrounded. She pushed herself to her feet. Her mouth worked a silent prayer for strength as she frantically searched for a means of escape.

"To what god do you pray?" Vala asked. "What god do you think can free you from us?"

Maere froze and looked hard at the man who had spoken to her. She squared her shoulders. "I pray to the one true God."

"She's a Christian," Jorvik said. "Raised by those nuns and priests we take such pleasure in visiting."

The men laughed.

"Not with that wild spin of hair," one of them called out. "Or with that body." Grimnir grabbed Maere's arm and pulled her forward. "Before the sun rises, I'll have her praying to me!"

They all laughed again. Visions of ancient martyrs meeting their demise arose in Maere's mind. Sweet Mother, was this to be her fate? To be sacrificed as a whore to these men? To be used until there was nothing left of her, then abandoned to die? Well, she would not go down without a fight!

Maere sucked in her breath and, before the Northman could react, slapped him soundly across the face. The stinging sound pierced the night air and silenced all of them. Grimnir shoved her to the ground, knocking the breath out of her.

"Enough!" Jorvik said. "Take her back to the camp."

Grimnir nodded as Maere watched him intently, struggling to catch her breath. In one swift motion, the man reached down and yanked her to her feet.

Jorvik tucked his dagger into his belt. Then, with one movement, his fist connected with Grimnir's jaw. Maere screamed as Grimnir struggled to keep his footing and still hold onto her. He steadied himself and eyed Jorvik.

"Now let us return to camp." Jorvik said, looking pointedly at Grimnir. His hand rested once again on his weapon's carved handle. "And if she escapes again, it is you I'll hunt down, not her."

CHAPTER TWENTY-THREE

Dylan groaned as he rolled onto his back. He cracked opened his eyes and, as they focused on the ceiling of the grotto, he watched for a moment the play of sunlight against the craggy surface. It was morning and dew-scented air filled the small cave. He sat up and looked to his right. Maere wasn't there. He pushed himself to his feet.

Finding his legs weak and wobbly, his head spinning, Dylan braced a hand against the wall to steady himself. He was as weak as a babe. He closed his eyes for a moment and focused on the task at hand—locating Maere. Slowly, his strength began to return, and his head cleared. Dylan opened his eyes again and looked about the small cave. Maere was nowhere to be found. She was gone!

He touched his index finger to the center of his forehead. *Calm down*. She may have just stepped outside to see to her privy. Dylan rubbed his jaw as he yawned. He froze. His beard was starting to thicken, not the stubble he would have expected after a night's sleep. He raised both hands to his face and ran his fingertips over his cheeks. *Sweet Danu*. How long had he slept? By the feel of it, two or three days.

"Sir?" a woman's voice called to him from beyond the grotto. "Are you about?"

"Maere? Is that you?" In four strides, he was at the opening. He rested a hand at each side of the cave entrance and leaned forward. "Maere?"

"She's gone," the voice said. A young woman with dark blonde hair stepped from the cover of the prayer bushes. She wiped at the tears streaking her cheeks. "I fear greatly for her."

"Where is she?" Dylan lowered his hands and stepped out of the grotto. "And who are you?" He paused, recognition sweeping over him. "Wait. I know you. You were at the abbey, with Maere, in the chapel."

"What you say is true." The woman nodded and bowed her head slightly. "I am Seelie."

Images of the fire filled Dylan's mind along with memories of Morrigu and her interference. Maere's recent disappearance smacked of the goddess's meddling as well. "How is it you come to be here? Do you know what has happened to Maere?"

"I can guess." Seelie folded her hands in front of her and stared at them while she spoke. "I was standing in the courtyard at Saint Columba's when Maere's uncle arrived. He said he'd come to claim her, he did." She shuddered. "Strange choice of words, don't you think?" Seelie looked at Dylan. "He had Vikings with him too. The priests denied the uncle entry and sent him on his way, but not before telling him Maere was no longer at the abbey. I ran away so I could warn my friend." She narrowed her eyes. "Those *Northmen* pulled her from the cave and carried her off."

So, it wasn't Morrigu, but Eugis who was behind Maere's vanishing. "What else do you know?"

Seelie straightened. "Only that I would have followed them and fought them all to save Maere if they hadn't been on horseback and moving so quickly." She pointed to a clearing in the tree line surrounding the cave. "They went through there."

Despite two days and nights of sleeping, Dylan suddenly felt drained. How long would this game between him and Eugis go on? He already knew the answer, before the question was even fully formed in his mind. Until one of them had taken Maere and her power. At least the Vikings had traveled into the forest. He'd be able to ask the trees which path they'd taken. He turned his attention back to Seelie. "How did you find this place?"

"When I left the abbey, I prayed to the Lord for guidance, that I might find Maere. He sent a messenger to me, a large black bird, who guided me to this very spot." Seelie made the sign of the cross over her breast. "A true miracle I witnessed."

Dylan slammed his hand against the rock. *Damn! So Morrigu is involved.*

Seelie jumped. "Have I offended you in some way?"

"Not you." Dylan's expression darkened. "Another offends me in unimaginable ways." He nodded. "How long have you been here?"

"A day and a half. I hid when the Vikings arrived and broke into the cave. After they left, I tried to wake you, but you would not be stirred, so I simply waited. I prayed you would soon awaken, that we might travel to rescue Maere."

"Is there anything else you might know about Maere you can share?"

"Have I not been forthcoming? I've told you what I know." Seelie glanced away.

"You know something more." Dylan forced her to look at him. Her eyes met his and, for a brief moment, he ventured into their blue depths. "I can see it in you."

Seelie tried to look away, but Dylan held her gaze. She sighed, resigning herself to telling the truth. "She's not like us, sir. I was beaten and raped by the young monk Bertrand you saw at the chapel. I somehow found the strength to get to Maere. And when I did find her, I died in her arms." Seelie closed her eyes in the remembering of that night. "She saved me, Dylan." She looked at him. "She brought me back to life."

Dylan released Seelie and turned away from her. This was beyond anything he'd been taught of those triple-blessed. Maere could bring back the dead? Was it a one-time occurrence, wrought of the anguish of watching her friend die? Or could she actually draw on the powers of the nether worlds and return those lost in death? Whatever it may be, Eugis must have found this out. It was no wonder he was still so intent on being the first to have her, the one to share her power.

He faced Seelie. "You need to return to the safety of the abbey. I'll find Maere."

"There is nothing for me there. The abbess is dead, perished in the fire. Those remaining believe me to be evil because of my friendship with Maere," Seelie said. "I cannot return. I would go with you, that I might help Maere and give back a small amount of the help she so graciously granted me."

"So be it, then, as long as you can keep up the pace." Dylan turned and walked away, stopping just short of entering the grotto. Imprinted on the stone, as if left behind by a lightning strike, rested the image of a raven in flight.

"Morrigu." Dylan placed his hand over the likeness. "This is not over, Goddess," he whispered harshly. "I will find my betrothed. Then I will find you."

"Where are you taking me?" Maere demanded. Already they had ridden for two days and her body protested at being made to ride again after only a short rest. Jorvik slid up behind her and grabbed the reins.

"Why do you keep asking? I cannot see what difference it makes to you," he said, as he pulled the chestnut mare about.

Maere gritted her teeth. It took all of her self-control to keep from elbowing the man in the gut. She supposed it would do no good, though. He was twice her size and then some. "I would simply like to know where my fate lies."

Jorvik chuckled. "I thought you Christians didn't believe in fate, that you put all your faith into your god's will."

Maere turned slightly, surprised. "How do you know so much about us?"

"I've been to many monasteries in my time here."

A gold ring on his right hand glinted in the morning sunlight and caught her attention. The metal was ornately fashioned and set with emeralds, a cross incised on the larger center stone. "So I see," she said tightly.

Jorvik raised his hand and admired the ring. "Yes, priests might take a vow of poverty, but this monastery had many riches." He lowered his hand. "The one who owned this had no use of it where he was going."

Images of priests and nuns being hacked to death by this plague from the North filled her vision. Would she be killed too? Would she suffer the same fate as her brothers and sisters in Christ? Maere's stomach lurched. Would she die at the hand of this menace same as her mother and father had all those years ago?

She clasped her hands together to steady their shaking, silently chanting an old matin prayer over and over, *Lord, from the fury of the Northmen, protect us.*

Maere looked deep inside herself for some last vestige of courage. If only she could believe in herself like Seelie believed in her, then she'd have the strength to face this man and not be intimidated by him. If only she could find the power again that possessed her when her friend was dying.

What was it about her these men wanted? First Dylan mac Connall took her from the abbey and then this Viking steals her from Dylan. *Could it have something to do with the healing of Seelie?* Maere shook off the thought. It made no sense. There was no way for them to know of it.

Then an idea came to her. Did she dare play it out? If these Northmen were as pagan and superstitious in their beliefs as she'd heard, it might just work. Perhaps she might even scare them into freeing her.

Maere cleared her throat. "I've seen you before," she said, as casually as she could.

"You can't have," Jorvik replied. "Not before I captured you."

"I tell you true. I saw you even before that." She glanced back and caught his eye. "I've seen you many times."

"And where would you have seen me?" He tightened his hold on her, his breath hot on her neck. He whispered in her ear, "For I would have surely remembered one as comely as you."

Maere stiffened and swallowed the bile rising in her throat. "I dreamed of you, Viking. I dreamed your coming."

"Impossible!" Jorvik thundered.

"Nay, not impossible. I saw you," Maere insisted. "I saw you riding out of the mists of the forest and to the abbey. I saw you hovering near the edge of nightfall, a tall thin man—my uncle—at your side." She turned her head and lightly touched the scar on his arm. "In my dreams, I saw her touch you. Here."

Jorvik pulled up his steed. He grabbed Maere's shoulders and twisted her to face him. "You lie!"

He was furious but his protest was in vain. Maere already saw in his eyes what she had hoped for: A trace of fear.

CHAPTER TWENTY-FOUR

Dylan gathered his things in the pilgrim's grotto then hoisted his pack onto his shoulder. He stepped outside and stood in the fresh morning air, taking a deep breath to settle his thoughts. It was time to end this conflict with Eugis. It was time to claim Maere as his and his alone.

"How will we know where to go?" Seelie asked as she reached behind the petition bush and gathered the few belongings she'd brought with her.

Dylan didn't respond. He walked the perimeter of the clearing around the cave, inspecting the paths that led to it. He stopped in front of one. "You say this is the one they took?"

Seelie nodded.

Dylan walked to the largest oak tree which stood on the edge of the forest, directly opposite the cave entry. He slowly rubbed his hands together, bowed his head, and said under his breath, "Show me, Grandfather Oak. Show me my betrothed." Dylan leaned forward, placed his hands on the tree, and gently touched his forehead to the trunk. In a flash, the amber blood of the tree flowed through him and the history the oak had witnessed filled his thoughts. There were simple farmers carrying their goods, robberies, murders, lovers inter- twined with each other, battles. It took some time to sort through it all, but Dylan finally found Maere there in the images.

In his vision, he saw the Norseman break the seal on the cave, enter, and leave in a northerly direction with a sleeping Maere. Dylan balled his hands into fists and dropped them to his side. Their home, Tintagel, was to the north. Eugis must have determined he'd take Maere there for safety. The Vikings were most likely meeting him thereabouts. He stepped back from the oak and whispered his thanks, offering blessings to the tree for a long life free from disease and the interference of man.

Dylan backed away and bumped into Seelie, knocking her to the ground. He turned and extended his hand to her. "Is there something you wanted?" he asked.

Seelie rose and shook the dirt from her brown homespun gown. "I wished to see what you were about." She eyed him for a moment. "What were you doing? Maere said you were evil." She took a step back. "Were you up to some kind of Devil's magic?"

He smiled and shook his head. "You and Maere are very similar, do you know that?"

The young woman eyed him warily but didn't reply.

"How I can explain this?" He leaned against the trunk. "Simply put, I was talking to the tree."

"Talking to the tree?" Seelie took another step back.

Dylan nodded, smiling.

"And what did she say?"

"Well, *he* doesn't talk, really. I simply saw what the tree saw. And that was—among other things—a group of Vikings taking Maere north of here."

"But I saw them going west, not north. Perhaps the tree does not know for certain."

Dylan laughed. "A moment ago, you thought me a demon for talking to a tree, now you think it might be giving me wrong information?" *Very much like Maere indeed.* "At first they moved along the path you indicated, but the tree can see farther than we can, given its great height, and saw them take a turn north." He adjusted his pack. "Come, we've already lost too much time and I won't lose another moment with this conversation."

He entered the westerly path out of the clearing and took a quick look behind him. Seelie was standing there, rooted, staring.

"Either come or stay. I care not which you choose, but I won't wait or slow down for you." Dylan turned around and began walking again. He grinned when he heard the soft footfalls of Seelie, running to catch up with him.

"I TELL YOU EUGIS, he betrays you."

"Those crazy Northmen have a strict code of honor, Goddess. It is said they never go back on their word." Eugis ran his hand along her bare side, pausing on the soft curve of her waist before continuing down along her rounded hip.

"Unlike many an English mortal I've had the displeasure of knowing," Morrigu said.

"You're thinking of Dylan mac Connall, aren't you?" He looked up at the stars. "What could have possibly attracted you to that young whelp?" He shook his head. "Particularly when there are more able and experienced men around."

Morrigu stiffened. "'Tis not your business, Eugis." She rose from the bed of pine boughs they shared under the arc of clear night sky in a forest near Tintagel. "You are incapable of understanding, with that human mind of yours."

Eugis rose up on one elbow. "Try me."

The goddess turned around to face him, her eyes glowing red. Eugis opened his mouth to speak but when his eyes met hers, he thought better of it.

"I said no. I will not explain myself, nor my feelings, nor my actions to any man, be he god or mortal!"

Eugis rose to his knees and raised his hands, palms out in supplication. "Forgive me, Goddess. I only sought to offer you comfort."

"I am the maiden, the mother, and the crone. I am the raven of death. The men of the battlefield fear me, crying out for their mothers when my form approaches. I have power beyond your ken and yet you seek to comfort me?" She snorted. "You don't even possess the capacity to listen when I tell you there is treachery afoot in your hirelings."

He bowed his head and clasped his hands together to still their shaking. "I meant no disrespect. I only spoke from my limited knowledge of the Vikings." He dared a quick look at her face. "If you say there is a problem, then there must be a problem." Eugis motioned toward the sky. "Just as surely as the stars shine."

Morrigu's glare melted into a smile, her lips red and glistening. "Jorvik has indeed turned against you. He rides away from here, away from this meeting place."

Eugis cursed.

Morrigu allowed a small smile to cross her face. "I am pleased, then, that you will listen to me where the Norseman is concerned."

"Of course," Eugis said quietly. "I'd be a fool not to."

"A fool indeed." Morrigu approached him where he sat and lowered herself to his lap. She ran her hands through his thick graying hair, soothing him. When his eyes half closed, she grabbed a handful of hair and yanked his head back, hard. She leaned over him, her breath hot on his face, pleased to see fear in his eyes.

"Now that we have this little matter settled, perhaps you should prepare yourself to worship me again." She relaxed her grip and urged him forward as she eased backward. "Worship me. And afterward you may seek the girl and your revenge against the tall Northman." Morrigu smiled. She kissed Eugis, biting his lip and drawing blood. "And perhaps your revenge against Dylan mac Connall as well."

CHAPTER TWENTY-FIVE

The Norsemen rode steadily along in the early morning light. The heavy clip clop of the horses' hooves scattered sand and flattened water grass as the men neared the coast. In the distance, a horn sounded, its tone long and low. Two short blasts followed by one longer one. And again. Two short blasts, one long one. A second horn joined the monotonous chorus.

The Vikings pulled up their horses and stopped. Jorvik held up one hand to silence his companions.

"What is it?" Maere asked.

"Quiet," Jorvik hissed. He cocked his head ever so slightly, turning his ear toward the soulful sound.

The horses skittered when the horns sounded once more. Two short. One long.

Jorvik raised his eyes to the luminous sky. "What have you done, Goddess?" he shouted. He raised his fist, shaking it in fury. "What have you done to my father?"

"WILL the trees really tell you where the Vikings took Maere?" Seelie asked as she lifted her brown nun's habit and stepped high over a fallen log.

Dylan smiled, more to himself than to the young woman. He answered over his shoulder, "Aye. They'll tell me." So full of questions, this one was. She reminded him of someone he knew once, a fey child with copper hair and freckles across her nose. He clutched a hand to his heart and whispered, "I will find you, Maere." He looked up to the sky, which was just beginning to lighten. "I swear it."

"Did you say something?" Seelie called. "Were you talking to me?"

"Just to the gods."

"To the gods?" Seelie stopped walking. "Don't you mean 'to God' as in the one true God in heaven?"

Dylan turned around and laughed, his dark eyes crinkling at the corners. He ran his fingers through his hair and lifted his face to the warmth of the early sun.

"Tell me, Seelie. What did you do—what did your family do—before you entered the abbey?"

Seelie looked at him, confused. "My family farmed the land." She stabbed at the forest floor with her foot. "But they were poor and I was one of their youngest children. They could only afford a marriage dowry for my eldest sister, the rest of us were sent off to different abbeys where the dowries were much less." She took a deep breath. "I was given away when I was nine."

Dylan closed his eyes, his face still turned toward the sun. "Do you recall your mother and father burning fruits and vegetables in the hope it would give them a better crop?"

She thought for a moment, digging into the recesses of her mind. "Aye. That I do." Her eyes lit up with memory. "Mama made honey cakes for us to eat."

"That was the feast of Beltane you remember, Seelie." Dylan opened his eyes and looked into hers. "The day is reserved for paying homage to Beltos so he'll look favorably on the people in the coming crop year."

The light in Seelie's eyes quickly faded. "You mean we were worshiping a pagan god?"

"Not pagan or Christian." Dylan said, his voice softening. "Just one of the spirits with whom we share the land."

Stunned, Seelie stood still for a moment. "You are telling me these beings exist?" She looked up at Dylan. "You expect me to believe this?"

Dylan shrugged. "It matters not to me what you think to be true.

But you've come to understand I can communicate with trees. And you've witnessed Maere's powers, have you not?"

Seelie nodded.

"Why should this be different? I was there when Maere was born. She was blessed with her abilities by the goddess of the lake." *The same who haunts me now.*

"How can you know this? Even if you were there when she was born, how can you know anything about this supposed goddess's blessing?"

Dylan looked away. The images of Maere's birth night were as fresh in his mind as if they'd just happened. Him, a small boy with wild hair, standing near the stream when he heard his name called out. And there she was—the most beautiful thing he'd ever seen. She talked to him and her voice was like a song. There was no indication then of the trouble he'd find in Morrigu's embrace all these years later.

"I know because the goddess told me this."

"You have spoken to such beings?" Seelie asked, her eyes wide.

"I have." He hoisted his brown leather pack and slung it over his shoulder. "And you have seen only the tip of it." Dylan frowned as his thoughts moved again to Morrigu. "There is much evil still to be dealt with, this much I can tell you." He turned and continued down the trail.

Seelie hung back for a moment, considering the man and his words. Something stirred the bush beside her. In the span of a heartbeat, she leapt forward and ran to catch up with him.

"WOULD you have me chase the Vikings down?" Eugis asked. "I hope that is not your plan." He picked at his nails. "It would seem foolhardy to me. Dylan is a more amenable prey."

Morrigu rolled onto her stomach. "Put another log on the fire. I grow cold this fall morn."

"You? Cold?" Eugis shook his head in disbelief as he reached for the wood. "The way you go around here without a bit of clothing, I thought the weather never bothered you."

Morrigu pushed herself up like a cat, crouching on all fours, and leveled her gaze at Eugis. "What do you know of it?" she hissed. "I am whatever I choose to be and at this moment, I choose to enjoy the warmth of the fire."

Eugis raised his eyebrows, but kept his thoughts to himself.

Morrigu rose slowly into a long, languid stretch. She shook her head and her black hair slowly lengthened and swept around her body in long tendrils, forming a cloak. "As for Jorvik, I do not suggest you chase him down." Her smile dripped with sweetness. "Unless, of course, you seek to end your life now."

Eugis grunted. "Very odd sense of humor you have."

She smiled wider, displaying an even row of sharp white teeth. "It is one of my assets, don't you think?"

He turned away from her gaze. She was playing with him and it wasn't sitting well this morning, this talk of death. Did she know something he didn't? *Idiot. Of course, she does. She is a goddess, after all.*

Eugis looked back at Morrigu and found her now lying down beside him. Oh, she was ripe for the picking all right. Tightness grabbed his belly and worked its way down to his loins. He savored the pressure of his growing erection, the thought of forcing her legs apart and plundering her wet prize.

Morrigu glanced at his crotch. "I see I've distracted you from the matters at hand."

Eugis leaned down on one elbow. "You are a distraction unto yourself, goddess." He ran his hand lightly over her belly. "Tell me, did Jorvik realize his task? Does he possess Maere? Or is she still with Dylan? What should I do?"

"Am I now a fortune teller?" She brushed his hand away. "Have you debased my station so?"

"No, it's nothing like that," Eugis protested. "I only seek your counsel. Does he have my niece?" Morrigu didn't respond. He stared at her, but her face was completely void of any thought or emotion.

Yes. Morrigu definitely knows something. "You say the Vikings have turned from here. I will venture to guess they do not have Maere then, that Dylan still has her." He watched the goddess, but her expression gave no clue as to whether he was on the right track. "I'll send two men to intercept them and bring her to me. Is that what you would have me do?"

Morrigu raised her arms and stretched. She quietly said, "Do not push me too far, man. There are things you must discover on your own."

CHAPTER TWENTY-SIX

"Where is my father?" Jorvik demanded as he rode into his people's camp. He swung a leg over his horse and dismounted in one quick motion, moving so fast Maere fell forward on the horse's neck. She grabbed a handful of mane before sliding off sideways. She steadied herself and found she was alone except for the one called Grimnir standing nearby.

A man walked past—looking her over—his disdain obvious. Maere pulled her cloak tighter around her as another man ventured near. This one stopped for a moment, grinned slyly, and moved on when Grimnir gave him a playful shove.

"Jorvik's done well this time, eh?" The men shared a laugh.

Maere moved sideways along the horse, away from the pair who spoke a language she didn't understand. Every so often they would gesture toward her. Nervous, she fidgeted with the ties of her wrap and forced her attention away from the men. A colorfully dressed woman came near, her arm outstretched, offering a cup. Maere smiled gratefully as she accepted the water and drank it down. The women were about the same age, but the Viking was taller and wore her hair in many braids tied with copper ornaments. Maere gestured toward the shiny discs. "Beautiful," she said with a smile.

The Northwoman touched her hair quizzically for a moment, then nodded in understanding. She removed one of the ties and handed it to Maere. "Are you certain?" Maere asked. The woman continued to hold the item out. Maere took it, turning it over in her hand. The warm copper glowed with the morning sun. She bowed her head in thanks as the woman walked away.

Maere watched as she entered a long wood structure covered with thatch, one of many in the camp. Blankets, serving as doors, were pulled back, allowing a view inside. A small cook fire smoldered in the center of the building. Off to one side were two or three cots, on the other, a loom and stacks of wooden bowls and utensils. *Not so different from us.* But if that were true, if they were so similar, why so much fighting and distrust? Why did these Vikings insist on overrunning their lands and taking from them what they so obviously already possessed? *Perhaps it wasn't about things as much as it was about the land?*

"Come," Grimnir said, startling her out of thoughts. When Maere didn't immediately respond, he grabbed her arm and dragged her along behind him.

Jorvik was at the center of the camp and his people were gathering about him. There was something in their demeanor, she sensed. *Fear? Of Jorvik?* She couldn't be certain, but they were definitely holding something back from him.

"Where is my father?" Jorvik asked the crowd. There were no answers, only silent stares and heartfelt expressions of grief. He stopped and scanned their faces, one by one, each man, woman, and child.

A gray-haired woman cried, dabbing at her eyes with a thin, supple scrap of suede. Jorvik approached her. Taking one gnarled hand into his own strong one, he knelt before her on one knee. "Tell me, Ragna, wise elder. Are my fears founded?"

The old woman stared into Jorvik's eyes for a moment, then turned her head in the direction of the rocky bank. Jorvik looked down, fighting to steady his emotions as he followed Ragna's gaze. Slowly, he rose and began walking toward the water. Toward where the lifeless body of his father now rested.

Those who weren't following Jorvik quickly surrounded Maere. Hands reached out—seemingly bodiless—there were so many. Touching her all over—her hair, her arms, the green wedding tunic she still wore.

One burly man dared touch the freckled skin of her fair face. Maere jerked her head this way and that. Still, the hands reached for her. "Make them stop, Grimnir." She received no response. "Please."

Grimnir stood for a moment before stepping between his charge the burly man. "Oluf leave her be or you will have to answer to Jorvik."

"The great Jorvik," Oluf said with a sneer. "You're like a little boy hiding behind his skirts."

"I do not hide," Grimnir said calmly, his eyes narrowed on the burly warrior. "He is my leader and therefore I respect his wishes. This girl is not to be harmed in any way."

Oluf grunted and cast one more glance back at Maere, then stalked off. Grimnir said something in their native tongue to the other villagers, an order by the sound of it. They turned and filed away, until only a small child remained, a girl with blonde braids and a red woolen apron. Grimnir proceeded to unpack the horses, keeping a watchful eye on Maere and the child.

Maere smiled at the girl and crouched down. She held out her hand, palm up, in greeting. The girl looked from the hand to Maere's face and back to her hand. She smiled back, dug in her apron pocket, and pulled out a small flat stone with a hole in the center and placed it on Maere's palm. Maere gasped and dropped it like a burning coal. *Another cursed charm!*

"No, I don't want it." Maere shook her head.

The girl's smile faded as she picked up the stone.

A vague vision flitted from the edges of her memory of another little girl with a similar stone, giggling with pleasure at the magical world she saw through the hole in its center.

"I'm sorry," Maere said, reaching for the little girl's hand. "My name is Maere. What is your name?"

"They call me, Sassa."

"Sassa. What a lovely name. What does it mean?"

"Divine beauty."

"Well, you certainly do resemble an angel," Maere said.

"What's an angel?" Sassa asked, plopping down next to Maere.

"Angels are lovely spirits who live with God in Heaven. Sometimes, he sends them out to deliver important messages to us."

"Oh, that sounds like a very important duty." Sassa tapped her chin. "It's like when grandma Ragna asks me to go to tell grandpa Ingar he is snoring too loud."

Maere burst out laughing and Sassa giggled too, clapping as she did so. The stone fell from her little hands to the ground.

"It is a very nice stone," Maere said softly. She picked up the stone and held it out to Sassa.

"You can have it. I have another one."

"Thank you," Maere whispered closing her hand around the stone.

Sassa crooked her finger to Maere to lean closer. "Want to know a secret?"

Maere smiled at the twinkle in Sassa's eyes. "Yes, I love secrets."

"The stone is magical. It was given to me by a fairy princess. She looked just like you. With hair like fire and sun kisses on her nose."

"What are sun kisses?"

"When the sunshine kisses you it leaves a mark on your skin." The girl touched Maere's freckles. "You've been kissed so many times the sun must love you the most."

"I am fortunate, indeed, to be so loved," Maere said.

"Yes, you are."

Ragna called out to the girl.

Sassa sighed. "Grandma is calling me to supper."

"Well, you must go, you need to eat to grow up strong."

"Oh, I don't need to grow up."

Maere smiled, thinking the girl was playing again. She kissed the tip of Sassa's nose. "Thank you for passing the time with me and for my lovely gift."

Sassa touched her nose. "Maybe I'll get a sunshine kiss too."

"Maybe."

The little girl skipped away.

A shout rang out in the distance. Others were heading toward the water's edge. "What's going on?" Maere asked Griminir, who'd just returned from setting up Jorvik's tent.

Grimnir grunted. "It's not your concern."

"But—"

"Nothing you need to know," he said. "You will attend with me and keep your mouth closed." He grabbed her arm again and started walking in the direction of the others. This time, Maere stood her ground, refusing to move. Grimnir turned around, his eyes narrowed.

"Remove your hand from me," she ordered.

"I will not." He gave her a tug, fury twisting his face. "I won't be punished for you running off again."

"Sir, my arm is sore and bruised. And I am too tired to run away," she said. When he didn't loosen his grip, Maere continued, "I swear by all that is holy I will not run off."

"What you and I consider holy are two very different things."

Maere raised her chin. "What does it matter? If it is holy to me, then I will not lie against it."

Grimnir studied her for a moment, then let go of her arm. "If you turn out to be Loki in women's clothing, I will hunt you down and kill you. Do you understand?"

She glared at him, then walked toward the crowd. Grimnir followed a few steps behind. "You think you could catch me only because your leader did before. I would not be so foolish again," she called over her shoulder. "I would take a moment beforehand and dream you gone from here."

"Witch," he muttered.

Maere fought to keep back a smile, lest he see it and grab her again.

As they reached the gathering, she spotted Jorvik at the center and made her way to him. He stood quietly over a neat rectangular pile of sticks and branches, surrounded by large stones.

In the middle of the formation, on a berth made of wood, lay the body of an old man. Dressed in brown and white furs, a bronze helmet on his head and a silver hilted sword clasped in his hands, Maere thought he looked ready to rise at any moment to do battle.

Jorvik met Maere's eyes, his glistening with unshed tears. "Go away from me. You have no place here."

Her gaze swept over the dead man and returned to Jorvik. The resemblance was very close. "This is your father," she said softly. "This is why you needed to return so quickly. Because you heard he had died."

"I needed to come back quickly to prevent his death, not witness it." He turned away and whispered, "I know this is your work,

Morrigu." Then Jorvik pulled his dagger from its sheath and sliced his palm. He held his fist high in the air, blood dripping freely onto his father's funeral pyre. "The wind will carry the message of my Valkyrie soul, my song of battle, to you." He unclenched his fist and held his hand open to the sky. "I will seek you out, Goddess. It is not over between us. If I have to die in the process, I *will* avenge my father."

CHAPTER TWENTY-SEVEN

The moon rose slowly, its face embraced like a lover by streaky clouds tinged with orange. Dylan threw another log on the glowing embers that remained from the fire he'd made earlier in the afternoon. If it were up to him, they'd still be on the trail. They were so close to finding Maere. He felt her presence as a tangible thing deep in his soul. He saw her fair face and her wild hair flying about her. He saw the agony in her eyes as she struggled to remember anything of her past life, unsure if she should trust the stories he'd told her.

But the rain of the previous day had soaked Seelie clear through and by this afternoon she was thoroughly chilled. He couldn't leave her behind to fend for herself, so they stopped for the day to let her rest and dry her clothes. He'd offered her a shirt from his sack. She twisted her wet hair into a knot and wrapped a thin piece of wool around it as a covering against the cool night air.

He rose and walked to the low branches of a hawthorn tree to check her clothing for dampness. Feeling the seams, he nodded to himself. Good. They would be dry by morning.

Dylan glanced over to where Seelie lay near the fire. She was sleeping and, from the looks of it, would sleep straight through the night. That was a good thing. She needed the rest for their journey.

Nearby, an owl hooted. "Has someone died, my friend?" Dylan whispered. "Or is it death you bring with you?" A fluttering of wings and the bird was gone. Dylan sighed. No answer. Not that he had truly expected one, but stranger things were known to happen in his world. He smiled ruefully and shook his head. *An understatement, to be sure.*

Looking toward the fine sliver of moon highlighted against the now-indigo sky, he uttered a simple prayer. "Nimue, look over my love and keep her safe 'til we are together again."

Dylan walked back to the fire and sat cross-legged. He pushed his black hair out of his eyes and picked up his leather pack. Opening it, he dug deep inside. He closed his eyes and felt around until his hand touched what he was looking for. Carefully, he pulled out the tattered linen cloth. Placing his sack beside him on the ground, he spread the fabric across his lap. Dylan caressed it and raised it to his face, inhaling the long-gone fragrance of a little girl he once knew. A little girl who smelled green like the trees, talked to the fays, ordered him about, and healed with just a touch.

His hand moved to the center of the material where a jeweled brooch glinted in the firelight. It was the pin Maere's family had given her in honor of their betrothal. Dylan smiled at the memory. Maere had looked utterly terrified when she entered the gathering with her mother and father on that Beltane night so long ago. He remembered winking at her and wondering what she was thinking as Manfred made the announcement...

"Before the sacrifices begin, I have something to say," Manfred had said. The gathering grew quiet as their leader arranged his family in front of him. He gestured for Fox mac Connall to join them, who in turn pulled Dylan along by the arm. Fox was a big, burly man with thick arms and muscled legs, a warrior, used to fighting. His hair, as black as his son's, was tied into a knot at the nape of his neck.

Maere covered her mouth as she giggled nervously. Rhea squeezed her shoulder to quiet her and leaned forward to whisper in her ear, "Hush, child. This is important."

"But Ma," Maere said, "Dylan looks like a scrawny bird next to his Da!" Rhea smiled and patted her on the head. Dylan elbowed Maere so she'd be quiet.

Manfred continued. "Tonight, I announce the joining of our two families." He took Maere's hand in his left, Dylan's in his right. With great solemnity, he placed their hands together and took a step back. "Tonight, I announce the betrothal of Dylan mac Connall to my daughter, Maere cu Llwyr."

Murmurs of approval reached their ears. Maere managed a shy glance up

at Dylan. He sensed her looking at him and gently squeezed her hand. Oh, he
could only imagine what the girl had been thinking, so full of ideas was she…

But it was not to be. Eugis, in his bid for power, murdered their families and carried Maere off. All these years, Dylan lived on the memories, quenched his thirst with the promise of retaliation. He'd finally found her, only to lose her again. He buried his face in the linen, already stained with countless tears, and quietly added more.

"BLAST THIS," Maere said under her breath. She'd been trying for what seemed like ages to unfasten the sinew tethered tightly around her ankle, binding her to a large central column of the longhouse. Grimnir had deposited her here. Whatever the knot was these Vikings used, it defied her nimble fingers. It seemed as if the more she fussed with it, the tighter it became until—her nails torn and bloody—she finally gave up.

She sighed and leaned against the column, watching the cook fire for a moment. Seeing the play of flames made Maere uneasy, as it had for as long as she could remember. Looking for a distraction, she dug around in her pocket and was surprised to find the circular stone given her by the Viking girl. Maere turned it over and over in her palm, feeling the smoothness of it against her skin.

She opened her hand and held the talisman out to the fire. The mottled golden quartz picked up the color of the flames and glowed. It was much like her own necklace, the one Dylan had forced her to look through and see those devilish beings.

But were they really devils? The miniature woman had seemed harmless enough. She shook her head. She was truly going daft to even contemplate such thoughts.

Maere considered the stone again. Should she? After all, what harm would it do to look through the hole? If nothing else, it would put her mind at rest that such small beings didn't exist—surely that black-hearted Dylan mac Connall had cast a spell to make her see them.

Muffled voices outside the blanketed opening told her she wouldn't be alone for long. Spying a scrap of sinew on the floor near her, she grabbed it, tied it through the center of the stone, and slipped the makeshift necklace over her head. She would find time later to investigate the matter of little people and dark spells.

A man pushed back the woven fabric hanging in the doorway and stood in the portal for a moment.

Maere scrambled to stand, recognizing the burly warrior named Oluf. "What do you want?"

The man's pale blue eyes gleamed in the firelight. He was shorter than Jorvik and the other warriors, but he was heavy, with arms like clubs.

"I've developed a terrible itch," he slurred, raising a skin to his lips and guzzling it down. He stalked closer to her, grabbing his crotch. "And it's in need of scratching."

"Grimnir ordered you to stay away from me. Jorvik will have your hide."

Oluf snorted and drank again, wiping the droplets of wine from his mouth. "You think I fear Jorvik? The great and mighty warrior? He steals from your rich churches and nobles and brings it back here to share with his people." Oluf spat. "He keeps nothing for himself. He is weak, not strong."

Maere glanced at the opening. She had to get there and call for help, but the tether would only allow her to move so far.

Oluf grinned as he stalked closer, with the caginess of a wolf moving on its prey. His intent shone in his eyes, the firelight reflecting a feral light within them.

Maere pulled at the tether but it wouldn't budge. She glanced all about her for something that would keep the man away. For heaven's sake, there wasn't even a stick of firewood within her reach.

Oluf stopped his advance and leered. Lifting the skin, he took another long swig.

"Stay away from me," she said, holding up her hand.

He chortled. His hand snaked out and he yanked her against his chest. She screamed and kicked out, trying to squirm out of his grasp. He roared with laughter. "You are only making me more excited." He rubbed himself against her and she almost gagged at the press of his hardness. "This will help relax you, my flame-haired beauty." He grabbed her chin and brought the skin to her mouth.

Maere managed to free an arm and slapped the wine away. It landed on the floor, the reddish contents spilling out like blood. The sight transfixed her. Blood. There was something about it that shook her memory. In her mind's eye, she glimpsed a bowl filled with the dark liquid, held by a man whose hands were covered in it. A hot burning sensation began to build in the pit of her stomach.

Olaf had stumbled back but now he moved forward again and grabbed Maere by the shoulders.

"Get away from me!" Maere shoved at him. But the man was a mountain, unable to be moved from his intent. The heat in her stomach traveled up to her chest and down her legs. The internal fire spread out her arms and rushed through her head. "Sweet Jesus," she whispered. "I am on fire."

Maere pressed her hands on Oluf's face and his eyes widened in shock. The heat was intensifying. Maere broke out in a sweat. The fire centered in her hands—a white glow emanating from them.

It's happening again. Just like with Seelie.

Maere had somehow brought Seelie back to life. Her power had come from her grief and love. But what of Olaf? This time she was feeling rage and loathing. She had no time to ruminate. All she wanted was to stop him from attacking her. She pressed her hands to his cheeks, unable to stop the flow of fiery heat through her hands.

"You are a witch!" the drunkard gasped. He tried to pull away, but he could not move. All he could do was stare at her in horror.

Her eyes grew wide as the power overtook her body. She couldn't fight it. Whatever magic it was, it owned her. It possessed her soul. Her sight grew narrow and was confined to the face in front of her.

"Don't ever touch me again," she snarled. The heat surged through her and out her hands, flinging the heavy warrior away. Oluf yelled as he flew across the tent and landed with a heavy thump against Jorvik's leather packs.

Maere held her hands out in front of her, palms up, and studied them as if they belonged to another person. Slowly, she turned them over. The heat was gone from both her hands and her body. The intensity of the light abated. She dropped to the floor, drew her legs up under her gown, and wrapped her arms around them.

"What goes on here!" Jorvik stepped into the tent and took in the scene before him. In the blink of an eye, he understood what had happened. Maere was rocking back and forth, still tied to her tether and Oluf was moaning at the other end of the tent.

Jorvik roared in rage and grabbed the warrior by his boots dragging him out of the tent. "Bastard! This is the last warning you will get." Jorvik called his men over. "Take him away. I'll deal with him later."

He walked back into the longhouse and crouched down in front of a shaking Maere.

Maere looked up, dazed, as if seeing Jorvik for the first time.

"Are you all right?" he asked.

Maere hesitated before speaking. "I don't know what happened."

"I heard a scream, and I saw a flash of light," Jorvik began. "When I got here, Oluf was writhing in pain over there and you were huddled here, rocking back and forth. Did he attack you?"

"He-he tried, I fought him off."

Jorvik snorted. "You certainly did."

"I don't know what is happening to me."

"Neither do I, but whatever you did to him, I approve."

Maere couldn't help it. She burst into tears.

"Oh, by the gods, save me from a woman's tears." Jorvik blew out a breath and gathered her in his arms. "You did something good. You should be proud of yourself." He patted her on the back, as he tried to console her.

"I suppose so." She sniffed, wiping the back of her hand over her nose. "But I don't know how and why this is happening."

"Neither do I, but right now both of us need to get some sleep." He took out his dagger and sliced through the sinew binding her leg.

"Thank you," she whispered.

He grunted and handed her a fur robe. He motioned at the fire. "You can sleep here and be warm."

She nodded, wrapping the fur around herself.

"I will sleep there." He pointed to the entrance of the tent. "Rest. You will not be bothered again."

Maere lay down and closed her eyes, the weariness of the past few days overwhelming her. Jorvik's actions had surprised her. She found herself trusting he would keep her safe. For tonight at least.

Before blessed sleep claimed her, she thought of Dylan and prayed he was safe. Dylan would understand what was happening to her. He would help her through this.

I'll find my way back to you, Dylan. I will.

CHAPTER TWENTY-EIGHT

D ylan rose early the next morning. He'd slept fitfully, the night filled with dreams and nightmares. Seelie was still sleeping as he picked up his bag and headed to a stream nearby. The water would be cold, but it was what he needed to clear his head so he could focus on his quest.

Reaching the gentle stream, he disrobed, pulling his shirt over his head and dropping his breeches to the ground, and entered the cool clear water. He leaned into the soft current and let it take him along its path. Water droplets clung to his lashes as he closed his eyes. Images of the water goddess came to him unbidden. She had been resting beneath the surface of the water the night Maere was born.

"Dylan," she had called out softly to him. "Come to me." And so he went, a boy of four, to see the pretty lady of the lake. She'd granted him the magic of the trees that night and he thought there could be no one more beautiful than she, with raven hair and silver eyes.

Except Maere…his stomach twisted and he opened his eyes. No, he had to stay the course and not be weakened by feelings. His first priority was to avenge the deaths of his loved ones and to keep Eugis from taking Maere's power…

Dylan stood and scooped up a handful of sand from the bottom of the creek and scrubbed his body with it. Diving under, he rinsed and returned to the surface, pushing his hair out of his eyes.

He left the water and dressed. The air hung heavy around him as he started back to camp, as if it would push him back into the water. *Magic? Perhaps. Perhaps only a portent of more rain.*

Returning to camp, Dylan found it empty. "Seelie? Where are you, girl?"

He checked the hawthorn bush. Her clothing was gone. Dylan paced the clearing, checking behind each and every tree and boulder. Seelie was nowhere to be found.

"Now what?" he called out to the sky, knowing deep inside who was to blame for this. "What new trial have you set for me, Morrigu?" The day would come when he would face down the goddess. It might be his death, but anything was preferable to being a pawn in her game.

Dylan pulled his thoughts together and focused on the hawthorn bush. Seelie must have been here, when she dressed. Would his magic work here? Though large in size, the hawthorn wasn't exactly a tree. It could do no harm to try. He spread his hands over the bush, letting them rest lightly against the dark green leaves. "Tell me, good plant, what happened here this morn?" He took a deep breath and closed his eyes. "Show me Seelie."

Images flooded Dylan's mind. He saw two men ride in on horses, and one dismounted, and approached Seelie. The men were large and dirty and wore the fur and leather clothing of the Picts. Seelie sat up. "What do you want?" she asked, her eyes darting from one man to the other.

The one nearest to her spoke. "We don't want no trouble from you." He took a step closer. "Master Eugis says we're to bring you with us."

"What?" Seelie stood. "Why would he want me?"

"Aren't you the girl Maere?" He stepped closer. "He has need of you." The other man, still sitting atop his ride, guffawed.

"Maere, you say? And Eugis sent you?" She touched a finger to her cheek as if in thought.

"He is tired of waiting for those cursed Vikings to do his bidding." The man tapped his chest square in the middle. "Sent us, he did, his own country-men, 'cause he knew we'd do better."

"But how did you find me?" She folded her bedding as she talked. It was obvious to Dylan that she'd been trying to extend their stay, in the hope he would return soon to help her. He never should have left her alone.

"The goddess said those northern ones cheated Eugis, but she didn't say more than that. He decided you'd be out here somewhere, with a black-haired man, so here we've come a-tracking. You are Maere?"

"Aye, 'tis me." Seelie placed the bedding in a neat pile.

"You'll give us no trouble, then? You'll come nicely?" He glanced about him. "Where is your companion?"

"If you mean the man who stole me from the abbey, I've escaped from him," Seelie said. "I would very much like to see my uncle and will come quietly. Please, let me dress first." She gestured toward the hawthorn. "My clothing is there."

The man walked back to his horse and mounted. "Be quick."

And so Seelie took her clothes and walked behind the bush. As she dressed, she spoke quietly to it. "Dylan, I hope you can see this. I hope you can hear me." She glanced at the men. "What I do is in hope of giving you time to find Maere. Do not come after us." Seelie finished dressing and adjusted the scarf she'd put on the night before, making certain her blonde hair was still covered. "Stay away. I will be fine."

The taller rider trotted over, helped her atop his horse, and the three left the camp.

Dylan opened his eyes. He wavered, uncertain whether to ignore Seelie's command and follow her anyway or continue his search for Maere. Seelie was brave, but she didn't know Eugis, didn't know what he was capable of doing. It was strange that Morrigu apparently hadn't let on that Maere wasn't with Dylan. By the sound of it, she was playing Eugis as well, sending him scurrying this way and that in his bid for power.

Dylan decided he'd not let Seelie's sacrifice be in vain. Without a backward glance, he headed into the forest in search of his betrothed.

"Finally," Eugis said, as his men approached.

"We brought her right to you, as quick as we could," the tall one answered. He dismounted and pulled the young woman off his horse and shoved her toward his master. "You didn't tell us she was so comely."

"Did either of you touch her?" Eugis's face grew dark. "Tell me now!"

"No, sir. Not that the thought didn't cross our minds." He grinned widely.

Eugis stared hard at the trio a moment longer before turning his attention to the woman before him. "It's been a long time, niece." He ran a finger along her smooth cheek and down her chin. "Have you missed me?"

Seelie slapped his hand away. "You'd do well to keep your hands to yourself."

"What I'd do well with is to make you my wife." He smiled and spread his arms wide. "Am I so hard to look at? Would it be so difficult to bed me?"

"What have we here?"

Eugis turned to find Morrigu approaching.

"Forgive me." He bowed his head. "I didn't hear you arrive, Goddess."

Morrigu dismissed him with a flick of her wrist. She stepped closer to Seelie, who instinctively took a step back. "Hold her," Morrigu said to Eugis. Her eyes locked with Seelie's for a moment before traveling the length of her body. "Does she have any identifying marks?"

Eugis thought for a moment. "None that I can remember. Why do you ask?"

"Are you certain this is the girl you're looking for?" she said, offering a smug smile.

A jolt of panic shot through Eugis. He released his hold on Seelie and walked around her, looking her up and down. "Tell me your name, girl."

Seelie met his stare head on. "Maere."

"What of your parents?"

"What of them?"

She was defiant enough, that was certain. He stepped closer to her, their feet almost touching. "Tell me about them. What do you recall?"

"I don't remember much. Only that they were murdered by Viking invaders." She squared her shoulders. "And that you, kind uncle, rescued me and brought me to the abbey. Isn't that correct?"

Eugis turned and put his arm around Morrigu's shoulders, leading her away from Seelie. "That's the story as the girl knows it," he said. "The abbess herself told me last I checked that Maere had never recovered her past memories."

"Maere could have told her story to anyone, could she not?"

He considered this. "Why are you suspicious when victory is so close?"

"Why did you send your men to do your bidding, not believing Jorvik succeeded in his task?"

Eugis fought back frustration. "You told me he betrayed me. You told me I couldn't trust him, that he'd gone north instead of after Maere as instructed."

"I did not. I told you to decide for yourself as to the trustworthiness of the Vikings." She shook off his arm. "Last we talked, you did trust them."

"But I thought more of your words," he said. "I value your counsel and came to believe Dylan and Maere awoke and escaped the cave themselves, that Dylan still possessed the girl."

Morrigu smiled that terrible knowing smile of hers. His face blanched. He'd been tricked!

Eugis called out to the men who had brought Seelie to him. "Was there anyone with this woman?"

"She was alone, said she'd escaped from a man."

"Did she fight you?" Eugis ran a hand through his hair, fear gnawing at his gut.

The man shrugged. "No fight. She gave herself up peacefully."

"What?" He looked sharply at Seelie. "You were never given to going quietly anywhere you didn't want to go."

"But sir," the man said. "It's like I said. She came willingly."

"Is that true?" Eugis asked.

Seelie's hands began to tremble as she nodded ever so slightly. "There was no fight because it was my choice."

"Eugis?" Morrigu said. "Doesn't our Maere have red hair?"

Seelie froze.

"Yes, she certainly does. At least, she did as a child."

"Then it should still be some shade of the color, wouldn't you say?" Morrigu raised an eyebrow.

Eugis reached out and ripped the woven scarf from Seelie's head, sending her long blonde curls tumbling about her face. He grabbed her by the chin. "I can't imagine your hair would have turned so light over the years." Seelie tried to pull away, but Morrigu was standing directly behind her now.

"Tell us who you really are," she whispered in Seelie's ear. "Maybe then we'll let you live."

Seelie's eyes grew wide. "I suppose it makes no difference now if I tell you. They're already to the other side of the country."

Eugis grabbed a handful of hair and yanked Seelie's head back. He put his mouth near the young woman's face. "Who? Tell me who you're speaking of or I'll snap your neck."

Seelie swallowed, hard. "Maere. And Dylan. The Vikings took her. Dylan and I were tracking them. He's no doubt found her by now and they've escaped."

So Jorvik had succeeded. Eugis shoved the young woman to the ground and walked away, Morrigu's laughter ringing in his ears.

CHAPTER TWENTY-NINE

The sound of horns blowing in the distance entered Maere's dreams and stirred her awake. Someone came into the longhouse and approached her.

"You must come with me," Sassa's grandmother, Ragna, commanded. She wiped her hands on her woolen tunic and waited.

Maere stood and rubbed her eyes. In the dim light, she noticed Jorvik was gone. Where had the tall Viking retreated to at such an early hour?

Ragna tossed her single long gray braid over her shoulder and spoke again. "We must make haste."

"Where are you taking me?" Maere asked as she stepped gingerly to the doorway, her ankle still tender.

"Not for you to worry over." Ragna pushed the cloth aside and held it open for Maere.

It was still dark, probably an hour or two before sunrise, and a thick mist hovered above the land. Several small fires dotting the campsite broke the ghostly cover in spots. Fire. Maere shuddered and looked away.

As her eyes grew accustomed to the night, she saw people gathering at the edge of the makeshift village, near Jorvik's father's body. The old woman tugged at Maere's sleeve, indicating she was to follow her. "Come. It is almost time."

"Time for what?" Maere asked, her eyes finding the fires once again, wishing them away.

"Time for the funeral. Everyone must attend, be they kin or not. It is a sign of respect for the dead and his family."

Maere jumped at the deep male voice speaking from behind her.

She turned around to find Jorvik, clothed in his battle armament, talking quietly to one of his men. A breastplate of black metal with stags hammered in relief spanned his chest, thick leather jerkins covered his legs, silver and copper bands circled his upper arms, and his sword and dagger hung low at his waist. He was more formidable than ever, if that was possible.

"You appear to be going to war, not to honor your father's memory," she said softly.

"You know nothing of how we honor our dead. You know only your Christian ways." Jorvik's eyes narrowed and Maere realized the sadness they carried. She shouldn't have spoken so.

He turned toward his father's body. "When a Norseman sends you to the Great Hall of Valhalla, you know it. My father's spirit will receive a hearty send-off befitting his station."

Maere opened her mouth to speak, but her attention was drawn by Sassa, who was being escorted into the center of the group. She was made to stand near the body. The villagers stepped back, forming a circle around her and the men who served as her escorts. Four of them positioned themselves around her. Then they bent down, two taking an arm, two taking a leg, lifting the young girl until she was suspended flat on her back in mid-air.

"What are they doing to her?" Maere asked, a feeling of dread creeping up her spine.

Jorvik waved his hand to silence her. She turned to Ragna. "What are they doing to Sassa?"

Ragna's eyes filled with tears. "She is being prepared to join her master."

Join her master? What did that mean? But it wasn't long before the meaning became clear, as another man approached the girl, dagger raised.

"You cannot do this," Maere screamed. She turned to Ragna. "Sassa is your granddaughter—" She suddenly understood Sassa's cryptic words the day before. *I don't need to grow up...*She grabbed Jorvik's arm. "Make them stop. It's not right."

Jorvik shook her off. The man with the dagger looked at Jorvik questioningly. Jorvik nodded his approval and the other continued.

Speaking words Maere could barely hear, let alone understand, he approached and circled the men, stopping in front of each of them to mutter an incantation. When he finally stopped before Sassa, she was smiling. Smiling, of all things! Maere couldn't believe it. This child was actually welcoming her death!

Oh, dear Mother, what have they told her? She thinks this is going to be an adventure!

The dagger was raised and, in one swift motion, the girl's throat was slit ear to ear. Her eyes widened and her mouth worked as if to form words. Blood spurted and gurgled from the wound, soaking the ground.

Ragna gasped. The tears streamed down her face as she continued to stand in stoic silence, staring ahead.

A long buried memory shot through Maere. She swayed and Jorvik caught her.

"She felt no pain," Jorvik whispered. "She went willingly to help my father in the next world." He held Maere's arms, helping her stay upright.

Maere watched, transfixed, as the thick red liquid seeped into the dirt.

"It was a great honor for her to die so," he added.

Maere shook her head to clear it. What was the girl's blood trying to tell her? What should she know? The girl, now dead, was placed perpendicular to Jorvik's father, Otto, at the foot of the stone bier. The men who had held her were now busy stacking branches and logs all around and over the pedestal, careful not to cover the faces of the dead. The circle of people moved closer and closer until they stood in a triple ring, the nearest of them about nine feet from the bier.

A battle cry—deep enough and frightening enough to make a faint-hearted man fall over and die—sounded from behind Maere. She clapped her hands over her ears and turned around. From her spot, at the outer edge of the third circle, she watched Jorvik dip an arrow, its pointed end wrapped with a rag, into one of the many fires around them. With another scream, he launched the projectile. It landed squarely on top of the bier, and was followed by another and another. And other Norsemen joined him, lighting the early morning sky with flaming arrows. Soon, the wood caught fire and began to blaze.

Maere froze. She stared into the fire, watching as the flames grew higher and higher.

Run! Fire isn't safe. It has never been safe.

And why is that?

I don't know. I don't want to know.

You have to know. Look at it. Look into it. You have to understand. Why is it not safe?

Maere did as her mind bid. She stared hard, fighting against her instincts to turn away. Then the funeral scene faded away and she saw another time, another fire. A frightened little girl. A desperate boy. Uncle Eugis. Her mother and father. Dylan's father.

Dear Blessed Mary! Her mother and father! And Fox mac Connall! Garroted. Blood everywhere. Soaking the ground. Filling the ceremonial bowls. Covering Eugis's hands.

Eugis's hands.

Eugis. Father's brother. Her uncle. Beltane fires everywhere.

Bodies committed to the flames in sacrifice. Ma and Da. Dylan's Da.

Maere shuddered, her legs weak, her entire being wracked with grief held so long within. She wrapped her arms around her shoulders. Looking up at the sky through her tears, she saw it all so clearly now. Vikings did not murder her family. Eugis did. Dylan mac Connall had spoken the truth.

And where was Dylan this night? Where was her dearest childhood friend, her betrothed? Was he safe?

She glanced at Jorvik. He stood near her, staring into the fire, his eyes brimming with tears.

A hot flush surged through her. Moving with intent and strength of purpose, her power rising within, she easily pushed her way through the outermost ring, past the middle ring, stopping only at the last ring of warrior-men. Murmurs rose among the Vikings and joined the roar of the fire.

The warriors held her at bay, refusing to let her pass. "Tell them to move, Jorvik," she called out above the growing din. "I do not wish to harm them."

"Do not let her pass," Jorvik shouted to the men. And then to her he said, "It is not fitting for you, a woman and an outsider, to step inside their circle."

Enough! The word echoed in Maere's mind. "Enough!" Maere shouted aloud. The heat coursed through her once again. With a touch, the men found themselves separated.

Stealthily, Maere approached the fire, as one would approach an enemy. In truth, it was an enemy. An old one who had never let her rest, one which taunted her to remember when she could not.

But she remembered now.

Without a second thought, Maere strode into the inferno now raging over and around Otto's and Sassa's bodies. Women screamed, men shouted. Maere heard their muffled cries through the dense call of the flames, but it didn't matter to her. She felt no pain, no heat, as the brilliant white light of her gift filled her, swirled around her, and kept her safe.

Maere shoved aside the wood and took Otto by the hand. With her free hand, she touched Sassa's cheek. The fire grew brighter and stronger and blocked Maere's form from the Vikings.

"What was she thinking?" Grimnir rushed to Jorvik's side. "She didn't even cry out when she entered the fire."

The words stuck in Jorvik's throat. He could only stare in shocked disbelief.

A flash of green light—the color of life itself—shot up from the bier and lit the sky. The flames parted beneath the eerie glow and out walked the girl, then Otto, then Maere. The entire gathering of Vikings went quiet, the circle parting without a sound, allowing the three to pass. Were these spirits?

Jorvik fell to his knees in front of the old man. "Father? Can it really be you?"

Otto smiled and touched his son's head. "It is I, son. I tell you truly. I was in the Great Hall one minute, with Sassa serving me wine, then here the next." He nodded at Maere and his eyes shone with gratitude. "This Light Elf brought me back to you." He stretched his arms out at his sides and addressed his people. "Back to all of you!"

And with his announcement, for the first time since he'd walked out of the flames, the villagers dared to approach him. Reaching out, they touched his clothing, his beard, his face. Others watched Maere in wonder. A Light Elf in their very midst! Such a blessing from the gods was always hoped for, but never expected.

Sassa tugged on Maere's hand. "Are you one of those angels you told me about?" she whispered.

Maere knelt before her and held the girl's face in her hands. "I don't know. But I can tell you this, I am so happy to see you."

Ragna ran to them and swooped Sassa up in her arms twirling her around.

"Grandma why are you crying, aren't you happy to see me?"

"I am my sweet child. I am so happy." The old woman turned to Maere. "I thank you with every fiber of my being."

Maere's eyes swam with tears as she watched Ragna take Sassa's hand and walk with her back to their home.

A man handed Otto a skin of wine. He took a long drink and wiped his mouth with the back of his hand. A cheer went up as the crowd surrounded him and led him to a smaller fire where they could all sit and hear the tale of his great adventure through the gates of death and back.

Jorvik looked at Maere, amazement clear on his face. Her clothing was intact. Her skin as fair as a flower. Not even her hair was singed. There was no sign whatsoever of what she had been through. "What manner of woman are you?"

Maere stood before him. "A woman who values her freedom above all else." She gathered her loose hair and knotted it at the nape of her neck. "One who now knows her truth."

"Not Sister Maere?"

"Nay. Not Sister Maere. I'm no longer ignorant of my path in this life." She smiled and gently shook her head. "You must promise me something, Jorvik."

"Anything."

"I respect and honor your ways, but please believe me when I tell you that our loved ones will pass on one day. And when they do, they will be greeted with love by those who went before us. We do not need to sacrifice our living for the dead. Sassa is a good child. She will make a good wife and mother one day to a lucky man. Please make sure she is wed to a good one."

"I promise it will be so."

"And can you do one more thing for me?"

"I can do a thousand-and-one-more things for you, Maere," he said with a warm smile.

Maere understood at that moment Jorvik was not the same man who had kidnapped her. Or perhaps he had reclaimed the man he truly was. She smiled back. "Will you let me leave?"

Jorvik took her small hands into his much larger ones. "Blessings on you, woman." He glanced at his father, where he sat in the midst of the crowd. "For what you have brought back to me. I will prepare a beautiful mare and supplies for you that you might ride free from here."

"Thank you."

Jorvik's pale eyes stared into hers. "I know 'twas that evil, the one called Morrigu, who claimed my father's life before his time. If I ever cross paths with her again, she will know my wrath. But you, little one, you must be wary of that raven. She is not through with you yet."

CHAPTER THIRTY

"This is how you would rescue me, Dylan mac Connall?"

Sleeping under the bough of a great pine, Dylan stirred slightly. Maere spotted an owl feather nearby. Stifling a giggle, she picked it up and tickled the end of his nose.

He swatted at the feather. Maere tickled him again. He sneezed and bolted upright, his black hair hanging in disarray over his gaunt face. The fierceness of his expression made Maere drop the feather. Suddenly unsure of herself, she rocked back on her heels and waited for him to speak.

Dylan stared hard at her. "Your trick won't work, Morrigu."

"Morrigu?" *Was he still asleep, speaking his dreams aloud?*

"Do not play with me, Goddess. I know your schemes and I tell you this one won't work," he insisted. "I am filled to the top of my head with your deceptions. You play us as if we were poppets." Dylan rubbed the sleep from his eyes and pushed his hair away from his face.

Maere sat down near him on the ground. "You think I'm *Morrigu*?" Had the man gone daft in her absence?

Dylan didn't reply. He continued to watch her every movement with great skepticism. Unnerving, it was.

"I tell you true, Dylan mac Connall, I am not your goddess." She crossed her arms. "Check inside yourself. You'll know it's me."

He searched her face with those piercing black eyes of his, recognition slowly coming over him. He reached out and lightly touched her cheek in wonder. "'Tis you, isn't it, girl?"

She bristled. "I said as much, didn't I?

"But how?" he asked.

"The Viking, Jorvik, was grateful to me for helping his father. He set me free. My first thought was to return home." She glanced at him and smiled, her eyes twinkling with mischief. "My second was to find you. As it turns out, I found you before finding my home."

He raised an eyebrow, his own smile playing about his lips.

Curse him. He'd been such a gangly, graceless boy. Why'd he have to grow into such a compelling man? One so easy on the eyes? Would he be as easy on her heart? If he were to know the full truth, finding him had been her only thought, not that she'd ever admit as much.

"I would have you know I am no longer the ignorant girl you discovered at Saint Columba's."

"What do you mean?" His expression hardened. "Did the Viking harm you?"

"Is there something wrong with you that I must repeat everything I'm saying this morn? I said I'm no longer ignorant. I didn't say I was no longer innocent." She raised her eyes to his and her irritation melted away, the energy between them flowing like a tangible thing.

"You remember."

Maere nodded. Then she searched the blood red sky of morning, the sun still low on the horizon, touched and protected for the moment by the earth. "Yes, I remember." Once again, she saw in her mind the torturous murder of their kin, and herself as a young girl, being torn from everything and everyone she'd ever known and ever loved. She met his eyes. "I know now you spoke the truth to me." A tear ran down her cheek. With a gentle touch, Dylan swept it away.

"I myself have cried countless nights," he admitted. "For my father. For Manfred and Rhea." He sighed. "For you."

"For me?" His words stirred something deep inside.

"For what was to be between us." He closed his eyes. "Tell me, Maere. Can it ever be?" He opened them again, and waited for her reply.

Maere studied the man sitting cross-legged opposite her. Was there any of the young boy she had known left there? Perhaps in the wildness of his hair or his barely- contained energy. But his eyes were different, so different. These were eyes which had seen the dark side of things, eyes that seemed a thousand years old. "In you, I see the boy who once was." She touched his hand where it rested on his knee. "But what of the man he has become? Him, I don't know. Just as you can't possibly know the woman I've grown into. How can we honor vows spoken when we were children when we have no ken of each other?"

Dylan picked up a dried, bare tree branch. With a deft hand, he traced a line along it. Pine needles sprang forth where there were none a moment before. He waved his fingers over a pile of dried pine needles and they began to smoke, then flames appeared. The small fire danced and cast long shadows on the craggy trunk of the tree. He studied the branch and its new leaves. "This is your Christian resurrection story, isn't it? The dead coming back to life? It is the same with you, I imagine. The recovery of your memory is a resurrection of sorts. You are neither Maere the young girl full of mischief, always ordering me about—"

"Ordering you about?" Maere interrupted.

He smiled. "Yes. And you are neither the young woman who left the convent. You've been born anew, as has this branch." He handed it to her.

Maere twirled the branch between her fingers and inhaled deeply of the pine scent. "Knowing what I now do, I don't believe I can claim the Christian faith any longer." She shook her head ruefully. "They would beat me now in hopes of driving the Devil's magic from me."

"Is that what you think?" Dylan leaned forward, resting his elbows on his knees. "What you have is from the Devil?"

She smiled. "Nay, Dylan. 'Tis truly a blessing."

"Tell me what happened."

Maere quietly related the story of her capture by the Vikings, and her first days in the camp. "And then, at the funeral, they spilled a young girl's blood in sacrifice. It spoke to me from the earth, prodding me to remember another time when blood flowed." She stared off into the distance. "The pyre was lit and flames burned high and bright, touching the sky." Maere focused on Dylan. "I never knew why I was afraid of fire—could never remember—until this moment. It was then my mind returned to me, as if a trap door were thrown open." She shook her head. "A miracle, it was. Everything rushed back to me. And once I remembered who I was—what I was—I had no choice. I had to save them."

"Save who?"

Maere shifted, restless under the intensity of his gaze. "Jorvik's father. And the young girl, Sassa. The fire would've destroyed their bodies. I brought them back."

Dylan swallowed hard. "You returned them from death?"

Maere turned her face toward the small fire and nodded. "Jorvik released me in gratitude." She gestured. "And gave me this mare to ride." Her eyes filled with tears. "No one should lose a mother or father, or a child, to the fire. No one."

Dylan moved closer and placed his arm around her. "It's all right, girl. It's why you were blessed with the gift." He gave her a light squeeze. "Do you recall the story of the night you were born?"

"Parts of it," she whispered. "Tell me Dylan. Tell me of our people."

"You are of the Keltoi tribe, the Dumnonii. On the night you were born, three signs appeared and showed us you would be very special. The water goddess appeared in the stream. A white foal was birthed at the same moment as you. And when you were brought out to your father, a hawk flew overhead." He smiled. "You were a pretty bairn, your hair as red as the sunset."

She dropped her head onto his shoulder and he pulled her against him. "It was that very night I promised your da I'd always look after you." He gently brushed his lips against her forehead. "You're safe now, Maere. I won't let any harm come to you."

"Nor I you," she whispered. Her eyes slowly closed until her breathing was even and she was asleep.

In the silence of the early morning, Dylan quietly scolded himself. He had believed he was cold enough to use Maere as revenge against Eugis. But she stirred in him feelings he had long forgotten, long suppressed. By the moon herself, he loved this woman. He could see into her soul the same as he could the heart of a tree. The strength and goodness she possessed were a soothing balm and he longed to wrap himself up in it, wrap himself up in her.

Before he could think of nothing but revenge, now he could think of nothing but getting her as far away as possible from Eugis. To keep her safe from harm, even if it meant keeping her away from himself as well. And he would do this, soon. But there was one thing nagging his conscience.

He would have to tell Maere of Seelie's fate.

CHAPTER THIRTY-ONE

"Do you believe you can hide from me?" The low deep voice circled her dreams, hovering about the edge, faceless. "You will be mine. It is fated."

The black figure moved fully into view, the mist of the night swirling around his feet. He stretched out his hand—blood dripping from his fingers formed a pool on the ground. From the bloody earth sprang forth another hand. It twisted and grabbed at the air. "Do you remember this?" Maere looked closer at the hand. It bore her father's ring, the double raven crest of cu Llwyr.

She crouched down. *Papa?* She leaned closer and the hand grabbed her arm. She screamed and struggled against its grasp, fighting to pull away. A woman sprang forth from the pool of blood, still gripping her. *Morrigu!* Wearing her father's ring!

No! Maere clenched the wrist with her right hand. She raised her left hand toward the man in black, the man she now realized was her uncle. *You will not have me!*

Eugis laughed loud and long. The goddess released her as the dream faded.

Maere awoke covered in sweat, her breath uneven and ragged. She lay still for a moment and stared at the sky, forcing herself to calm down. The remnants of the dream danced in front of her eyes, the haunting laughter filling her ears. *How long must I run from him? Will I ever be free?*

Dylan, sensing her movement, rose up on one elbow and turned toward Maere.

"He's coming," she whispered.

He didn't need to ask of whom she spoke. He already knew.

JORVIK REMAINED QUIET, hidden by the dense underbrush, and listened. He shifted, watching Maere now, the same as he had since he'd released her.

She'd argued at the time she left him she needed no help, no protection. He thought better of arguing with her and sent her on her way. He'd already made the decision to follow her himself and see to her safety.

Dylan was talking now and, from the looks of it, Maere was none-too-pleased. He moved forward to hear their words.

"What do you mean Eugis has Seelie? How can that be?" Maere rubbed her eyes roughly, smearing angry tears across her cheeks. "We left her at the chapel. How did she find you in the first place?"

Dylan's expression was grim. "Morrigu led her to the grotto. When I awakened, she insisted on coming with me to find you."

Maere turned on him. "You shouldn't have let her!"

"As if I had any choice in the matter." He snorted. "The woman is as stubborn as you."

Maere sank to the ground and pulled her knees against her chest. "We have to find her."

"Agreed. But first, I would get you to Tintagel where you'll be safe." Dylan rolled his blanket and tied a strip of leather around the middle. "I won't endanger you any longer."

"'Endanger'?" Maere's head shot up. "It's *my* choice to be here, not yours."

Dylan reached for her hands and pulled her to her feet. His eyes never leaving hers, he spoke. "You are in more danger than you realize. Not just from Eugis, but from me as well." Maere searched his eyes but he looked away. "My intentions have not been true." Hard as the truth was to tell, he had to tell it anyway. "At the beginning of my journey, I sought you out more to be used as bait than to lay claim to our betrothal."

"Bait? What in Heaven's name are you talking about?"

"You say you remember your past." Dylan was frustrated and angry, more with himself than with her. "Do you not remember the part about your powers being transferred to whomever you first bed? Have you no ken of that piece of history?"

"You make no sense, man." Maere jerked her hands free.

"I make perfect sense. And this is the truth of it. The first man you take to your bed will share in your powers, maybe even take them entirely from you. It's uncertain exactly what will happen," Dylan explained.

"I care about none of this." She crossed her arms and tapped her foot angrily. "Why are we even speaking of it? Finding Seelie is our concern now."

"Haven't you figured it out? This is why Eugis captured Seelie, mistaking her for you. This is why he murdered our parents and took you away. It's why he's tried to kill me. He wants you for himself. He wants your power."

Maere closed her eyes. The man who had haunted her dreams for as long as she could remember teetered on the edge of her internal vision. The evil one she had seen had never been Dylan. It had been her uncle all along. But was he so intent he'd take his own niece to bed? Oh, of course he would. He'd already murdered his own kin so what would incest be to one such as him?

Maere stared hard at the man before her, his body nearly quaking with emotion. "So, tell me Dylan mac Connall, what part of this demon plan is yours? Where do you fit in?"

He swallowed, forcing the guilt back to the recesses of his conscience. "At first, I thought to use you to catch Eugis. You were coming of age, so I knew he'd come for you. Or I thought I might simply take you to bed and the powers would be mine. His plan would fail either way. He'd be dead or you'd be no use to him."

Dear Mother. He was as evil as Eugis in his scheming. She didn't know this man after all, not like she had started to believe she did. He could not be the Dylan she had grown up with. "And what is your plan now, sir?"

Dylan relaxed a little. "Only to see you to safety. Then to rescue Seelie and return with her to Tintagel where you'll be."

"And why have you changed your mind?" Maere circled him. "Surely you could take me any time? I am no match for your strength." She stood before him, hands on her hips, defiant. "Do it now, man." She raised her chin, saw the challenge she placed before him, the anger, reflected in his expression. "If you dare."

Dylan yanked her by the arm and pulled her tight against him. One hand cupped the back of her head, the other held her hands together behind her. His lips met hers, rough, punishing, filled with all the longing and hate and love he'd bottled up inside himself these many years.

Maere pulled away and sneered. "Your father would be so proud of you, Dylan."

She saw her words hit him like a blow to his gut. He dropped his arms and pushed her away. "Get your things. I'm taking you to Tintagel." He eyed her. "No arguments."

Jorvik smiled to himself. Maere possessed a strong spirit. She would make a fine bride for the young man. His thoughts pondered the young woman Seelie. She seemed important to Maere. Knowing Eugis, she would most likely not live long enough for Dylan to take Maere to Tintagel and return.

As long as Maere was with this Dylan, and they kept to the less-used trails, they'd be safe. They wouldn't need his protection to make their way home. He still owed Maere for returning his father to him.

He stood and stretched, then walked silently back to his horse. He'd find this friend of the girl's and return her to Maere. Alive.

CHAPTER THIRTY-TWO

Dylan struggled to concentrate on the path before him, but the woman who clung to him made it damn near impossible. He shifted a little on the horse, trying to move forward so Maere's soft breasts wouldn't be pushing against his back. *By the gods, it did no good!* Her well-formed body continued to sway and bounce in unison with his as she slept.

He cursed silently. All his plans for Eugis's retribution had practically flown away when he'd laid eyes on Maere.

He'd been fearful of what he'd find when he entered the convent walls, worried she'd be a shell of her former spirited self. Instead, he found her a vision in the glow of Magrethe's candles, beautiful and rounded, and as headstrong as when she was a child. The woman Maere had become took his breath away. Suddenly he was alive with desire such as he'd never known, even with Morrigu.

Dylan squirmed again, glancing down at the legs hugging his. Spots of creamy skin showed through the tears in her woolen stockings. His hand moved, hovering, ready to touch, to caress. He knew in his heart and soul she'd be warm and as soft as down. His body roused and Dylan cursed out loud this time, dropping his hand back to the reins.

Behind him, Maere stirred. "Did you say something?" she asked sleepily.

He felt her yawn and rub her eyes. "Talking to myself," he grumbled. The motions of her arms made her breasts move against his back that much more. Even through the layers of clothing, he believed he could detect her nipples growing firm and hard.

Dylan took a deep breath. *Steady yourself, man. You'll never make it to*

Tintagel with your sanity intact if your thoughts keep wandering in this direction. Maere moved again, sliding against him as she righted herself in the saddle. His entire body stiffened.

"What's the matter with you?" She pushed at his back with both hands. "You're sitting strangely and it's not at all comfortable."

"Well, I'd hate for the lady to be discomfited," he growled. "Shall we stop for the night so you might rest yourself from such a grueling ride?"

A sharp retort hovered on the edge of her tongue. No doubt the sour mood the man woke up in was still upon him. She supposed it didn't make any sense to bait him, except that it might make her feel better. "Who do you think you are to speak to me so?" she demanded. "Try as you might, you do not intimidate me, Dylan mac Connall. Keep your evil temper to yourself!"

Dylan pulled the horse to a halt and jumped down. He turned to reach for Maere but she was already sliding off the opposite side. Their eyes locked for a moment, then her feet touched the ground and she was hidden behind the mount. "Do I need to remind you again what gives me the right?!" In two strides he was around the horse. She ducked out of his reach and scurried to the front of the mare, hugging its thick neck. Maybe she should have kept her thoughts to herself after all.

"You will stay away from me, sir."

"It's time you understood I'm not the boy you ordered about." He gave a disgusted snort. "I do as I please and you'd do well to remember that." He grabbed the horse's reins and led it over to a patch of grass and underbrush.

Maere watched him warily as he removed their belongings from the animal and made the camp ready for the night. Was he ignoring her now? Common sense told her to let him be, he was in a foul mood and nothing would right it with the possible exception of a good night's sleep. But common sense lost the argument in her mind. She stomped to where he was tying the reins to a tree. "What you don't understand is I am a lady now and you will behave as such in my presence." She turned away, caught sight of the rising moon, and her mood suddenly shifted. "So beautiful," she murmured. A distant memory of the moon goddess and her stories washed over Maere. "Nimue watches over those she loves."

Dylan said nothing. She faced him. His features were shadowed in the growing darkness, except for his eyes. Those eyes! The Devil himself would wish for such piercing, black eyes. But what was that she spied in them, if only for a moment? Tenderness? The anger within her faded. "Dylan?" she whispered.

He drew a ragged breath. "I watch over those I love as well."

She searched his face before presenting him with her back, lest he see the emotions coursing through her. "What are you saying?"

Dylan lifted her heavy braid and his warm hand brushed the back of her neck. Maere shivered with the touch. He caressed the length of hair, loosening the leather tie when he reached the end. Moving with a gentle purpose, Dylan untangled the coppery mass until it hung in waves about her shoulders. "I believe you know what I'm saying," he whispered against her ear.

Maere turned to him again, her face alight with the glow of the moon, her eyes glittering like emerald stars. They were his undoing. He lowered his mouth to hers, ever so slowly, to give her time to protest. But, oh, how he prayed to the gods she wouldn't! "Tell me now if you would stop this."

Maere laughed a little. "Stop a kiss? What harm can there be in a small kiss?"

Dylan's hands swept over her shoulders and up the side of her face, cupping it. "You might have been in a convent for many years, schooled by virginal women, but I think you know there won't be just one small kiss between us tonight."

Her body swam with such feelings—tingling and vibrating all at once, building a hot tension deep in her belly. *No!* She had felt the heat build with Oluf and she ended up tossing him across the room. She would not hurt Dylan. She loved him too much. Maere pulled away.

She loved him.

"I would not hurt you, Dylan." She took another step back.

He laughed. "I do not believe you will."

"You don't know. Oluf, a drunken warrior from Jorvik's village, attacked me and I sent him flying across the room."

Dylan moved toward her, tamping down his rage at this Oluf's actions. Maere had been through so much. He wanted to calm her fears. "I'm sorry he tried to hurt you."

"Why, you had nothing to do with it."

Dylan's lips quirked up in a smile. "Your ability is powerful. But you fear it."

Maere nodded.

"Tell me true, did you want him to touch you?"

"No. Of course not! Why would you ask me such a thing?"

Dylan took another step until he was standing so close he could feel the heat of her body radiating out, touching his. He knew she felt his, too, by the way her eyes darkened. "Do you want me to touch you?"

Maere blushed. "I don't understand what your question has to do with any of this."

"Really?" She was suddenly the shy, quiet Maere he'd sometimes glimpsed when they were children. He smiled. "Don't you see, Maere? It would make sense your power would protect you from an unwanted attack." He caressed her cheek. "But if it was something you wanted, it seems that would be a different story."

"I see." *Sweet Mother, but his nearness was maddening.* She licked her lips. Ah, mistake that was, as she watched Dylan's eyes leave hers and travel to her mouth. "Dylan?"

"Yes?"

"What are we going to do?" He had spoken to her of protecting those he loved, like Nimue. Did that mean he loved her? Was it possible to love someone you'd been separated from for so many years? She searched her own heart and realized that, yes, it was possible. The wild boy had grown into a strong man and she loved him still.

"Well, I know what I'm going to do." His hands were in her hair again. "I hope you're going to return the gesture." And with that, his lips caught hers, gentle, searching. By the gods, the woman was sweet. He groaned and deepened the kiss.

As soon as his mouth took hers, Maere was undone. Her body caught fire, and it spiraled through her, burning until she thought she'd die in the flames. It licked at her, teased her, forcing her to beg for release from its wicked taunting.

Dylan raised his head, his voice hoarse when he spoke. "Tell me now if you would stop this, Maere. Else, I will have you this night. You will be my wife in truth, and I will love and protect you 'til the end of my days."

Maere looked at him with all her love. "I will be your wife, Dylan. I give myself to you. Willingly and with love." She reached up and pulled him into another kiss. "Always with love."

They held each other close, their breath intermingling, reveling in the feel of each other's body. His—hard, tense, muscled. Hers—soft, yielding, eager. Slowly, Dylan released Maere from the embrace and led her to the sheltering boughs of a nearby pine. He dropped to his knees, spread the quilt, and offered his hand to Maere. He held his breath, part of him still fearful she would turn from him.

Maere's senses danced, alive and heightened. The caress of the gentle night breeze touched her face where Dylan had only a moment before. Desire ran over and through her body. She took a step toward him.

Wings beat overhead and she froze.

An owl hooted nearby and Maere relaxed a little. Nimue's messenger. Something tickled at the edge of memory. A portent of death, wasn't it? Nimue sent the owl to gather the souls of those she would have with her. Maere shook off the ill feeling, focusing once again on Dylan.

Then a fierce beating again, much too strong for an owl. Panic replaced desire as Maere looked up. *What in sweet Jesus's name?*

Maere screamed as thick, scaly talons dug into her shoulders and lifted her from the ground. Dylan was on his feet and rushing toward her. In the span of a heartbeat, she was carried off into the night by a huge raven, not a trace of her left behind.

CHAPTER THIRTY-THREE

Maere writhed in pain as the sharp claws of the great bird gripped her. She swung at the raven, each movement bringing even more agony, more blood.

"Release me, Morrigu!" she pleaded, but the bird-goddess only cawed at her mockingly and tightened her hold. Maere looked down. The wooded land moved fast beneath her swaying legs as they made their way through the night. "Where are you taking me?" Still no answer, only more evil caws.

What of her power? Where was it now when she needed it? Maere forced herself to concentrate, to try to bend the magic to her will. But she was weak, from loss of blood and sheer terror. Darkness hovered at the back of her mind, closing in on her like a black plague. *No! I must stay awake.* But like the goddess, the darkness was too strong for Maere. *Sweet Mother, will I ever be free?*

DYLAN KNEELED beneath the massive pine where he had prepared the marriage bed only moments before, his body shaking. Futility descended upon him. How could anyone fight against such odds as a goddess and her magic? He stared at the trunk's rough bark, Maere's screams still echoing in his ears. The gentle tree quivered as it bent its tip to touch the ground near him. A silver-needled branch swept by, then a green pinecone dropped and rolled to a stop in front of Dylan.

Through eyes blurred by tears, Dylan reached out and touched the pinecone, closing his fingers around it. Immediately he felt its energy —the resin flowing like life—restoring him. This child of the pine filled him with its hope. He quietly thanked the great tree for its gift as it slowly righted itself.

Dylan held the cone gently in both hands. A glow emanated from its center. It levitated above his palms and began to twirl, taking on the appearance of a full-grown tree, in miniature. He closed his eyes and merged with the memory it held inside. It was from near the top of its mother. It had seen Morrigu taking Maere away! And it knew the direction the goddess flew. The direction he must now travel to bring his beloved home.

"MAERE? CAN YOU HEAR ME?"

Maere stirred, opening her eyes slightly. The bright morning sun cut through the trees and found her. She quickly shielded her eyes. A woman grown and still the sunlight teased her. "Yes?" Her throat dry and sore, the words came as barely a whisper.

A sigh escaped the person kneeling over her. A cool gentle hand caressed her forehead and smoothed a tangle of hair from her cheek. "It's Seelie, my friend. Seelie." She tipped Maere's head forward and spilled a little water into her mouth from a clay cup.

Maere coughed and wiped her mouth with the back of her hand. She rolled to her side, groaning, and tried to force her body into a sitting position, but even the slightest movement brought pain. By the gods, her shoulders were on fire where that devil bird had sunk its knife-like talons into her. *By the gods? Dylan was having an influence.* Panic returned and she focused on Seelie's face. "Where is Dylan?"

"It's Dylan you're worried about and not yourself? If you could see what I see you'd change your mind, quick." Her tone was light, but her eyes were wide with concern. "You're hurt Maere. You need to think of yourself right now."

Was it a trick of the goddess or was Seelie, in truth, here at her side?

It made no sense Morrigu would bring her to her friend. She had to see for herself. Moving slowly, Maere pushed past the pain and rose up on her elbows. She steadied herself and looked over the woman kneeling before her. Her heart jumped. "Oh, Seelie. 'Tis you. I feared you were long dead." Tears fell freely down Maere's cheeks, leaving streaks in the dirt that dusted them.

"I am a slave, but still alive, as you can see," Seelie said, hugging Maere to her until the tears slowed. "You're in Eugis's camp. Morrigu brought you here last night," she whispered, turning her head sharply at a sound in the forest. "I can't stay but a moment. I don't know what your uncle might do if we're found together."

Seelie gently released Maere. She dipped the edge of her wrap in what remained of the water and washed Maere's face. "There, now. Much better." Footsteps sounded nearby. Seelie jumped to her feet, head down, her shawl pulled tight around her face. "I must go. I'll come see you when I can."

"No, Seelie, wait. I don't understand." Maere extended her hand to stop her but Seelie was already out of reach, heading toward one of the crude structures bordering the encampment. Her strength drained, Maere eased herself back down. Eugis's camp? *Sweet Mother*, she prayed. *Have mercy on my soul.*

"You are good to me, my goddess," Eugis said. He stood away from his niece, off to the side of the small cluster of tents and fires, and observed her as she talked to her friend.

"True," Morrigu said. She touched his chin, forcibly drawing his attention back to her. "I believe it is time you showed your gratitude."

Eugis glanced from Morrigu to Maere, his need growing. His eyes found Morrigu's and knew the need wasn't for her. It was for the power Maere would bring him.

"You hesitate," Morrigu dropped her hand. "Would you consider denying me my rightful due?" Her face held no emotion, but her words carried a deep and dark undercurrent.

He lowered his mouth near hers. "Nay, Goddess. I would worship you for now and always." His breath caressed her lips. "I thought to complete the task at hand and meet you as you deserve, as your equal."

Morrigu laughed. "My equal? Do you believe you could ever be my equal?" She grabbed the back of his neck and kissed him hard, punishing him with the intensity of it. Releasing Eugis, she flicked her black hair over her shoulder, revealing a full bare breast. "You will fulfill me now." She ran a sharp nail along the back of his hand, drawing blood.

Eugis shuddered, his body gone cold. "My mistake." He opened his arms wide and the goddess stepped into his embrace. He covered her mouth roughly with his own. Let Morrigu say what she would, he knew the legends. His magic would grow a thousandfold when he mated with Maere. He shoved Morrigu to the ground and she laughed out loud. He smiled as he lowered himself, his eyes on the body of the young woman who would make him all-powerful.

CHAPTER THIRTY-FOUR

"I see your friend has found you." Eugis nodded his head in Seelie's direction.

Maere's eyes flew open. She sucked in her breath. Here was the uncle before her, the one who killed her mother and father, killed Dylan's father. The uncle who had taken everything from her and wanted even more. She swallowed a wave of nausea and stared hard at him.

He squatted down but still towered over his niece by a head. "No words of welcome for your father's brother?" He leaned in more closely, as if inspecting her. "Or did the nuns cut out that unruly tongue of yours?"

Maere backed away from him, pain shooting through her shoulders. She didn't get far before she found herself up against a boulder and could move no more.

Eugis touched her cheek. "Do you even remember me, I wonder?" He let his hand fall to her injured shoulder. "You were so young when last we saw one another."

Maere shoved his hand away. "Aye, I remember." She met his eyes. "Everything."

"Well, then." He dropped back on his haunches and smoothed his tunic. "Know this—I loved my brother, but I had no choice. He forced my hand."

He blamed her father? "I see no truth in what you say," she spat, her anger growing. "My mother and father were not at fault. *You* are the murderer."

"So you would think." Eugis put out a hand, in supplication. "If Manfred had taken my counsel, none of what happened would have been necessary. He chose to ignore my words. The deed is on his head, not mine. He betrothed you to mac Connall's boy when I knew 'twould be best if I were to be your husband. Best if the powers stayed within our family."

Eugis stood and Maere's eyes traveled up the full length of him. They stopped at his heart, then his eyes. She realized he truly believed his tale. He believed he had no responsibility for those deaths.

"As your only living kin," he continued, "it falls to me to make certain you are cared for."

"I don't claim you as kin," Maere choked out. "All I had, you took away." Disgust ran over her like a cold chill. "You have toyed with me, haunted my nightmares. We are no relation. I am nothing like you."

"But don't you see? You could be." Eugis squatted down again, his face close to hers. "I can help you, niece, to realize the full extent of what lies within you." He nodded. "Yes, I can see you're interested. Come to me willingly and I'll raise you up beside me. We'll rule the Dumnonii." He laughed and leaned in closer, gripping her upper arms, his breath hot on her face. "Maybe we'll rule the gods and goddesses as well."

Maere looked away. "I am sickened by you."

Eugis released her arms and sat back. "Willing or not, it doesn't matter. Either way I'll have you first, before Dylan or anyone else." She brought her eyes back to his face. "That interests you, doesn't it? Yes, he's on his way, but he'll be too late."

Dread filled Maere. "What gives you the right to play with our lives?"

"I give him the right." Morrigu stepped into view. She looked the younger woman up and down. "This is what you would have?" she asked Eugis.

"True, you are more beautiful than she, dear goddess." He stood and ran his hand up and down Morrigu's arm in a slow caress. "But that's not what draws me to her. You know that."

Maere's eyes narrowed. She felt the heat building in her belly, and took a deep breath, fueling it. "Let me leave, Eugis, before anyone is hurt."

Eugis laughed. "She threatens us?"

Morrigu took a step forward, her head tilted, silver eyes staring. "Her power builds. I can sense it." She turned to Eugis. "She has not learned how to control it, nor will she until she shares herself. Her rage at you has triggered a reaction." She laughed out loud. "You have your hands full with this one."

"She's but a girl and no match for me," Eugis replied.

Morrigu chuckled. Black feathers appeared along her spine. She turned her head, loosening her neck muscles, and her hair turned to inky down. "Believe what you will." She stretched her arms and cascades of feathers dropped from their length until she was enveloped by them, her human attributes only evident in her face, hands, and feet. "I find myself bored with this. She distracts you when I deserve your full attention."

"Not so," Eugis protested. "Do you not still seek revenge against Fox's son?"

"I tire of the game." Morrigu raised her arms to the sky and took flight. "I seek another, younger man who will worship me properly."

"Dylan," Maere whispered.

"Mmmm. So it would seem to you." The goddess looked down at Eugis as she circled overhead. "This much I will share with you, Eugis, before I take leave. Make sure this one's drugged but good before you take her virginity. Or poisoned and dying, whichever way you like it." She smiled at Maere then looked back at Eugis. "For I tell you true, if her mind is not incapacitated in some way, she'll kill you before you have a chance to enter her." With a loud flapping of wings, Morrigu shot up toward the sun and vanished.

Maere tilted her chin, ignoring the bright sunlight as she considered the goddess' words. She looked at her uncle. "Let me go now and I will leave you be."

Loud laughter burst forth from him.

"You find me amusing?"

"Aye, girl. Again, you would threaten me. Perhaps you don't recall I'm a Dyrrwed High Priest with magic of my own?"

"I recall you used your position to threaten and intimidate others to do your bidding against Dylan's family and mine. That is the only magic you possess, the ability to control those less learned." Maere looked away, her eyes watering. "Or those who would trust you."

Eugis crouched near Maere and ran a finger along her cheek. When he reached her jaw, he cupped her chin with his palm and pulled her forward. "You forget something else I have."

Maere struggled against his grip, but he held tight.

"What is her name? Seelie?" He watched intently. "Does it not matter to you what happens to her?"

Sweet Jesus. Panic ran up Maere's spine. "What are you saying?"

"I know you're not stupid. You understand well enough my intent." He stood and pushed his graying hair out of his eyes. "Now then, I will take my leave. There's much to prepare before our ceremony." He bowed mockingly toward Maere, "'Til tonight, my lady." He turned and walked away.

As she watched Eugis leave, Maere forced thoughts of Seelie and Dylan from her mind, concentrating instead on the heat of her power. She worked to force it into something tangible she could use against her uncle, but it wouldn't budge. Nothing.

Frustrated, Maere lay on her side and pulled a thin blanket up tight about her. If she was to be blessed with a gift, why couldn't it have been something she could use whenever she wanted rather than finding it available only when least expected? Perhaps it was best this way—for if she could do as she pleased to whom she pleased, she'd most likely end up like her uncle. Or Morrigu.

CHAPTER THIRTY-FIVE

From the crest of a small hill, Dylan watched Eugis's men as they moved to and fro. A small group stopped to talk, gesturing toward the west end of the camp. Dylan squinted against the glare of the setting sun in an attempt to see what they were pointing at, but he could only make out shadows against the bright rays. He sat back for a moment, catching his breath. He'd traveled fast and furious over the land, stopping only to check his path against the memory of the trees around him. Morrigu, in her raven form, had flown many miles quickly but it took him a full day of hard riding to finally reach Maere. And Eugis. He clenched his jaw. He'd send the man into bloody oblivion before it was all said and done.

Dylan moved slowly to his right, toward what appeared to be a clearing just beyond the stand of trees bordering the camp. By the time he'd reached the area, the sun was low on the horizon, a faint red glow tingeing the clouds above. But there was enough light for him to see where the men had pointed, and why they had been in a hurry.

The clearing held a large flat gray stone surrounded by stanchions of white rock. Wreaths of mistletoe hung from the stone pillars and a garland of oak branches was strung about the center stone. Seeing no one about, Dylan ventured into the middle of the circle and ran his hand over the flat stone. A carved spiral spun out from the middle and touched stylized carvings that created a border around the edge. The central spiral was stained. Dylan leaned closer and, even in the near-darkness, recognized it for what it was: blood.

A sacrificial altar. This is where Eugis would bring Maere. No, he corrected himself, where Eugis would *try* to bring Maere. Dylan would not allow for the possibility Eugis might still win after all these years.

A muffled sound from behind interrupted his thoughts. He turned quickly, but not in time to raise his arm against the blow coming down on him. The last thing Dylan saw was Eugis, smiling in the background, as he crumpled to the ground.

ALONE IN THE DARK, Maere huddled against the stone post she was strapped to, the warmth of the sun still radiating from it. Quietly, she watched the play of the fire as it danced and cast its colors against the night; the reaching and shifting of the flames was mesmerizing. Where she had only looked at fire in fear before, she now saw its beauty and awesome power. In truth, she believed part of the flame lived within her, left from when she'd walked through it to save Jorvik's father and Sassa. If only that power would come forth, she could defeat Eugis. But what of Seelie? Knowing her uncle, he'd already given orders that if Maere harmed him, or tried to escape, her friend was to be killed on the spot.

She shifted, restless in mind and body, her thoughts a silent prayer sent on the wind to her betrothed. *Dylan, stay away from this place. I can't be responsible for your destruction too. We've seen too much death together. Please, if you can sense my words, stay away.*

A tent flap on the other side of the fire flipped open and a short, sturdy man emerged. Maere couldn't make out his features as he walked toward her but his hands alternately balled into fists then relaxed where they hung at his side.

He stopped in front of her. Maere looked up. "It's time," he said.

Maere glanced down at the ground for a moment, then at the full moon where it danced low in the sky. She took a deep breath. "Nimue." The name of the moon goddess came out barely a whisper on her exhale. "If you are the last sight I see, I am grateful, for you are beautiful."

The man shifted from one foot to the other. "Now."

"Aye," Maere replied. She rose to her feet. She held her bound hands out toward the soldier. "Cut my bindings."

He took a step back. "I will not! You won't work your magic against me!"

Maere sighed. "I seek only to face Eugis with some pride in place."

"Your pride be damned. If you're so powerful, release them yourself," he said. "I'll not be turned into some dark phouka who roams the night, stealing souls by one such as you."

"Is that what you think I can do?" Maere cocked her head and looked the man in the eye. Yes, there was fear there. There was a time when no one feared her. The people of her village only loved her and welcomed her into their homes. "Believe what you will, then."

The man grunted. He walked in a wide arc around her to cut loose the tether holding her to the stone. He grabbed the length of rope attached to Maere's wrists and gave it a good jerk. She stumbled forward and fell to her knees. He laughed as he pulled her upright. "Maybe the stories about you aren't true after all." He took a step closer, his confidence growing. "Seelie tells me you saved her life. Is it true?"

Maere smelled sour mead on his breath. "Where is she? Is she safe?"

"For now." The man grinned. "She'll be kept alive until Eugis is through with you anyway, just so he can be sure you won't try anything."

"I gave him my word." Maere bristled. "I said I'd not harm anyone as long as Seelie remained safe."

His eyes glinted as they swept over Maere's face and form. He gave her lead a rough pull. She stumbled again but kept her footing. "Maybe I'll be asking your uncle for you when he's had his fill."

Anger swept through her. Men and their talk of taking her! The man gave the tether another jerk but she didn't budge. He looked afraid again.

Power flowed from the soles of her feet into the ground, rooting her to the spot. She would survive this, she promised herself. Eugis would not steal her power. She would not allow it. The legends said there was a chance only a sharing took place, not that she completely lost her power. She straightened her spine. Yes, she would come through this,

Eugis be damned. She stepped forward. "Lead me to this place. Now." The man nodded and began walking, keeping his distance.

Sixty yards through the camp and into the forest, they entered the clearing. Maere stopped at the edge and looked around her. Candles placed all around cast tall, flickering shadows against the trees. Mistletoe wreaths decorated the stacked stone pillars, a grim reminder of the fate of her and Dylan's kin at Eugis's hand. The flat altar in the center had been draped with white linen cloth, so finely woven she could see a large spiral carved into the stone surface beneath it.

A whimper pulled her attention to her left. There, bound tightly to a tree, was Seelie. Their eyes met. Maere willed strength and courage into her friend.

"I'm so sorry," Seelie mouthed. Maere understood. She nodded slightly, a faint smile on her lips.

"Welcome, Maere," Eugis said as he entered the clearing, his white priestly robes flowing about his thin body. "Come." He opened his arms. "Come to me."

Maere hung back, her resolve fading. Her breathing grew fast and shallow.

Eugis's face was a dark shadow beneath the hood of his ceremonial cloak. "Bring him forward!" Two men stepped into the firelight, dragging an unconscious Dylan between them.

"What goes on here? Have you killed him?" Maere jerked at her bonds, held tight by Eugis's man, until her wrists were bloody. "Let me go!" she cried out.

"Tie him up. There. At the foot of the altar," Eugis said. "That should give him the best view." He looked over at Maere. Her hair was wild and blood from her wrists stained the front of her tunic. She was a frightful sight. Didn't matter. His plan was falling into place, even without Morrigu's help, blast her goddess hide. Maere would soon be dead and he'd have her powers added to his own. They said at the abbey she could raise the dead. Too bad she wouldn't be able to help herself that way.

Maere felt Eugis's eyes on her. She dragged her gaze away from Dylan to him.

"What say you, niece? Shall we get started?"

CHAPTER THIRTY-SIX

"Do I have a choice?"

"None whatsoever."

"Then dispense with your false manners, Uncle, for I have had my fill of you and your game."

Eugis smiled. "Ah, not yet, you haven't. But soon."

She looked up sharply. His eyes took on an unnatural glow—from the fire or his own evil, Maere couldn't be certain. Eugis motioned to the man who held her tether. He nodded and pulled Maere forward, half-pulling, half-dragging her to the altar.

Eugis approached from the opposite side, his face still shadowed by his hood. He reached out one hand to Maere while with the other he drew an *athame* from the embroidered sash that bound his Dyrrwed robes.

"Give me your hand," he said, the small knife raised.

Suddenly, Eugis's followers emerged from the outer darkness and gathered into a circle outside the stone stanchions. Maere warily looked about. Some wore branches imitating the horns of the forest god. Some had oak leaves woven in their beards. All held the sacred mistletoe in their hands. Each also held a tall torch fashioned from a tree branch, the end wrapped with rags and dipped in oil. In silence, they touched their torches to the ceremonial bonfire, before taking their places. The smell of burning animal fat gagged her.

Just beyond the circle of men and fire were Seelie and Dylan. Her friend and her love, tied to an ancient and gnarled oak hanging like a canopy over them. Seelie's face was drawn, as if she were holding her lips tightly together to keep from crying out.

Dylan was motionless, his head resting on his chest. *Is he still breath-*

ing? Maere felt certain her own heart had stopped beating for an instant.

Eugis took a torch from one of his men and stepped up to the altar. "I call on the father, the brother, the great god of the forest," Eugis said, raising the torch high.

Maere slowly turned to face him. His empty hand was still outstretched, waiting for hers. She met his eyes. "Let them go," she said quietly.

"Give me your hand!"

"Let Seelie and Dylan go, and I will do whatever you ask of me."

Eugis's eyes narrowed. He gave the torch back to his man and strode over to Dylan. He slapped the unconsciousness man across the face. Dylan stirred. Eugis grabbed a handful of black hair and yanked Dylan's head up.

"Maere?" Dylan's voice was a ragged whisper.

In one swift movement, the sharp point of the ceremonial knife was piercing Dylan's neck. Tiny drops of blood formed and glistened in the torchlight. Dylan grimaced.

"Stop it!" Maere said. "Harm him and you'll get nothing from me."

"I believe I'll get everything from you. Perhaps even more," Eugis said. He released Dylan's head, wiping the thin blade on Dylan's sleeve. The younger man dropped back into unconsciousness as Eugis returned to the altar. "When will you realize you are in no position to bargain, Maere?"

Eugis reached across the stone and grabbed her left hand. With a swift movement, he sliced across Maere's palm. Shocked, Maere tried to pull her hand away, but Eugis was prepared, and held on tight. He sliced his own left palm and placed it on hers, mingling their blood. He smiled as it pooled on the altar, soaking the center of the cloth, radiating out along the spiral toward the edges.

Eugis whispered, "Our marriage bed."

Maere's cheeks grew hot. She looked over at Dylan. *Sweet Mother, should he awaken . . . He cannot watch this.*

"At the very least, have the decency to remove your men from this place," she hissed. "And Dylan."

"Do you not know that when a king beds his wife there must be witnesses to her purity?"

"You are not a king and I am most certainly not your wife."

Still clasping her bloody hand, Eugis pulled her onto the altar.

Seelie struggled against her bindings. "Do not do this!" she pleaded.

Maere looked at her. "Please. I beg you. Look away."

"Nay, we'll have none of that. I want all to see my prize." Eugis motioned to the guards near Seelie and Dylan. "Bind their foreheads to the tree that they might better enjoy the sights before them."

Then, with a quick flick of the *athame*, the cloth at Maere's breasts parted. Another flick, and her belly was laid bare, her clothing and undergarment cut clear through. Still another flick and one shoulder of her robe fell away.

Embarrassment flooded Maere, but she held her ground and stared at Eugis, making no attempt to cover herself. She heard Dylan's groan. Was he awake? No, she would not allow herself to look in his direction. It was because of her that her parents were dead, it was because of her that Dylan's father was gone. Abbess Magrethe too. All were dead because of her.

"You would torture me this way? I'll not give you that joy, Uncle." As she spoke, she yanked her robe down from her shoulders, letting it fall away from her body, leaving only what was left of her shift.

"Still trying to rule this ceremony, I see." He shook his head and leaned toward her. "What of this power of yours I've heard so much about? Where is it now when you need it?" Eugis gestured to the man at his left, who came forward and handed his master a bronze cup in the shape of a horn. Eugis swirled the liquid around, chanting. "Perhaps your power knows I am your true mate and therefore it will not harm me. We'll soon find out."

Maere recalled Morrigu's words. "You would poison me, then? Am I to be shocked? If so, know I am not." As strong as her words were, her courage was waning. Where was her power this night? Why would it not come forward? "Truth be told, there is nothing you can do that would surprise me."

"Nay. Not poison." He made a sweeping gesture around the circle.

"You see, I've promised my good followers you would be their reward for helping me this night." He gestured with the cup. "This will only relax you. And bind your hateful tongue."

The man who had brought her to the clearing grabbed her jaw and forced her mouth open. Eugis held the cup to her mouth, trickling the potion down her throat, smiling as she choked and swallowed.

A strange warmth spread through her. It touched her head, her belly, her legs. Maere struggled against the potion. She couldn't focus. Her limbs grew heavy, as did her head. Panic ran through her as she suddenly recalled her mother and father's behavior the night they were murdered. Eugis must have given them the same potion, made from mistletoe.

"There, now. You're feeling more amenable, aren't you?" Eugis took a step forward and caught Maere as she swooned. He lifted her and laid her out on the bloodied linen. Chanting, he cut the wrist bindings and straightened her arms down at her sides. In a singsong voice, he beckoned the god of the forest, Robin, the green man, Jack-in-the-Woods, calling to him by every name sacred. As he called forth the Horned One, he walked to the foot of the altar and took hold of Maere's ankles. With one swift motion, Eugis yanked her legs apart. Maere had no power to fight him.

He grinned. "Now we can truly begin."

CHAPTER THIRTY-SEVEN

From the depths of Dylan's unconscious mind, a dream emerged. He was at Kate's cottage in the forest, sitting at the sturdy old table, a cup of broth in front of him. He raised the cup to his mouth, the scent of onion and herbs filling his being as surely as the warm liquid would.

As he made to drink, a gnarled hand darted in front of him, knocking the cup to the floor. "What?" Dylan stammered, leaping to his feet. He looked up and there she was—his mentor, teacher, mother, friend. Kate's face was even more lined than he remembered, and her dark eyes bore into him.

"Nothing better to do, boy, than sit around and feed yourself?" she asked, her stare fixed on him.

Dylan glanced around the room. It was as tidy as ever, a warm fire burning in the hearth, drying flowers and herbs hanging from the beamed ceiling. "Is there something you wish me to do for you?"

She simply continued to look at him. Dylan shifted nervously. What could she possibly want? Then it dawned on him. He'd been away for a long time and hadn't greeted her properly. He held his arms out and took a step forward. "You're wanting a hug, I see."

A wooden spoon appeared in her hand and, before Dylan could blink, Kate swatted both of his hands with it.

Dylan yelped. "What did you do that for?" he asked, rubbing his knuckles.

"You are supposed to be rescuing your betrothed. Not hiding away in a useless dream!"

Dylan froze. He remembered. Maere. He had to save her. As the vision of Maere's face filled his mind and heart, that of the cottage and

Kate faded. He slowly opened his eyes to the muffled cries of his beloved. Eugis was hovering over her, his men huddled close around them, the light of the torches casting an uneven glow.

Seelie whispered, "Are you awake?"

Dylan's head ached. He tugged at the rope and realized they were bound to the remnant of an old tree. Dylan stilled his mind and body, letting all thoughts take flight, and opened up to the tree. The energy imprint left behind swirled through him, healing his wounds, strengthening his awareness.

"Can you hear me?" a deep voice whispered to him.

"Aye, tree, I hear you well."

"I'm not a tree, man. Have they taken your senses?"

Dylan turned his head slightly. It wasn't the tree speaking to him, but a tall Northman instead.

Bleary-eyed from the mistletoe, Maere stared over Eugis's shoulder as he towered above her. "Nimue," she whispered to the bright moon. "Nimue."

An owl hooted in the distance. Once. Twice. A third time. Each sound moving closer and closer to the clearing. "She answers," Maere murmured. "Thrice. Someone will die." *'T'will be me.*

No fight left in you?

Maere's head lolled to the side.

You can defeat him.

"Nay. 'Tis too late." She forced her gaze to her uncle and watched his motions as if in a dream. "Even now, he rips off his garments."

You are stronger than this. The power is within you, girl. Reach for it.

Maere swiped at her ear. "Leave me be. I'll die as my betrothed is even now dying. At least then we will be together."

You would see Eugis win?

Winning. Losing. In the end, it matters naught.

From somewhere in the dark, a sharp slap stung Maere's cheek. She opened her eyes. Eugis's dark form was almost on her, readying to rut like a wild animal and take everything.

Another slap and her head snapped to the other side. But her eyes were open this time and it wasn't Eugis who had hit her.

"Who taunts me so?" Maere cried out. "Who has struck me?"

220

Here girl. Look here.

Maere followed the voice. An owl sat on the branch of a tree. Its eyes boring into her.

You will survive this. Maere heard the owls's words in her own mind.

And you will know the full extent of your power. There are those who would help you.

Beyond Eugis and his men, right outside the edge of the gathering...Maere glimpsed a tall form. *Jorvik! How could it be?*

The raven returns. The owl spoke again in Maere's thoughts.

In the blink of an eye, the raven swooped in and transformed into Morrigu.

"I knew you couldn't stay away." Eugis smiled. "I knew you'd come back to watch the deed." He poised himself for entry. One quick shove and all the power he'd ever dreamed of would be his. His! Then Morrigu would worship him.

"I think not," she sniffed, reading his thoughts. "That is not the way it works. When you seek to become as one with the gods and goddesses, there is a price to pay. 'Tis the way it's always been, and always will be. You above all others should know that."

Eugis straightened, his mind racing. Had she not encouraged him to seek out his niece? To make a bid for her power? "Let me finish here and then I'll worship you as you deserved to be worshipped." He forced what he hoped was a calm expression. "I will love your body with the full of my passion."

Morrigu smiled her thin sharp smile. Eugis had seen that look before. There was little time before she would make good on her threat. He must have Maere's power now...

"No!" Dylan's voice pierced the night sky. The dead oak to which he had been tied sprang to life in an instant, expanding and snapping Dylan's bindings. "No!" he shouted again. The oak tipped forward, spreading its branches around the altar, blocking Eugis's men. They fought against the tree, but it held them fast out of the way. Except for one who would not be stopped—the Viking.

Jorvik parted the way with his heavy sword, the glow of torchlight reflecting on the tip of the metal. He entered the circle and the oak closed behind him once more. He bounded forward, toward the altar, ignoring Dylan's shouts. Ignoring the goddess, who had turned her seductive smile toward him. He struggled to see past the few of Eugis' followers who were still gathered near the altar. *By Odin!* Would he get to her in time?

The great owl hooted and swooped toward Maere.

Morrigu angrily shrieked as the owl perched on the altar and dropped a feather on Maere's head.

CHAPTER THIRTY-EIGHT

I n that moment, clarity returned to Maere as if a heavy veil had been lifted from her mind. The spirits of all those women who had come before her, those who had been born under the triple sign of the goddess, surrounded her. Drawing strength from the ancestors, she was born anew.

"No," Maere hissed. The fire within her sparked and grew, fueled by these spirits, fueled by her anger and pain. She kicked at her uncle and the man stumbled back. Maere sat up, swung her legs over the side, and slid to the ground. She took a step forward, the bright light of her strength filling her.

She turned her head slightly to nod at Dylan, Jorvik, and Seelie. Jorvik took a step back and bowed his head. She looked down at her hands and realized she was glowing, lit from within by her power.

Dylan pushed past Jorvik, his eyes taking in her torn garments. He pulled off his cloak and wrapped it around Maere's shoulders. "Let us leave this evil place, my love."

Eugis scrambled to his feet and drew himself up straight. "She will not leave. I will yet have her and claim her power. She is mine."

Maere trembled with anger. She was her own woman, in charge of her fate, not to be controlled by any man. She took a shuddering breath. The spark within her fanned, growing into fire, fully evolved. She felt more alive in this moment than since she was a small girl, since before her parents were murdered.

Murdered.

She drew her shoulders back and stabbed a finger at Eugis. He screamed and skidded across the ground, slamming into one of the stone pillars. He forced himself up and raised an answering hand toward her. A wave of magic touched her. It wasn't strong, though. Not like hers. With a flick of her wrist, she raised him off the ground. Higher and higher he traveled, his eyes wide with terror. His fear mattered not. She'd see to it he could not harm her again. See to it he could harm no one else she loved.

"Maere!"

Her resolve faltered as Dylan stepped to her side. He touched her shoulder and her hand dipped slightly.

"You will not dissuade me from this. I will see him dead," she whispered, her voice husky and strained.

"You cannot do this."

She laughed. Who was he to tell her what she could or could not do? "You are the one who has sought revenge all these years. You searched me out as a token to be used in exacting vengeance. Now you would tell me to let him go?"

"I would tell you not to commit murder. It isn't worth the damage your soul would suffer. You would become as he is." Dylan nodded toward Eugis, still hanging above the ground, trapped by Maere's magic.

"He tells the truth." Jorvik was now standing on the other side of Maere. He nodded at Dylan. "Remember what you did for my father and Sassa. You carry the gift of life within you. Not death."

Seelie came forward. "If not for you, I would be dead. You healed me, Maere. You saved me."

Their words reached deep down inside Maere. She looked first at Jorvik, then to Seelie, and, lastly, to Dylan. Her eyes met his—those dark piercing orbs glowed with the reflection of the very moon herself. She understood why the others were trying to convince her not to kill Eugis, but not Dylan.

"Look at me. Look at what he has done to me." She swept her free hand over her body. "My clothes, torn away. My body, laid bare for all to see." She shook her head. "He tried to take what I would freely give to the man I love. And you would reward him for this?"

"Of course, I would not!"

"Your power is for healing," Jorvik said, his deep voice soft and soothing.

Dylan nodded at Jorvik and added, "Not for killing. Go inside yourself. You know this."

Maere faltered as Dylan's calming voice washed over her. She lowered her arm, thereby lowering Eugis to the ground, his body limp and exhausted from struggling against her magic.

Morrigu walked forward and screeched in her raven's voice, "Finish him!"

The four of them stepped back. Dylan slipped his arm protectively around the shoulders of his betrothed.

"Would you let this one's sweet words turn your mind?" Morrigu glanced at Dylan. "He knows nothing. Finish Eugis and realize your *true power*."

Jorvik stepped between Morrigu and Maere, his hand on the dagger tucked in his leather belt. Maere touched his arm. "'Tis all right." She turned to Morrigu. "Nay, Goddess. No matter how much I might wish him dead, these who are dear to me speak the truth. I cannot kill."

Morrigu tilted her head and eyed the young woman. "From the instant of your birth until now, you have not cared for the taste of blood, have you?"

"Why are you here, Morrigu?" Dylan demanded. "Did you come to celebrate Eugis's rise into stolen power? To force our submission to you and him?"

The owl, circling overhead, hooted and Morrigu turned at its sound. "I am merely here as an observer."

Seelie snorted and Jorvik looked over at her. He nodded, his lips curved up in a slight smile.

The owl hooted again and Morrigu waved her hand at it. Her body shivered as the transformation to raven began. The owl swooped in and landed on the hard-packed earth. It stared pointedly at Morrigu.

Morrigu sighed. "Very well! I'll tell them."

"Tell us what?" Maere shoved past Dylan and Jorvik and faced the goddess.

"The truth is, your power cannot be taken. This was an imagining by Eugis, and others like him. The hopeful dreams of small men."

Maere's eyes narrowed in understanding. "You allowed all of this to happen so I could claim my powers for myself. It was all needless. All this suffering. All for your selfish entertainment? You have toyed with our lives."

"I made you, girl. I was the goddess in the stream who blessed your birth." Morrigu shook her head. "You speak as if I have a care as to what happens to you. To any of you."

"You may be a goddess," Seelie spat. "But you are also a demon."

"Do not forget to whom you are speaking." She spread her arms and lifted from the ground.

Jorvik stepped in front of Seelie to protect her. "Do not meddle in our lives again, or I will call on Odin himself to turn you into a pile of feathers."

Morrigu's eyes narrowed. "You are a fool, Viking," she hissed. "I could have taken you to the heights of pleasure. And you prefer this pale creature?" She nodded at Seelie.

"I prefer a good woman to a conniving goddess; a creature who plays games at the expense of mortals and only believes in hate."

"Hate. Love. What you fail to understand is they are the same to me."

The owl hooted once more before taking flight.

Morrigu huffed. "Besides you have always had others watching over you." She turned to acknowledge the owl who hooted once more before flying away.

Dylan watched the owl take its leave, an awareness flickering through his mind. "You will leave us to live our lives from here forward Morrigu," Dylan said. "Or I am certain you will have to answer to that wise old bird."

"That owl is more trouble than she's worth. Besides I have no more need of any of you." She looked at Maere. "You have realized your true powers, which was the point all along. Your trial by fire is complete and the circle is closed."

The firelight glinted off Morrigu's feathers. With a rush of air, she shot into the night sky. Within the span of a heartbeat, she swept back down, straight at Eugis, her beak poised at his heart.

With a scream, Eugis raised his arms to protect himself. But it was too late. The goddess was too fast and too strong for him. Her beak pierced his heart. He cried out once more, then went silent.

Morrigu rose again into the night, Eugis dangling from her mouth like a broken poppet. With a loud and raucous caw, she released him, his lifeless body plummeting to the earth. It landed in the ceremonial bonfire, sending a shower of embers toward the sky, his body engulfed by the flames.

Maere watched in silence, drawing Dylan's cloak tightly around her. This time, she would not look away from the fire.

CHAPTER THIRTY-NINE

One by one, Eugis's men walked to the fire and tossed in the torches, oak branches, and leaves they'd worn for the ceremony. The man who had brought Maere to the altar opened his mouth, then shut it tight and turned away, moving into the dark forest. The others followed.

The flames continued to crackle and spew sparks into the air. There was nothing left of Eugis now except charred bone and the memories within those he had harmed.

Maere began to shake uncontrollably, her teeth chattering. Her strength waned and she collapsed to her knees.

Dylan squatted and touched her arm, searching her face. She was so pale. "You need to rest," he said softly. "I'm worried for you."

"I am worried for me too." She gave him a faint smile. "I don't understand why all this has happened."

"Nor do I. I don't know if understanding is possible. Not when it comes to the gods and goddesses." He helped her stand. "Come. For now, I would see you warm and safe this night."

Maere clasped his forearm and he pulled her to her feet. There was such strength in this man. Had it always been there? She searched his face and, for a brief moment, beheld Dylan as a boy, his big noisy feet traipsing through the forest. She held on to that memory, that day so long ago when he had pledged to watch over her and keep her safe, as she allowed herself to be led out of the clearing and to a nearby tent for the night. "Stay with me," she said.

"Always," he replied.

JORVIK WATCHED Dylan and Maere leave the fire. He started to follow them back to camp when a movement caught his eye. He turned. It was the young woman, Seelie. He cleared his throat and she looked up at him, her blue eyes clear even in the darkness.

"Thank you for helping Maere. For helping all of us," she said. She picked up a blanket lying near the bonfire and wrapped it around her. "I am chilled." She looked up at the moon.

The Northman took a step sideways and stood up against her. Seelie moved away. "Wait," he said. "You needn't be afraid. I stand here only for you, to share my warmth."

A smile played at Seelie's lips. "Did you mean what you said earlier to Morrigu?"

"Aye. I've seen enough of magic in my life. I need no goddess or elf or magician to warm my heart or body," he said softly.

She nodded. Maere had told her he was a good man, one who could be trusted. And there was something about this giant warrior with hair the color of spun gold. Something that called to her heart. Could it be possible? They barely knew one another. But he had helped save them.

He touched her hand. "I would have a woman I can trust." Jorvik turned to her and searched her eyes. "I understand. We have only just met. But you risked your life to help your friend. You are a brave woman."

Although she blushed at his words, she placed her hand over his. "Will you tell me something about yourself?"

"I am not an easy man, but I would lay down my life for the people I love. Tell me something about you."

"I am a stubborn woman, but I will always protect those I love."

He laughed. It was so full of warmth, Seelie fell in love with him at that very moment.

"We are well matched it would seem," he said.

"Do you think you could love a woman who was raised with different beliefs from yours?"

"I know I could love a feisty, fair-haired elf who would do anything to help her dearest friend."

Seelie grinned and, standing on her tip toes, she kissed his cheek.

Jorvik smiled and pulled her into the warmth of his arms. Seelie knew she was home.

CHAPTER FORTY

The journey to Kate's cottage was quiet and peaceful along the forest path, save for the sounds of the birds and the wind rustling the leaves high above. Samhain was drawing near and a nip of autumn touched the air.

After that night, Maere had wanted only to be alone, wouldn't see anyone, even Dylan. Gone was her anger, burned away in the bonfire along with Eugis's body. She was exhausted in so many ways. The pain of losing her parents and being taken away from her home had made her forget who she was. Maere had needed to rest. And to remember. She needed to reclaim herself.

But she stirred when Seelie and Jorvik were readying to leave for the Viking camp, and it was time to say goodbye. She wrapped her arms around Maere, and the two young women held tight to each other.

"I shall miss you terribly, my dearest friend," Maere whispered.

"We will see each other again. And we will celebrate our happiness and our children will laugh and play together."

Seelie's words were with Maere still and, combined with Dylan's gentle care, were helping her to heal all those painful memories. She could have cast away the hurt with her magic but, as Da had told her all those years ago, "Some wounds aren't so easily healed."

"Maere?" Dylan's voice startled her out of her reverie. He smiled when he caught her eye. "See? Up ahead." She followed the direction his hand indicated. There, nestled among the pines, was a small, weathered, wood and sod cottage. Dylan drew his horse closer to hers. "Kate will be pleased with our visit."

"You're certain she won't find us an intrusion on her solitary ways?"

Dylan laughed. "I can tell you with certainty our arrival will be no surprise to this one. It was probably her idea all along we should stop here before heading to Tintagel and she only wants us to think it's ours."

A few minutes more and the pair were in front of Kate's modest home. Dylan swung his long legs down from his horse and tethered it to a post. He offered a hand to Maere and she slid down as well, coming to rest with her back against the horse's side, Dylan directly in front of her.

He brushed aside stray hairs which had escaped her braid, and offered a long caress down her cheek and the side of her neck. "You are beautiful," he whispered as his finger touched her lips.

Maere dropped a gentle kiss against his fingertip and offered a small smile. But before she could move away, Dylan let his hand fall to her shoulder. It made its way around to the back of her neck, massaging small circles, easing the tension. Maere's head drifted back and he gently kissed the base of her throat. She gasped in pleasure as he continued to kiss along her shoulder, his lips warm and moist against her skin. With a sigh, his lips claimed hers, gently at first, teasing, tugging. As Maere responded to him, Dylan deepened the kiss, marking her with his love.

"Well, isn't this a pretty picture for an old woman's tired eyes."

Dylan's head shot up. He glanced down at Maere, her green eyes dark with emotion. He cleared his throat. "Greetings, Kate. I see your timing is as good as ever, despite your advanced years." He squeezed Maere's shoulder, then dropped his hand to hers and clasped it. Turning, he bowed to his teacher. "This is Maere cu Llwyr, my betrothed."

Using her cane for balance, Kate hobbled over. With a quick motion that belied her age, she swatted him with it. Dylan yelped. "What was that for?"

"For not getting here sooner. Look at her." She motioned to Maere, still leaning against the horse. "She's near-to-exhausted and you would dally out here with pretty words and kisses." Kate reached for Maere's arm. "Come, dear. I've a warm fire inside and some hot stew for your belly."

Maere glanced at Dylan. He sighed. "She's right, as always. Go with her. I'll tend the horses."

With a nod, Maere allowed herself to be led to the cottage. At the door, Kate glanced back. "You can be such a man sometimes, Dylan. I thought I raised you better than this." With a cackle of laughter, she slammed the cottage door shut.

BY THE TIME Dylan had fed and watered the horses, it was near dark. He felt a twinge of sadness as he walked to the only home he'd known since his father died. What would time have brought to his and Maere's families, were it not for Eugis's interference?

A long, deep sigh escaped him, and he drew himself up. There would be no living in the past, only the present. And he would make the best of the future, one that contained Maere once again. Ah, but he was thankful to the gods and goddesses he had her back, safe from Eugis. He meant to make good on his promise to Manfred and would continue to protect her for all of their days.

He stopped and looked up at the sky, faint lights from distant stars beginning to appear. Crossing his arms, Dylan leaned against the doorway. There, rising above the trees, a small sliver of moon glowed bright. "Nimue," he whispered. "Maere always prayed to you when we were children. I pray to you now." He took a deep breath and let it out slowly. Sorrow tugged at him, at his heart. "Please, Goddess of the Moon, see my love whole and happy. See her free of her sadness and pain." After a few more moments, he turned and entered the small dwelling.

Inside, he found Kate at the table, spinning yarn from the pile of loose wool resting in her lap. The simple wood bobbin jumped up and down with a twirling motion, making small tapping sounds against the old plank floor. It was a comforting sound Dylan remembered from his childhood. And there was Maere, curled up on a straw cushion by the fire and covered with a thick blanket, fast asleep.

"Sit, boy," Kate said quietly. "There's warm cider in the pitcher there. Pour us both a cup." She gathered up her spinning and tucked it aside, in a tree-bark box near her feet. She then turned in her chair and faced Dylan. Kate reached for his hand and Dylan met hers halfway. She smiled. "'Tis good to have you here again. I have missed you."

"I have missed you as well. But I have a feeling it hasn't been that long since you saw me." He raised the cup to his lips and took a long drink.

"Whatever are you talking about, boy?"

"I see an owl feather on the arm of your chair."

Kate looked down and cursed. "Damn feathers. Now don't go spreading idle gossip about that. I was just helping out where I could. Someone needed to remind the blackbird to stop sticking her beak where it doesn't belong."

Dylan chuckled and then grew serious again. "I promised her Da, Kate, I'd keep her safe. And I couldn't. She's been through so much. I failed her all these years."

"You did not fail me, Dylan." He and Kate both turned to find Maere sitting up, her legs drawn close against her breast, her arms wrapped around them. "You are a good man and I will never blame you for what happened."

"Maere—"

"Nay. Let me speak, Dylan."

She stood and walked toward them. The firelight cast a warm glow about her body. Or was it her magic? It mattered not, she held him transfixed.

"These past weeks I've been wracked with guilt that I was the cause of all this— the death of our loved ones, Eugis's evil. All because of the circumstances of my birth. I fear what I carry inside will always cause those who demand power to hunt me down." She poured herself a bit of cider, holding the cup tight to keep her hands from shaking. Maere took a deep breath and continued. "But I have been dreaming while I slept just now. And in the dreaming, I've come to understand, at least in a small part, that I need not blame myself." She touched

Dylan's face. "And you shouldn't fault yourself either. 'Twas none of it your doing."

"That's where you're wrong," Kate said.

"I'm not wrong. Dylan is not to blame," Maere insisted.

"Not that part. The part about fearing what you carry inside. What Eugis and men like him do not understand is you must give of yourself freely and with love." She waved her hand. "Your magic can't be taken or forced away in any manner. It can only be shared when you are ready for the sharing."

"Eugis destroyed our families and now he is dead because of his thirst for power." Dylan shook his head. "And I'm glad of it."

"Agreed." Maere touched the back of his hand. "We can't let him— or what he did to our families—continue to rule us."

Dylan covered Maere's hand with his and the weight of the past ten years fell off him as easy as a cloak. He kneeled by her and took her hand in his. "I love you, Maere cu Llwyr."

She smiled and nodded. "And I, love you Dylan mac Connell."

"Will you be my wife?"

CHAPTER FORTY-ONE

"Aye, my love. I'll be yours." Maere planted a gentle kiss on Dylan's lips. He leaned forward to take more but Maere pulled away with a soft giggle. She turned to Kate. "Will you do the hand-fasting for us?"

The old woman's eyes twinkled. "I would be honored." She went to a small chest tucked in a corner of the room and pulled out a handful of multi-colored yarns.

"You're certain this is what you want?" Dylan asked.

Maere poked him in the rib with her finger, making him jump. "Don't be arguing with me, Dylan mac Connall. I have powers, you know."

Dylan rolled his eyes. "You see, Kate, already it starts." He laughed. Here was a glimpse of the old Maere, the girl who chased fays and played hide-and-seek with the sun. He hadn't realized how much he'd missed her until now.

"Clasp your left hands together," Kate said as she approached the pair. As they took each other's hands, the old woman wrapped the yarns around them, from wrists to fingertip, chanting of the colors, "Blue for understanding, yellow for harmony, brown for healing, white for protection." She glanced up and winked. "Red for passion, green for fertility." When she finished with the binding, she turned to Dylan. "Dylan mac Connall, state your purpose here this night."

His eyes met Maere's. "I take you to be my wife. Beginning this day and beyond, for all time."

"Maere cu Llwyr, state your purpose here this night."

She smiled at Dylan. "I take you to be my husband. Beginning this day and beyond, for all time."

Kate placed her hand over the couple's. "As witness to this hand-fasting, I grant that you are truly wed." She unwound the yarns and put them back in the chest. Turning around, she found Dylan and Maere standing there, smiling at each other. "Are you needing my permission to kiss the girl now, son? You seemed to be doing a fair job earlier today." She laughed as she headed toward the door of the cottage.

Kate took her cloak down from a peg and wrapped it around her shoulders. "I've been needing to gather herbs by the light of the moon. I'll be gone this night, back on the morrow." She winked again. "So don't be waiting up for me. If you get my meaning."

"By the gods, old woman," Dylan said, "we get your meaning." He released Maere's hands and went to his teacher. "But it'll be cold tonight. Are you certain about this?"

She patted his arm. "I still have my cave. Filled it myself just the other day with fresh supplies and wood for a fire." She winked. "I had a feeling you might show up."

Dylan laughed and opened the door. "Out with you then! And be sure to knock when you return." He shook his head and closed the door. He went to Maere, took her hand, and led her across the room. "Come. I will show you where I grew up." He pushed aside a curtain and revealed his small chamber, the cot against the wall, his desk still stacked with his sketches and writing. With a piece of burning tinder, he lit the few candles in the room.

Maere went to the desk and picked up one of the drawings. She was reminded of the scroll Dylan had brought to the anchorage, the one with her face on it. And here was another. And another. All drawings of her. She turned to him. "What does this mean?"

"It means I did nothing but dream of you from the day you were taken from me." Dylan pulled her into his arms. "I have something for you." He reached into the pouch at his waist, pulled out a piece of fabric, and handed it to her. "Do you remember this?"

As Maere unfolded the stained and torn fabric, a flash of knotted gold caught the candle flame and glinted. Her hand flew to her mouth. "Oh, Dylan! I thought I'd lost this forever." She unpinned the garnet brooch and held it to her heart. Visions of her parents and the night they gave her this gift came to her. The night she and Dylan were betrothed. "How?" she asked.

"When I tried to pull you away from Eugis on that night, your mantle tore. All these years, I've kept it safe for you." Dylan took her into his arms again, holding her tight against him. He kissed her.

Maere gently laid the brooch on the desk and wrapped her arms around his neck, meeting his passion. He scooped her up and carried her to his bed, gently placing her on top of the coverlet. He stood above her and pulled his shirt over his head. Maere reached up to touch him. He gently guided her hand away. "Touch me now and we'll be finished before we start," he whispered, his voice husky.

He untied his leggings and braes, letting them drop at his feet. All that remained was his undergarment and that beautiful gold torque his father had given him their betrothal night. Maere reached up again and pulled him down. He fell gently atop her and covered her mouth with his.

Such fire Maere had never known! Not even when she burned with her power could it match this joining of their mouths. Searching, tongues touching, filling her with the greatest of desire.

Dylan rose slightly on one arm. She leaned up to catch his mouth, but he moved his head, eluding her. "Are you sure you're ready? I would not rush you, love."

Maere answered by unfastening her dress and easing out of it. "Will you be helping me with my shift, or do I have to do it myself?"

A low growl came from the back of Dylan's throat as he claimed her mouth once more. His hands swept up and over her sides, then back down again. He found the edges of her shift and helped pull it over her head.

Maere undid the last of his garments and he kicked them off and out of the way. She ran her fingers over his chest. When Dylan moaned, she grew bolder and allowed her hands to travel further down his body, claiming him with a tight squeeze.

"Sweet Danu," he whispered between kisses. Leaving her mouth, he traveled down her throat, sucking and nibbling until Maere was writhing beneath him. Going lower still, he cupped her full breasts with his hands, kissing first one, then the other.

Maere let out a ragged sigh as her senses took over, lost in this moment of pleasure. "What magic is this?" She was breathless as his hands traveled over her belly. "Dylan," she whispered his name a thousand times over. "Dylan."

She pulled him roughly to her, claiming his mouth once more. Instinctively, Maere began to move her hips against his. "Take me." Dear Mother, the fire would consume her. "Now."

Dylan groaned again. With a single movement, he was inside her, swaying his hips side to side, savoring the feel of this woman, his love, his wife.

Maere moved against him, meeting his passion with her own. And as the tension continued to build in her, so did her power, until the two were as entwined as their bodies, hearts and souls touching. "Ah, love," she cried out as the light enveloped them. Higher and higher she went, taking Dylan with her, the light of her magic consuming them both.

"I love you, Maere cu Llwyr," he whispered.

"And I, you, Dylan mac Connell," she whispered back.

A NOTE FROM THE AUTHOR

I hope you enjoyed *Pagan Fire*, Book 3 in the Oracle Dreams Trilogy. If you'd like to leave a review, please visit Amazon.com.

I love to hear from readers! You can contact me through my website at www.teribarnett.com. While you're there, please go ahead and subscribe to my newsletter so you can stay up to date on new releases, special offers, and giveaways.

ABOUT THE AUTHOR

In addition to her Oracle Dreams Trilogy, Teri Barnett is the bestselling author of the Bijoux Mystery Series and the upcoming Lac Voo Mystery Series. Both cozy mystery series are set in sleepy tourist towns on the Lake Michigan shoreline. She's also the creator of Cats & More: Adult Coloring Book Series, a Reiki Master Teacher, and has written numerous non-fiction books about the practice and teaching of Reiki. Other non-fiction works include *How to be a Kickass Goddess: Twelve Steps to Owning Your Life* and the accompanying *Kickass Goddess Journal*, because you always need to journal when you're a Kickass Goddess.

All of Teri's books can be found on Amazon.

And if being an author isn't enough, Teri is also an award-winning artist and nationally recognized commercial interior designer who brings a lifetime of learning and exploration to her writing and workshops. Born and raised in Michigan, Teri currently resides in Indiana where she writes books, does cool art, crochets too many shawls and blankets, and hangs out with Black Cat Lou, her bossy black cat. BCL is the inspiration for Griselda, Morgan Hart's rescue cat in the Bijoux Mystery Series, who makes her debut in Book 2, *Mystics are Murder*.

When Teri isn't busy working on her next book or redesigning the world, you can find her doing the artist thing in her studio, tromping through the forest, hanging with her kids and grandkids, or riding through the corn tunnels of Indiana on her motorcycle.

You can visit Teri online at www.teribarnett.com to learn more about her books, subscribe to her newsletter, and/or just to drop her a line to say hello.

TERI BARNETT
COMPLETE BOOK LIST

ORACLE DREAMS TRILOGY
Historical/Paranormal Time Travel Romance Trilogy

Through the Mists of Time: Oracle Dreams Trilogy Book 1

In 1865 London, Valerie Sherwood Brooks embarks on a tour of Italy where she is catapulted back in time to the ancient city of Pompeii and into the arms of a mysterious man who will alter her very destiny.

With a romantic heart and yearning for adventure, Valerie is overjoyed at the prospect of leaving London for the excitement of Italy, even if it means traveling with her overly protective parents and rambunctious little brother. Despite a childhood accident that has left her in need of a cane, Valerie is determined to explore the ancient ruins of Pompeii on her own. But when an earthquake shatters their visit to the Old City, Valerie is hurled back in time to 79 A.D.

Thrust into a world of intrigue and danger, Valerie is forced into servitude in the grand home of the darkly handsome Christos Marcellus. As Valerie tries to keep her wits about her, she is torn between her complex feelings for Christos and her need to get back to her own time.

Knowing the coming eruption of Vesuvius will mean doom and destruction, Valerie is faced with a life and death decision. Will she make the right choice in time?

Shadow Dreams: Oracle Dreams Trilogy Book 2

In the village of Paran, in the peaceful realm of Keilah, Bethany M'Doro embarks on a voyage to the Earth plane, to the year 1875, in search of a man who has the power to save her or destroy her.

Widowed with a young daughter, Bethany M'Doro possesses a unique ability to see into the past and her clairvoyant gifts make her invaluable on archeological digs. Her team's most recent discovery—an ornate comb buried under a pile of charred bones—sparks a vision of the ancient evil cult of Eitel, known for stealing children's souls. Although it was believed the cult was destroyed centuries ago, Bethany senses it has been resurrected by a diabolical new leader.

Bethany returns home from the expedition, to discover her worst fear has been realized. Her daughter Sarah has gone missing along with several other children from the village. It can only be the evil cult Eitel. Desperate to find them, Bethany's visions guide her to the Earth plane, to Devil's Gate, Nevada in 1875. There she encounters Connor Jessup, the only man who has the power to help her. But Connor is tormented by his own personal demons and a tragic past that continues to haunt him.

Bethany now faces the greatest challenge of her life. Can she heal Connor and convince him to travel back with her to Paran to find Eitel's lair and save Sarah and the other children from certain death? Or will her daughter be lost forever?

Pagan Fire: Oracle Dreams Trilogy Book 3

In 883 A.D., in a secluded convent in Great Britain, Maere cu Llwyr embarks on a journey back to her home of Tintagel, Cornwall with a powerful warrior who claims to be her long lost betrothed.

Dylan mac Connall survived the slaughter of his family by a traitor to their clan. A young boy at the time, he was rescued by a wise woman who taught him the ways of magic and warned him of the perils that lay ahead if he chose a path of revenge. But Dylan can no longer heed the advice of his foster mother and is determined to avenge his family and find the spirited girl he loved in his youth.

Raised in an abbey by the Sisters of Saint Columba, Maere cu Llwyr is ready to take her full vows and become a nun. But when the warrior Dylan arrives and claims to be her rightful betrothed, Maere is shocked and wary of what her future will bring. A wee child when she was abducted from her village, Maere has blocked the memories of that horrific night. She has no recollection of the powerful ancient magic dormant inside her, or of the handsome man determined to unlock both Maere's mind and her power.

As Maere and Dylan travel back to Tintagel, they must face the mercurial goddess Morrigu, dangerous Viking raiders, and the traitor who destroyed their families. Can Maere and Dylan survive the battles to come and find their way back home and to each other? Or will they be forever separated by forces outside of their control?

BIJOUX MYSTERY SERIES

Romance is Murder: Bijoux Mystery Series Book 1

A dead diva, a rotten romance, and a town full of nosy neighbors…

Morgan Hart is home. A former homicide detective in Detroit, Morgan is back in her old hometown of Bijoux, Michigan to take over the reins of Sheriff from her dad, Able. The town has undergone quite a transformation since she lived here with new, kitschy shops along Main Street and a burgeoning tourist trade. Even the iconic pink Firefly Bed & Breakfast has jumped on the bandwagon and is hosting a romance writers' convention with some of the biggest names in the 'happily ever after' biz.

Morgan hopes to ease into her new job, new cottage, and new life – after all, Bijoux hasn't had a murder in a hundred years. But all of Morgan's plans go up in smoke when the biggest diva of the romance world is found dead.

As Morgan and her deputy, JJ Jones, begin their investigation, the townspeople have no qualms about telling her how to do her job, including Caleb Joseph, owner of the local bookstore who is far too nosy (and attractive) for Morgan's comfort.

With a murder to solve and the town in turmoil, Morgan will have to rely on her big city cop skills to catch a killer harboring a hate for happy endings.

Mystics are Murder: Bijoux Mystery Series Book 2

What do you do when your star murder witness only speaks 'Meow?'

Who could predict it would happen again? Morgan Hart didn't expect her first day as police captain of Bijoux, Michigan, the sleepy lakeside town where she grew up, would include a murder, even though that's just what happened. But with the killer behind bars, Morgan can take a breath and start painting her cozy cottage.

Or so she hopes.

When a fortune-telling mystic is found dead at Bijoux's Walk into the Light Psychic Gathering, Morgan and her deputy, JJ Jones, are called in to investigate. The trouble is Morgan's only witness is Griselda, a black cat with blood on her paws.

While every psychic in town claims to know what the cat 'knows,' Morgan relies on her own instincts to sniff out the suspects while dodging her conflicting feelings for local bookshop owner and town hunk, Caleb Joseph. And with her dad, Able's, upcoming wedding to Zoe Buffet, Bijoux's most famous clairvoyant and coffee cake queen, Morgan is under the gun to figure out which mystic is the murderer before the couple says I do.

Cupcakes are Murder: Bijoux Mystery Series Book 3

A cupcake conundrum, a culinary queen on the edge, and a cold-case killer on the loose...

Morgan Hart is settling into her job as police captain of Bijoux, the quaint and quirky tourist town nestled on the Lake Michigan shoreline. Murders have been solved, kittens have been rescued, and progress has been made in the renovation of her cozy cottage by the beach. Despite her grief and ongoing frustration over her husband's unsolved murder six years ago, Morgan hopes an overdue break in the case will finally lead to justice, even if it means exposing a betrayal that could leave her reeling.

Meanwhile, Morgan needs to keep a sharp eye on the upcoming Baker's Dozen Hometown Cupcake Bake-off and TV special hosted by British baking superstar Sassy McComas, aka The Queen of Cupcakes. Rumor has it, Queen Sass is secretly searching for a fresh face to host a new TV show and the competitors vying for the top spot include Bijoux's own pastry princess, Hannah Bellamy.

But when one of the top challengers in the Cupcake Bake-off turns up dead, Morgan has to sift through the evidence and stop the killer before they strike again and threaten to topple Queen Sass from her throne.

Pumpkins are Murder: Bijoux Mystery Series Book 4

A dead carver, dueling witches, and more tricks than treats...

Bijoux, Michigan is serious about Halloween.

Known as the most haunted town on the Lake Michigan shoreline, Bijoux hosts the annual Pumpkins and Poe Festival—the town's annual homage to Edgar Allan Poe and all things spooky. Pumpkin carvers from around the country flock to Bijoux, slicing and dicing their way into Halloween history. But when one of the carvers turns up dead with a jack-o-lantern on their head and a note with the word Nevermore scrawled in orange ink pinned to their apron, police captain Morgan Hart is called in to investigate.

After solving multiple murders at three previous Bijoux events, the beleaguered police captain steps into the fray once again, along with her down-in-the-dumps deputy, JJ Jones, recently ditched by his girlfriend, local cupcake maven, Hannah Bellamy. Meanwhile, Morgan's own "weak and weary" heart keeps getting tested by Caleb Joseph, owner of the Raven's Nest bookstore. The too-hot-for-his-own-good former Gothic Lit professor has made a hobby out of snooping around Morgan's cases.

It's up to Morgan to thwart various Halloween hijinks around Bijoux while preventing the town from panicking as she tries to catch a killer who's turned "trick or treat" into the darkest diversion of all—murder.

Mistletoe is Murder: Bijoux Mystery Series Book 5

Skeletons with secrets, prohibition pirates, and holiday hijinks…

Morgan Hart is hoping for a boring Christmas. After eight months of murderous mayhem in her hometown of Bijoux, Michigan, she just wants to snuggle under a warm blanket in front of a cozy fire, with a good book, a hot chocolate (extra marshmallows of course), and Griselda purring beside her. She might even work up the nerve to ask Caleb Joseph over for dinner. Cal, the attractive owner of the Raven's Nest bookstore, has become a good friend since Morgan moved back home to take on the job of police captain.

A bestselling mystery author, Cal recently purchased the old Lawrence Mansion on the edge of town and plans to throw a big Christmas Eve bash. But Morgan's holiday plans—romantic and otherwise—go up in smoke when dark and shadowy secrets are revealed during the clean-up of the 19th century-built home. Can Morgan and Cal uncover the ghostly truth or are they destined for a disastrous deck-the-halls?

CATS & MORE: ADULT COLORING BOOKS

Volume 1: Angsty Cats

Volume 2: Snarky Cats

Volume 3: Mandala Cats

Volume 4: Spooky Cats

Volume 5: Jingle Cats

Volume 6: Mystery Cats

Volume 7: More Mystery Cats

Volume 8: Coloring is Murder *(based on the Bestselling Bijoux Mystery Series)*

Volume 9: Cat Facts

Volume 10: Camping Tarot

Volume 11: Cosmic Cats

Volume 12: Crochet & Cats

NON-FICTION

Visit ReikiOne.com, PresenceandShadow.com, and/or SacredPriestess Journeys.com for more information.

How to Be a Kickass Goddess: Twelve Steps to Owning Your Life

What would your life look like if you owned it? REALLY owned it? Who would you be? How would you live? What would you do? In a straightforward, down-to-earth style, How to Be a Kickass Goddess: Twelve Steps to Owning Your Life takes you on a journey directly into You - everything you are and everything you can be. Now, grab this book and get busy. The world needs all the Kickass Goddesses she can get!

How to be a Kickass Goddess: Companion Journal

Beginnings: ReikiOne First Degree Manual

This manual covers the basics of Reiki training and practice, including history, principles, hand positions, and treatment guidelines. Also included is a brief introduction to the chakras and using crystals with Reiki.

The Deeper Journey: ReikiOne Second Degree Manual

The ReikiOne Second Degree Manual includes the three symbols traditionally associated with this degree, explanations and their use, methods of distance healing, sending Reiki through time and space, combining symbols for greater effect, the chakra system, the human aura, and a suggested reading list.

Reiki Master: ReikiOne Third Degree Manual Part A by Teri Barnett, Reiki Master Teacher

This book contains the 4th symbol, its use for Reiki treatments, a discussion of what it means to be a Reiki Master, and how to use crystal grids with Reiki.

Reiki Master Teacher: ReikiOne Third Degree Manual Part B

The Master Teacher Manual contains all the information your students need for stepping into Reiki Master Teacher - A review of the 4th symbol (plus additional data on this symbol), the 5th symbol for attunements, attunement instructions (individual and group), methods and ethics of teaching, getting in touch with your inner teacher, marketing ideas, an extensive reading list, and much more.

The Reiki Teacher's Handbook

A composite of all the ReikiOne Manuals, the Reiki Teacher's Handbook takes your teaching a step further. This book provides you with all the tools you'll need to teach Reiki. Written from the experienced perspective of a master Teacher of the Usui Shiki Ryoho method, you'll find this book adapts easily to other forms of Reiki and can grow with you as you progress on your teaching path.

www.ingramcontent.com/pod-product-compliance
Lightning Source LLC
Chambersburg PA
CBHW020056180626
46812CB00006B/2350